The Irish Goodbye

The
Irish Goodbye

A NOVEL

HEATHER AIMEE O'NEILL

HENRY HOLT AND COMPANY
NEW YORK

Henry Holt and Company
Publishers since 1866
120 Broadway
New York, New York 10271
www.henryholt.com

Henry Holt® and ⒽⒾ® are registered trademarks of Macmillan Publishing Group, LLC.
EU Representative: Macmillan Publishers Ireland Ltd., 1st Floor, The Liffey Trust Centre,
117–126 Sheriff Street Upper, Dublin 1, DO1 YC43

Copyright © 2025 by Heather Aimee O'Neill
All rights reserved.
Distributed in Canada by Raincoast Book Distribution Limited

Library of Congress Cataloging-in-Publication Data

Names: O'Neill, Heather Aimee, author.
Title: The Irish goodbye : a novel / Heather Aimee O'Neill.
Description: First edition. | New York : Holt, 2025.
Identifiers: LCCN 2025009221 | ISBN 9781250408150 (hardcover) |
    ISBN 9781250408174 (ebook)
Subjects: LCGFT: Domestic fiction. | Novels.
Classification: LCC PS3615.N443 I75 2025 | DDC 813/.6—dc23/eng/20250319
LC record available at https://lccn.loc.gov/2025009221

The publisher of this book does not authorize the use or reproduction of any
part of this book in any manner for the purpose of training artificial intelligence
technologies or systems. The publisher of this book expressly reserves this book
from the Text and Data Mining exception in accordance with Article 4(3) of the
European Union Digital Single Market Directive 2019/790.

Our books may be purchased in bulk for specialty retail/wholesale, literacy,
corporate/premium, educational, and subscription box use. Please contact
MacmillanSpecialMarkets@macmillan.com.

First Edition 2025

Designed by Omar Chapa

Printed in the United States of America

10 9 8 7 6 5 4 3 2 1

This is a work of fiction. All of the characters, organizations, and events portrayed in this novel
either are products of the author's imagination or are used fictitiously.

For my parents, to whom I owe so much

The Irish Goodbye

August 1990

Like everyone at the beach club that day, Maggie heard the crash. She jumped up from the sandcastle she was building and spotted her brother, Topher, diving off the bow of his skiff and disappearing into the blue-black water along the lighthouse's rocky promontory. A moment later, he resurfaced holding something she couldn't make out from the shore.

Alice, Maggie's middle sister, scrambled to the top of the rickety lifeguard stand and shouted down to Maggie, "Get Mom!"

Maggie hesitated. She wanted to see what was happening with her brother. Plus, she felt confident about her chances of winning the Port Haven Beach Club sandcastle competition. But when Alice shouted again, Maggie took off down the beach toward her family's house. She liked all the eyes on her as she ran, fists curled and arms pumping. From the dock, someone yelled, "Call 911!"

At the jetty that cut across the shoreline in front of her house, she scrambled over the rocks covered in slippery seaweed, slicing the inside of her ankle against a jagged edge. It stung, but she didn't stop. She hurried up the creaky stairs along the bluff and through the fence gate, calling for her mother. The geese fluttered their wings and scattered, frightened by her screams. She sprinted across the slope of lawn, wet from the sprinklers, and toward the white-and-blue clapboard Victorian, which suddenly seemed massive and terrifyingly empty.

She called out again, and to her relief, her mother appeared from the garden holding a paintbrush in her teeth and wearing her floppy straw sun hat. Her easel was set up by the lavender blooms she'd been painting all week, and splashes of red and blue covered her smock. She tucked her paintbrush behind her ear. "What's this about?" she asked.

"Something happened," Maggie said breathlessly. Her lungs burned from the running.

Her mother lowered herself to inspect the blood on Maggie's ankle. "Did you fall?"

Maggie shook her head and pointed to the bay.

"Is someone hurt?" her mother asked, standing.

Maggie wasn't sure. She'd heard the crash and then seen Topher dive into the water. Her oldest sister, Cait, was supposed to be on her brother's boat, but she hadn't seen her there. "The boat . . . Topher jumped in . . ." She grabbed her mother's hand. "Just come!"

Her mother untied her smock and chucked it in the direction of her easel, then raced past Maggie toward the beach club. At the dock, they found Topher helping Cait and his best friend, Luke, carry someone off his boat. Maggie tried to follow after her mother, but Alice yanked her by her bathing suit strap, and they stood next to the kayak racks with the club's camp counselors.

Waiters in black pants and white polos trickled out from the clubhouse to smoke cigarettes and watch. It seemed that no one knew what was going on.

"Is Topher doing CPR?" Maggie asked Alice.

Alice nodded.

Topher had practiced CPR on Maggie's favorite Cabbage Patch doll while training as a lifeguard, his big hands pumping the doll's puffy chest. She'd gotten annoyed with him then but felt proud watching him now. "On who?" she asked.

Their father rushed past them from the direction of the parking lot. He must have come from work because he was in his suit, but Maggie didn't know how he'd gotten there so quickly. He didn't acknowledge them as he rushed down the narrow dock.

"On Daniel Larkin," Alice finally answered.

Daniel was Luke's younger brother. He had given Maggie her first "toasted almond," a dunk in the bay and then a roll in the sand, at the Fourth of July barbecue a few weeks ago. Like Alice, he was starting the tenth grade at Saint Mary's that fall.

When the ambulance arrived, the onlookers scurried to the beach. Maggie gnawed at her thumbnail. The summer sky was bright, and she had to squint and hold her hand over her forehead to look out at the bay. For a while, it seemed to her like not much was happening; then, in a flurry, the paramedics loaded Daniel onto a board and rushed him off the dock. Luke leapt into the back of the ambulance and they closed the doors. The sirens blared, and just like that, they were gone.

At the dock house, Topher stood next to their parents, talking to two police officers. It was odd for Maggie to see her mother there in her loose linen shirt, her feet bare. All of Maggie's friends' mothers were younger and wore tennis whites, ate lunch at the clubhouse, and drank cocktails on the adults-only patio for happy hour.

Another police officer took pictures of Topher's boat, which bobbed gently against the dock's edge. There was a dent in the bow, Maggie noticed, and she imagined her brother was upset about that. He'd bought the boat that spring, all with his own money. It had been falling apart, but he'd rebuilt most of it himself.

"Why are the police here?" Alice asked Cait as she walked off the dock.

"I don't know," Cait said in a sharp voice, and turned toward the water. She hugged herself tightly, gripping the silver Saint Jude pendant she'd discovered in their grandfather's junk drawer years ago, anxiously chewing on it.

Maggie scanned the bay to see what her oldest sister was looking for, but all she found were a pair of sailboats scuttling across the horizon and boats anchored around the lighthouse for its annual fundraiser event.

"What's happening with Topher?" Alice persisted. "Is he in trouble?"

Cait turned back. "I don't know," she said again. But then, "Daniel was driving his boat. The steering wheel got jammed or something and they hit a rock by the lighthouse. I guess he flipped overboard."

Maggie watched her brother and parents on the dock. Her mother held Topher by the arm, and her father gestured toward the boat to one of the officers. Beneath Topher's aviator sunglasses, his face was shiny and red. She didn't understand why he'd be in trouble if he wasn't even the one driving the boat. Maybe Daniel should be in trouble. If he wasn't too hurt, she guessed. She imagined him returning to the beach club with a bandage around his head and everyone at camp making him a WELCOME BACK poster during craft class like they did when she'd had her appendix removed last summer.

Another police car arrived, and Topher and her parents walked off the dock toward the clubhouse.

"Where are they going?" Maggie asked, but her sisters ignored her.

Alice nudged Cait. "Why was Daniel driving Topher's boat?"

Cait leaned in closer to Alice. "Will you just shut up?" she hissed. Then she turned to Maggie. "Go find your camp group."

"Camp's over," Maggie said.

"Then go play with your friends."

Maggie started to protest—why did being the youngest *always* mean being left out?—but all Cait had to do was raise her brow.

Back at the beach, Maggie found she'd been left out of the fun there, too. They'd canceled the sandcastle competition, and all the popsicles were now gone. She sat at the foot of the lifeguard stand and finished reading

The Irish Goodbye

the last chapter of her most recent *Baby-Sitters Club* book, then followed her friends to the pool for a game of sharks and minnows. As they passed the clubhouse, she tried to spot her family, but the patio was empty, and she worried they'd left without her. Finally, Cait appeared at the pool's edge and told her to get her stuff.

Maggie walked back home along the pebbled beach with her sisters. They were quiet, and it looked like Cait had been crying.

"Where's Topher?" she asked. "And Mom and Dad?"

"At the police station," Cait said.

"Why?"

"We don't know," Alice said. "They could be at the hospital."

That made Maggie feel better. "I'm going to make Daniel a poster," she said.

Her sisters stopped and exchanged glances. Cait closed her eyes and puffed out her cheeks.

"Just tell her," Alice said.

"Tell me what?"

Cait opened her eyes again. She held on to the beach towel wrapped around her neck and straightened her back. "Daniel's dead," she said.

Maggie looked at her sisters, but they didn't say anything else, eyes fixed on the path ahead. There was so much Maggie wanted to ask, but she knew Cait would tell her to shut up like she had Alice.

Cait stepped over the broken shell of a horseshoe crab. "Everything's different now," she said.

And she kept on walking.

THANKSGIVING

2015

TWENTY-FIVE YEARS LATER

1.

MAGGIE

Maggie and her girlfriend, Isabel, crossed the border into New York. The drive from southern Vermont, where they taught at a boarding school, to Port Haven on the North Fork of Long Island, usually took Maggie about six hours, but it was the day before Thanksgiving and traffic was piling up. Maggie also hadn't accounted for the unexpected snowstorm making its way along the Eastern Seaboard.

Isabel picked through a bag of pistachios. "Prep me on your family," she said, and curled her long legs beneath her on the passenger side of Maggie's twenty-something-year-old Jeep Wagoneer. "Like a game. One word to describe each of them."

"Hmm—"

"No thinking," Isabel said. "What does Kerouac say about getting to the truth?"

"I don't know."

"Sure you do." Isabel snapped her fingers. "'First thought, best thought'!"

"That's Ginsberg."

"I told you you knew."

Maggie laughed, which relieved some of the pressure that had been building inside her. Not only was she bringing a girlfriend home for the first time, but something had happened that morning that had thrown her. Headmaster Cunningham, in his characteristically formal voice, had told her he'd like to speak with her first thing on Monday when she was back from Thanksgiving. He didn't specify what the meeting was about, but she'd avoided opening the calendar invite his secretary had sent because she worried it would reference something to do with her disastrous trip to Boston last weekend. She'd gone to attend an Anne Carson event at the Museum of Fine Arts and ended up seeing her ex, Sarah. Maggie had tried to put her anxiety aside for the visit home—she had enough to worry about with her mother meeting Isabel—but that proved more difficult than she'd expected. Throughout the drive, her mind drifted to Sarah leaning in to kiss her, and her stomach felt sour and twisty.

A sporty BMW behind them flashed its headlights.

"I think they want you to move over," Isabel said.

As Maggie switched lanes, the BMW zoomed past them, and the passenger stuck his middle finger out the window.

"Jesus," Maggie said.

"I like that you're a slow driver. It reminds me of my dad."

Maggie checked the speedometer, which was indeed hovering just above the speed limit.

When they'd first gotten on the road, she'd decided not to use the GPS on her phone because she didn't want a text from Sarah popping up while she drove.

Isabel relaxed back against the headrest. Her dark hair hung in a low-slung ponytail that made the car smell like coconut every time she adjusted it.

Maggie turned down the radio. "Okay," she said. "I'll play." It was better than stewing in her anxiety. "Let's start with Cait."

"And the word for her is—"

"*Fiery.*"

Other words might have been more precise—*explosive*, for one—but Maggie was trying to keep things positive, even though her oldest sister hadn't returned any of her calls recently. She hadn't even responded to Maggie's text about bringing Isabel home for the holiday.

"She was also always the prettiest," Maggie said. "Still is."

"I'll see about that." Isabel flashed her that wink Maggie found irresistible.

Maggie actually looked a lot like Cait. Whereas Topher and Alice took after their mother—all strawberry-blond curls and hazel eyes—Maggie and Cait had their father's straight brown hair, blue eyes, and lanky build. But Cait had some quality Maggie didn't, something that wasn't just about her full lips and smooth complexion. It was in the way she carried herself, almost like a warning. While it had gotten Cait attention ever since puberty, it wasn't something Maggie envied.

"Who's next?" Isabel asked.

"Alice," Maggie said. "Middle sister. The word for her is . . . *Mom*, I guess."

"Isn't that, I don't know, more like her role? Maybe the word is *maternal*?"

"She's such a mom. You'll see."

"Fine. What about your mom, then?"

Maggie had spent plenty of time that morning thinking about Nora. She knew her mother wouldn't be outright rude to Isabel, but her discomfort with Maggie being gay would make it difficult for her to be warm and welcoming.

"Nora is . . . *opaque*. I mean, I told you she was literally raised by nuns in an orphanage in Ireland, so she had it pretty rough." Then she said, "I've never felt like I've known her. Not really. Or that she wanted to be known."

"Doesn't everyone want to be known?"

Maggie held out her palm for pistachios. "I'm not sure if it's even possible to know someone fully." She cracked a shell in her teeth, and the nut popped into her mouth, salty and slightly stale.

"Maybe, but that's different from wanting to be known."

Maggie conceded.

"And your dad?"

"Robert." Maggie tapped the steering wheel. "For him, I'd say *obliging*."

Isabel laughed. "In a house full of women, what other choice did he have?"

"Well, it wasn't always that way, before my brother . . ."

Isabel shook her head. "Oh God, why did I say that?"

Traffic slowed to a stop and Maggie reached for Isabel's hand. "It's okay," she said.

After a long moment, Isabel said, "It's just, you never talk about him."

"Yeah," Maggie said, shrugging. "I know."

Isabel placed her hand high on Maggie's thigh and kissed her neck, sending shivers along Maggie's body. After what Maggie had done in Boston, she did not feel like she deserved any of Isabel's affection, and receiving it now was almost hard. Still, when Isabel leaned in closer and pressed her lips against Maggie's, she kissed her back—not only to avoid making Isabel suspicious but because it was exactly what she wanted to do. Isabel's breath smelled earthy and sweet: pistachios.

The blare of a car horn behind them broke the moment, and Maggie reluctantly pulled away from Isabel, put the car back in gear, and drove on.

* * *

Maggie first spoke to Isabel last winter while conducting phone interviews for the writer-in-residence program at Grove Academy, where she taught English. Isabel was her last call. Maggie had already favored Isabel's plays over the work of the other top candidate, a language poet who used only words containing the vowels *a* and *o*, but she approached the call cautiously.

Sarah, the mother of one of Maggie's students, warned her that choosing an openly gay writer might come across as playing favorites. It was a fair point, but since Sarah was also the married woman Maggie had been sleeping with for the past year, the irony of Sarah's cautioning about moral lines and clear judgment wasn't lost on her.

After Maggie and Isabel hit it off, chatting far past the half hour they'd scheduled, Maggie submitted her recommendation to the English department.

Coincidence or not, the next day Sarah called to tell Maggie that she'd confessed their affair to her husband, Frank, but that she'd decided not to leave him. Sarah had been the most constant person in Maggie's life for nearly a year, and the breakup was devastating, if not entirely unexpected. Sarah promised to protect Maggie and not tell Frank who the affair was with, but the fact that he was a trustee at Grove made Maggie paranoid about losing her job. Plus, Sarah's son, Oliver, was still in her class, and Maggie had to email teacher evaluations of his work to Sarah and Frank at the end of every quarter.

After a few miserable months of waiting for Sarah to change her mind, while having an unsatisfying, largely drunken fling with a bartender from town, Maggie finally met Isabel at a welcome ceremony the first week of summer school. It was a bluebell Sunday afternoon. Maggie arrived at the library late, dressed in the paint-stained overalls she'd worn to rip out the moldy carpet in the uninhabited cabin she'd recently purchased and was restoring off campus. She leaned against the back wall with her arms crossed and listened as Isabel read from a play in progress about her Venezuelan grandmother, who was a seamstress at the White House during World War II.

Isabel was not the California surfer girl Maggie had imagined. There was something almost somber in her beauty, and her long dark hair and high cheekbones reminded Maggie of the painting of an Indigenous woman that greeted visitors at the school's main entrance. Isabel's voice was raspy but sweet, almost masculine. She wore a white linen button-down tucked into worn Levi's, with a braided leather belt that wrapped around her waist twice. She was funny and charming and entirely self-possessed, and Maggie knew right away that she was in trouble.

After the reading, they all gathered in the garden outside the library. Maggie chatted with a few seniors there for the summer program but watched Isabel, too, with quick sidelong glances. She waited until they were alone to introduce herself.

Isabel filled a small plate with cheese and grapes, and Maggie handed her a pint of beer from the local brewery catering the event.

"I like your play," Maggie said. "Did your grandmother really work for Eleanor Roosevelt and read her tarot cards?"

Isabel was about to answer when a few faculty members approached, and the conversation turned to the recent announcement that the current English department chair was retiring. Maggie caught Isabel studying her more closely when someone mentioned talk of Maggie being the possible replacement. Though Maggie waved away the rumors, she hoped they were true.

After the event, Maggie and Isabel walked back from the main campus to the faculty residence hall.

"This is me," Maggie said when they arrived at her door. "There's a communal porch out back. I have some extra beers if you want?"

"I start classes tomorrow and haven't even unpacked, so I should probably—"

"Of course," Maggie said. "Some other time."

"Definitely." Isabel headed toward her door, then turned. "Oh, and my grandmother did claim she read Eleanor Roosevelt's tarot cards, but she never let the truth get in the way of a good story, so who knows?"

Maggie laughed.

Isabel pointed to Maggie's sneakers lying on her doormat. "You run?"

"Used to. It's been a while. There are some great trails around here, though. I have a map you can borrow."

"Why don't you show me?" Isabel said. "Maybe tomorrow after class?"

A laugh echoed from somewhere on the other side of the quad. The dining hall bell rang and drowned out the buzz of cicadas in the nearby bushes. The yellow lamps flicked on across campus as they did every evening at five p.m. The world around Maggie was as familiar as ever, and yet before her stood an enchanting woman asking her to go for a run tomorrow.

"I'd love to," Maggie said.

Maggie hadn't gone running in well over a year, but the next afternoon she led Isabel to her favorite trail along the back of the campus, exhausting herself by sprinting faster than normal in an effort to make a good impression. At the top of the trail, they sat on the rocky cliffs of a waterfall and chatted with two students who were on field study for their earth science class.

"The kids seem nice here," Isabel said as they walked back down the mountain. "I've never taught high school."

Maggie loved her students, a quirky and gifted cohort, and felt like a proud parent when she talked about them. Grove was her first teaching job out of graduate school, but she couldn't imagine ever wanting to leave the historic stone buildings and sprawling green campus. "They're great," she said. "Smart. They'll test you the first week, though, so don't be afraid to push back."

"Good to know," Isabel said, laughing. Then, more seriously, "Are you out to them?"

Well, that didn't take long. People were more likely to be surprised when Maggie told them she was gay than to figure it out on their own. Then again, most of the women she'd been in relationships with, including Sarah, regarded themselves as straight, so perhaps that played a part. She wondered what Isabel detected that gave it away, and glanced down at her outfit—running shorts and an old Grove T-shirt—as though it might reveal something.

"It's not what you look like." Isabel laughed. "It's . . . the way you look at me."

"How do I—"

Isabel fixed her dark, heavy-lidded eyes on Maggie.

"Oh." Maggie felt her face redden and tried to hide it by adjusting the brim of her hat.

The sun filtered through the canopy of eastern hemlocks surrounding them on the trail.

"Anyway," Maggie said. "I am. Out, I mean. I teach a seminar on contemporary queer literature in the upper school."

"And to think I had you pegged as an Austen or Woolf girl."

"Well, I dabbled in college." Maggie laughed. "But, really, don't worry about it. Everyone's cool here."

"I wasn't worried. Just curious."

They walked on until, suddenly, Isabel grabbed Maggie's arm and pulled her to a crouch. "Shh," she whispered. She placed one hand on Maggie's sweaty back and, with the other, pointed through the trees and around the bend to a deer and two fawns drinking from the moss-covered edge of a stream. The closeness of Isabel's breath and the heady scent of her sweat made Maggie feel like she was on the brink of something new, something she wasn't entirely sure how to name. They watched until a branch beneath Maggie's foot snapped, and the three creatures sprinted across the water without making a sound.

"They're like ghosts," Maggie said.

Isabel stood and reached for her hand, pulling her up.

For the rest of the summer, Maggie and Isabel ran together every morning, shared most meals, and drank whiskey on the communal porch at night, their thighs touching beneath the flannel throw they'd share when the temperature dropped after sunset. Isabel helped Maggie restore the wood-burning stove in the cabin, and Maggie acted out the part of Eleanor Roosevelt, mid-Atlantic accent and all, whenever Isabel staged a reading from her play. They made each other laugh and never seemed to run out of things to talk about.

Still, it felt safer to keep some distance. Maggie's crushes before had been consumed with urgency and angst. What unfolded with Isabel was different. There was a steadiness that almost confused her. Her first instinct wasn't to rip off Isabel's clothes, have sex, and then leave—she wanted something more, which scared her. She sensed the attraction was mutual, but her heart felt like an easy target, and she wasn't sure it was a good idea to get involved with another person from the school, especially with the chair position opening.

One rainy morning in August, she and Isabel went for a run to celebrate Maggie's thirty-fourth birthday. After, Maggie was home changing out of her wet clothes when there was a knock at her door. She opened it to find Isabel holding a chocolate cupcake with a candle and reached for the plate.

"Wait, wait." Isabel pulled a lighter from her back pocket and lit the candle. "Make a wish!"

Maggie met Isabel's golden-brown eyes, and thought *You* as she blew out the flame.

Isabel stepped into the apartment and stood close enough that Maggie recognized that something between them had shifted.

"What was your wish?" Isabel asked quietly.

Before Maggie could answer, they were kissing. Isabel's lips tasted like salt from the run. As they stumbled toward the bedroom, Isabel undressed her, kissing her all over, and then Maggie did the same to Isabel, revealing her long body, her hair dark and full. They lay on the bed together, skin on skin, and suddenly Maggie felt like she might cry. They stayed there for a long moment, lips hovering, eyes open, until Isabel took her chin, closed her eyes, and kissed her again—softly, then fully.

They spent that night, and every night after, together. Every night, that is, until last Friday, when Maggie went to Boston. Sarah had heard from a mutual friend that Maggie would be in the city and texted her a last-minute invitation to stop by for a glass of wine before the reading. Maggie hadn't spoken to Sarah in almost a year by then, but she made the decision, which she regretted immediately, to accept. She told herself it was a chance for closure, and she'd meant it.

A few days after Boston, on the evening before Maggie was leaving to spend Thanksgiving with her family in Port Haven, she brought a bottle of wine to Isabel's. Isabel had planned to stay on campus to work on her play throughout the break, but she was now considering heading to Connecticut for the weekend to visit friends.

Maggie searched Isabel's drawers for a shirt to borrow for Thanksgiving dinner. If they couldn't be together, Maggie wanted to wear something that smelled like her.

Isabel lay on the bed, a teacup of wine resting on her stomach, her head propped on a pillow.

"How about this?" Maggie said, holding up a navy fisherman knit sweater.

"Sure," Isabel said. "I'll give it an extra spritz of my perfume."

Maggie gave her a thumbs-up and sat on the bed.

"Is something wrong?" Isabel asked. "You seem off tonight. Or is it just that you're going to miss me?"

"I am going to miss you," Maggie said. Then: "But I also feel like you're being, I don't know, cagey." She crossed her arms. She knew her distrust sprang from her own recent indiscretion, but she couldn't stop herself. Her whole body buzzed with suspicion.

"Cagey?" Isabel sat up. "How am I being cagey?"

"*Just some friends* in Connecticut?"

Isabel laughed. "You're jealous!" She placed the teacup on the nightstand and tossed a pillow at Maggie.

"No I'm not." She threw the pillow back, and Isabel caught it with one hand, tucking it behind her head as she lay back down.

"I don't know what's gotten into you," Isabel said. She reached for Maggie's hand, pulling her closer until their foreheads pressed together. "I don't even want to go to Connecticut."

The Irish Goodbye

"Come with me, then," Maggie heard herself say.

Isabel sat up again. "Really?"

No, Maggie thought. She wasn't sure she was ready to introduce Isabel to her family just yet, but now that it was out there, what could she say but "Yes, really."

"I don't want to impose," Isabel said. "Would your mom be okay having me there?"

"Don't worry about that. I'll call her in the morning."

But Maggie was worried. Growing up, she and her mother had been close. Her parents were in their forties when she was born, and as she was the youngest, they weren't as overwhelmed with her as they had been with the older three. Maggie mostly spent her time as she liked: with her face in a book. It wasn't until she was in high school and the only one left in the house that Nora started to pay more attention to her comings and goings. Nora disapproved of how she dressed (like a tomboy) and who she spent time with (theater kids who dyed their hair and spontaneously broke into songs and monologues). When Nora first suspected Maggie was gay, she frog-marched her straight to Father Kelly, the family priest, who counseled Maggie to find salvation by simply not acting on her feelings. That was all it took for Maggie to stop talking to her mother about anything having to do with her heart. When she came out officially, years later, in college, her mother cried for months, and since then they'd settled into a deepening distance. Maggie had never mentioned Sarah to her parents, but she'd inserted Isabel's name into some of her phone calls home over the last few months. Though her mother never inquired further, Maggie tried to be grateful that, at the very least, her parents knew there was someone in her life.

The following morning, Maggie called home to say she'd be bringing Isabel for Thanksgiving.

"Will she not want to see her own family?" her mother asked.

Maggie's stomach tightened. "She'll see them in a few weeks for Christmas break."

"Oh, well. How was I to know that?"

Being there the whole weekend was beginning to seem like a terrible idea. "We might only stay Wednesday and Thursday nights," Maggie said. "We'll see how it goes."

* * *

Maggie gently nudged Isabel awake as she pulled off the expressway. The storm had picked up, but she was hungry and wanted to grab a late lunch in the village before heading to her parents'.

"Are you worried about your mom?" Isabel asked.

"I guess." Maggie had actually spent the last half of the drive still thinking about her meeting with Headmaster Cunningham, but that was the last thing she wanted to talk about. "Yeah, maybe."

"It's going to be fine. I mean, come on. It's 2015. We could legally get married now."

Maggie laughed, carefully turning onto the snow-covered, ostentatiously charming Main Street of downtown Port Haven. "Maybe when it's the pope sanctioning marriage equality and not the Supreme Court, my mother might be swayed."

Port Haven village was only a mile away from Maggie's childhood home. When she was younger, she and her sisters rode their bikes to the diner to get milkshakes. Back then, the village was just a narrow strip of brick buildings—Anchor Pizzeria, O'Reilly's Tavern, a bait-and-tackle shop, and Captain's Diner. There was always a smattering of tourists throughout the summer, but everything changed in the early nineties when the *New York Times* ran a feature about the town's "laid-back vibe" and "accessibility to Manhattan." They designated it "an old whaling port and seaside village on the eastern end of Long Island, without the Hamptons' pretension or price tag."

Within ten years, the town's summer population had tripled. Main Street was extended several blocks toward the beach, and it now boasted ice cream stands, a fudge shop, a winery featuring local vineyards, and more cafés than anyone needed. In the past year alone, two new farm-to-table and dock-to-table restaurants had popped up. Maggie's parents were always talking about a developer who was petitioning the town to open a beach campground along the harbor. But come November, most of the day-trippers were gone, and there was plenty of space outside the diner, where Maggie parked her Jeep.

As she searched for her wallet in her backpack, Isabel played with the faded mala beads that had dangled from the Jeep's rearview mirror ever since Topher taught Maggie how to drive when she was in high school.

"These are beautiful," Isabel said. "I've meant to ask where they're from."

Maggie studied the scuffed wooden beads in Isabel's hands. "New Orleans? Ashram in India? Dollar store in Chinatown?" She shrugged. "Choose your own adventure. They're my brother's. Or were."

"Ah," Isabel said. She released the beads.

"This was his car first," Maggie said.

"I didn't know that."

Topher must have told Maggie where the beads were from at some point, but the memory was long gone. She barely noticed them anymore. She pulled them to her nose, almost expecting to catch a whiff of the lingering sandalwood and vanilla of Topher's cologne, but all that greeted her was the smell of mildew.

"What would Topher's word be?" Isabel asked.

The word came to Maggie faster than all the others. "*Liar*," she said.

"Liar," Isabel echoed, but with a question in her voice.

When the word was repeated back to her, Maggie wondered if it was fair. Not because he wasn't one—he was—but because she was, too. They all were.

2.

CAIT

Cait swallowed a Xanax and fished her phone out of her tote while Poppy's Furby prattled away beside her. She had hoped her daughter would doze off once the plane hit cruising altitude, like her twin brother, Augustus, but Poppy was more interested in pushing every button on her seat and causing a mess with her sticker book and a bowl of warm rosemary almonds. All Cait wanted was two minutes of peace to read Luke's email, which had popped up on her phone during boarding, but the plane's Wi-Fi connection was dismal, and she could only catch the subject line—this weekend—and the first few words of the email—call me when you're settled . . .

"Mummy?" Poppy whispered.

Cait froze.

"Mummy!" Poppy nudged Cait's arm. "Stop looking at your phone."

Cait laid her phone on her lap. "Yes, darling?"

"I want to color."

Coloring. Perfect. Cait searched Poppy's backpack, relieved to find a

Wizard of Oz coloring book and a box of crayons. She was almost ready to forgive their nanny, Ruthie, who'd packed travel toys and snacks but forgotten Juju, Poppy's beloved stuffed elephant, which led to a complete meltdown at Heathrow security. Cait had bought the Furby at the airport gift shop despite—or maybe because of—Bram's recent warning that if Cait kept rewarding Poppy's tantrums, she would grow up to be just like her. A year had passed since Bram had finally signed the divorce papers, but Cait still resented him for the hell he'd put her through to complete the process, not to mention the astonishing cost of the lawyers.

As Poppy flipped through the pages to find one to color, Cait picked up her phone and tried to retrieve the email.

"I want you to watch me," Poppy said.

"Ooh," Cait said. "Lovely."

"You're not looking."

Cait put her phone down. "I am."

"It's Dorothy!" Poppy ripped the page out and handed it to Cait.

The entire picture was covered in Poppy's new favorite color: fire-engine red. All of Dorothy, the sky, the *yellow* brick road—it looked like a massacre.

"This one's for Grammy." Poppy held up a picture of Munchkinland.

"She'll love it," Cait assured her. "And maybe you can use different colors? Like the sky is blue and the brick road is—"

Poppy grabbed her red crayon. "I know, but I like red."

Cait buzzed the flight attendant to find out what was happening with the internet.

"It's not working," the flight attendant said.

Cait forced a smile. "Right. That's why I'm asking. Is it going to be fixed?"

"Let me check."

"Thanks," Cait said, and ordered a Bulleit Rye for herself and an apple juice and pretzels for Poppy. Over the last year, she'd traveled up to four nights a week while trying to make partner. She'd watch mothers board the plane with children the same age as the twins and fight back tears because she missed them so much. Now here they were beside her, and all she longed for was to be alone. Being a single mother of twins still felt like a joke the universe was playing on her.

For sure it had cost her the partnership at McHenry & Adams, despite all those nights away and bringing in more clients than any other associate two years running. "Look under the table," she'd told Raymond and Will last week when they announced that Neil made partner over her. "You're all wearing the same shoes. I quit." She drank two glasses of Veuve Clicquot at the Wolseley across the street, then went for a long walk in Green Park. She could not believe how many people were out and about, just strolling. *Don't any of you have jobs?* She was in no position to quit, really. She had some savings, but the divorce had made a sizable dent. She sat on a bench by a mother feeding her toddler apple slices. Drinking champagne on an empty stomach gave her a feeling of lightness she suspected would dissipate as soon as the reality of what she'd done sank in, and she'd have to make plans for what was next.

But so far, it hadn't. When she'd returned her laptop to the office yesterday, the morning was full of sunshine, and a feeling of liberation washed over her as she left for the last time.

"Here you go."

Cait smiled as the flight attendant handed her their drinks. She could almost see herself from another perspective. A confident, independent mother sitting in first class with her beautiful children. Bram may have been useless as a father, but at least he'd passed on his Dutch bone structure. *What a charmed life*, she imagined the flight attendant thinking.

"Cheers," she said, following the script, and clinked glasses with Poppy.

Poppy clutched the red crayon and made furious strokes across the page. Cait was about to show her, again, the correct way to hold a writing utensil, but she decided to let it go for now. Five years old is still a baby. Obviously she would be upset about Juju. Why was Cait always so hard on her?

The Irish Goodbye

But she knew why. Whereas Augustus was blessed with an easygoing temperament, Poppy was most like her. Not just hungry but bottomless.

Cait tried the Wi-Fi once more but couldn't get a signal. Frustrated, she set her phone on the tray table next to her drink, slid on her eye mask, and settled into the seat. The Xanax and whiskey were beginning to work their magic, and all the sharp edges softened. She wasn't sure how long she was asleep before Poppy jolted her awake, standing in the aisle with tears streaming down her face. Cait started to speak, but her words ran together in a garbled mess. She struggled to sit up, gripping the armrests to orient herself. "What's wrong?" she finally managed.

Poppy pouted. "I had to go to the loo. And you're going to be very angry at me."

Cait placed her hand on Poppy's cheek and checked her pants. "Did you wee yourself?"

Poppy pulled away, frowning. "No!"

"What is it, then?" She strove to keep her words clear and distinct, regretting the whiskey.

Poppy leaned against the seat in front of her, and the man in it stirred.

"Sorry," Cait said to him, and pulled Poppy onto her lap. "Why am I going to be angry?"

Poppy buried her face in her hands, and when Cait pried them away, Poppy mumbled something that sounded like *disown*.

"Darling." Cait stifled a laugh. "Whatever it is, I'm not going to disown you."

Poppy peeked her face out from behind her hands. "No. I dropped your phone. It's in the toilet."

Cait jerked up, and Poppy fell to the floor, where she let out a wail.

"Is everything okay?" the man asked.

"Yes, thank you," Cait said.

She started to lift Poppy, but when Poppy flung herself back onto the floor, she kneeled and whispered into her ear, "Stand up and stop making a fuss or—"

"I want Juju!" Poppy sobbed.

More people turned to see what was happening, and the flight attendant appeared behind the curtain to ask if Poppy needed anything.

"She's not hurt," Cait said. "She's just upset because . . . Can you watch them for a minute? I need to find my phone."

The flight attendant explained that it was not her job to watch children, but Cait hurried past her, locating her phone in the bathroom, wedged in the toilet's hole and soaking in some blue sludge. She used a clump of paper towels to retrieve and dry it off. Another flight attendant appeared at the door.

"Oh, dear," she said.

Cait turned on her phone, and a streak of obnoxiously fluorescent lines blipped across the screen before it blacked out. "Do you have any dry rice?"

"We don't have that."

A lump formed in Cait's throat as she wrapped her phone in fresh paper towels. She couldn't even remember the last time she had backed it up. Panic rushed through her body, settling into a helpless despair for everything she had likely lost. All those precious photos she had taken of the twins in the Cotswolds for her holiday cards. And what about the résumé she had updated in the Notes app and the contacts she'd been reaching out to for job leads? Had any of that been saved?

To make matters worse, she hadn't gotten around to buying a new laptop, and now she had no private way to read Luke's email or to get in touch with him during her visit to her parent's house that weekend. She and Luke had been trying to make plans to see each other, but nothing was definite yet, because she would have to sneak away from her family to make it happen.

She returned to her seat to find both kids sitting calmly and listening to audiobooks, which annoyed her nearly as much as it relieved her. The flight attendant patted Cait on the arm. "The internet's back up!"

"Great," Cait said. "Thanks."

The Irish Goodbye

The flight attendant tried to clear what was left of the watery Bulliet Rye, but Cait retrieved it and drank it in one gulp.

"I'll have another." She handed her the empty glass.

What was she thinking, telling Ruthie she didn't need her to come on the trip? But even before quitting the firm, Cait worried about money. Ruthie's wages. The twins' private school tuition, which Bram negotiated his way out of in the divorce settlement, because he made—what?—ten thousand euros a year less than her. The mortgage on the flat in Clapham. Even these three first-class tickets to New York had cost more than renting the house in the Cotswolds that October.

It wasn't just the money. It was how Alice would judge her for bringing a nanny home.

Cait could hear the voice of her therapist, Dr. Wagner, inside her head. *And what would that mean? For your sister to judge you like that?*

Since moving to London, Cait had mostly avoided holidays with her family, which had turned into subdued affairs where Alice and her mother cooked, and her father made a teary toast. Instead, she'd spend them with Bram's family in Amsterdam or would fly her parents in for the week before Christmas. Sometimes Maggie would visit for her winter break.

Things had been—*fine*. That's the word Cait supposed she would use to describe her life before Luke reached out to her last month, the first time in well over a decade. With her endless travel for work, and the weekends consumed with shuffling the kids from piano classes to soccer practices, she didn't have time to think beyond what was most pressing and urgent. She'd gone on a few dates on the rare night the kids were with Bram, but often she'd find herself in bed with a bottle of bubbly, hoping to stumble across a halfway decent Netflix series that she hadn't already binged.

Her social life was pretty much nonexistent. She'd never been good with female friendships, and her two closest friends in London were the wives of Bram's colleagues at Deutsche Bank. She'd quickly come to learn that leaving her marriage made her a threat—either an unwelcome reminder that their own marriages could fail or an image of freedom they secretly envied.

When she first met Bram at a party in law school at Columbia, she thought he was just another rich European grad student who casually referenced deep-water soloing in Mallorca and spent summers hiking Mount Fuji with his grandparents. He had grown up in Amsterdam, and his mother was half Japanese; he could speak Japanese, Dutch, German, and a beautifully accented English he'd used to seduce Cait away from all the meaningless flings and party boys she used to date. Still, she would have laughed if someone had told her in those early days that she would marry him. He was good-looking, and they had fun together, but he was often petulant, and his thirst for adrenaline reminded her a bit too much of Topher. She considered him just another fling. When he asked her to marry him—while taking tequila shots at a bar on the Lower East Side a couple of days after Topher died—she thought he was kidding, but she'd just been too vulnerable and disoriented to resist.

The first few years postwedding weren't bad. They settled into London and their jobs, traveled for both work and play. They lived independent lives, but that wasn't a problem until Cait decided it was time to start a family. They'd always talked about having kids, but now Bram wasn't sure he wanted them anymore. Eventually, he said he was willing to go along with it if it was important to her. It took a year for her to get pregnant, and in that time, they started fighting about everything—in particular, Cait's long hours at work ("Do you even have time to fit a kid into your life?") and whether to stay in London, which she wanted, or move to Amsterdam to be closer to his family, which he wanted. They both panicked when the first ultrasound revealed twins. Despite the night nurses and live-in nanny, the first few years were an exhausting sprint. She knew the marriage was over when she began to cringe at his touch. It wasn't just the sex that repulsed her. Her entire body revolted if he put his feet on her lap while they sat on the couch or if he tried to hold her hand as they walked down the street. She could no longer stand the smell of him eating his sardines and saltines, the curdled sound of his breathing—even his accent started to grate on her. Really, though, she just couldn't look fifty years down the road and see growing old with him.

She'd been the one to ask for the divorce, but when she shared with Dr. Wagner that she loathed being alone, he quickly scribbled something in his notebook. She still sometimes wondered what he'd written. She began to feel that while things with Bram had never been perfect, at least when they were together, there was someone to text when her plane landed or to wake in the middle of the night when the fire alarm malfunctioned and she had no idea how to change the battery.

She hadn't seen or spoken to Luke Larkin since the night of Topher's wake thirteen years ago. But back in September, she'd sent him a condolence card after learning that his mother had died. At the last minute, she included her email address and told him to look her up if he ever made it to London. A week later, his name appeared in her inbox.

c,
hello from the past.
i'll be on your side of the pond by way of morocco the last week of september.
martini(s) at dukes?
ll

After writing out at least half a dozen lengthy responses, she kept it simple:

Date? Time?

He wrote back immediately with the details.

She wasn't sure what to expect, seeing him again, but the moment he waved to her and stood up from the plush velvet wingback at Dukes, she decided she was going to sleep with him—again, not as a dewy-eyed first-timer. Why shouldn't she? They were adults now. Her parents were on another continent and his were no longer alive. They didn't have to answer to anyone but themselves. As much as she tried to resist it, she caught herself fantasizing about jetting off with him on some yacht now that he'd retired after selling the tech company he'd started right out of college.

Cait and her sisters had trash-talked him, surmising that Luke's parents probably helped him fund his company with blood money from the lawsuit after Daniel's accident, but she didn't know for sure. Luke lived in Boston and seemed to spend most of his time traveling the world on his sailboat and working with nonprofits, at least according to his LinkedIn. Not that she had stalked him or anything.

Those years under the sun had left their mark, and Cait was almost relieved to find he looked older than his forty-three years. His hair was streaked with gray, and his forehead lined with fine wrinkles. But he had the same relentlessly blue eyes with long, dark lashes that had mesmerized her as a teenager, and well beyond.

By the second martini, her hand was on his thigh.

"I was worried you wouldn't want to see me because of how we'd left things the last time," he said.

"Let's not talk about that," Cait said.

Why bring up what happened after Topher's wake, with her hand where it was? He hadn't attended the services but had come down from Boston to see her. She'd admitted that she often wondered if her feelings for him were just an unresolved adolescent crush or something more real. Her whole body ached with grief from the wake. But Luke had looked at her and said, "Go to London. Bram, the job, it all sounds right." And so she had.

Holding his hand now, she downed the last sip of her martini and leaned in closer. He had a slight scar on his upper lip from when they were in high school and Topher threw an errant baseball that Luke swung at and missed. Every time she saw it, she remembered how she'd held her cherry popsicle to his lip to keep the swelling down as they'd headed to the school nurse, and she'd teased him that there was nothing sexier than a popsicle mustache on a guy. The scar used to tickle her when they kissed.

"Do you have a room here?" she asked him.

Luke frowned. "I don't," he said. "And I can't stay long. I have a benefit for a grantee's NGO that I need to swing by. That's actually why I'm in town."

Cait sat back, embarrassed, and chided herself for being so presumptuous. For once, Bram had stepped up to watch the kids so she could have a night out, and she'd expected something different from the evening.

Luke stood to put on his Belstaff motorcycle jacket but stopped midway. "Will you be at the Folly for Thanksgiving?" he asked.

Cait looked up at him and smiled. "The Folly," she said. "I haven't heard anyone other than my family call it that in a long time." She felt an unexpected pang for her childhood home. A five-bedroom Victorian perched on a peninsula overlooking the Peconic Bay, the house had been in her father's family since the early 1900s. As the story went, Cait's great-grandfather christened the property "the Folly" because it was three stories tall and more than double the size of the neighboring beach cottages—and with only a wife and teenage son, what did he need with that much space? The original welcome sign, sea weathered and barely legible, now hung above the stone fireplace in the kitchen.

"I'll be in Port Haven cleaning out my mom's house that week," Luke continued. "Come home."

"This is my home," Cait said.

Luke looked around the room. "Is it?"

He kissed her cheek when he put her in the cab. She waited a few days to email him, letting him know she'd booked tickets. Again, he wrote back immediately.

i can't wait to see you

3.

ALICE

For every task Alice crossed off her to-do list, another popped up to take its place. She needed to meet the architect at her latest client's house to review the local safety codes for the renovations, her older son's basketball game started in less than an hour, and as she stood in the basement laundry room rattling off a quick prayer to Saint Anthony to find Finn's missing jersey, her mother called to say the catering crew had arrived at the Folly early to set up.

"They're not supposed to be there until tomorrow," Alice said. She pressed the phone against her shoulder as she rifled through the dirty clothes.

"I told them," her mother said, as if that settled it.

"Where's Dad?"

"Downstairs with his trains. He's no use."

Alice's father had retired last year as an engineer at the Brookhaven National Laboratory. He now spent most of his time hiking or rearranging his massive train collection in the basement.

The Irish Goodbye

Alice was furious that Cait had hired caterers for Thanksgiving dinner in the first place.

"I have to meet with David," Alice said.

"David?"

"The architect I've been working with at the Hickeys' for the last two months?"

"Of course," her mother said. Then: "Maybe you can swing by for a quick chat before?"

Alice wanted to say no, but she imagined her mother tripping on the flagstone and hurting her knee again. "I'll be there in a few."

She dug out Finn's jersey from the laundry basket, hidden under a heap of damp dish towels, and inspected a stain on the collar. Ketchup? Tomato sauce? Blood? She threw the jersey into the dryer along with some fabric softener sheets to mask the odor.

Upstairs, she found her husband, Kyle, in the garage, busy fixing their younger son's bike. His tools were meticulously arranged next to him like an army of obedient soldiers awaiting his command. If only he had the same level of enthusiasm for the rest of the house as he did for the garage. Kyle was the principal at Saint Mary's, where the boys attended school, and he had less than an hour between getting home that afternoon and taking Finn back for his basketball game. This was not exactly how she wanted him to spend that time.

"Do you have to do that now?" she asked.

Kyle tinkered with something on the wheel. "James needs to get off his electronics and move his body," he said. "This'll be good for him."

She could have used a hand getting ready for Thanksgiving, but the conversation she really wanted to have, about dividing the household chores more equally now that she was working again, was much larger and not worth getting into at this point. And, honestly, she didn't feel she was making enough money yet to justify asking for the help. She estimated she earned around ten dollars an hour if she added up all the time she spent working at the Hickeys'. She loved the work, though, and would have done it for free if she had to. Still, with her secret hope to go back to grad school for interior design, she knew she had to figure out a way to find more balance.

To remind him of everything she still had to do that day, she said, "I need to swing by my parents' to deal with the caterers before stopping by the Hickeys'."

Kyle checked the time on his watch. "They scheduled a meeting the afternoon before Thanksgiving?"

Alice had her own frustrations about the timing of the meeting, but she was desperate to please her biggest client, Georgia Hickey. It was a small project—the Hickeys' guest bungalow—but a rare chance to grow her portfolio, and if everything went well, Georgia had promised to introduce her to all her country club friends who needed a designer.

"I'll be in and out in no time," she assured Kyle.

Kyle nodded, but Alice worried he thought she was spreading herself too thin. Maybe she was. She couldn't remember when they'd last gone to bed together at the same time or enjoyed a glass of wine on the deck at the end of the day.

It was cold enough in the garage to see her breath, but Kyle wore only his suit pants and a white undershirt. His middle-aged paunch was becoming more pronounced, but his arms and legs were muscular from cycling. Affection spread through her as she watched him flip the bike right side up. *This is how he shows the boys he cares*, she thought. She walked over to him and kissed the top of his head. He reached for her hand and squeezed it once before returning to the task at hand.

In the kitchen, she found James in his karate uniform, leaning on the counter and picking at a bowl of fruit. There were times, like now, when he looked so much like a young Topher that she felt as if she were seeing her actual brother standing in front of her, with his shaggy mess of strawberry curls and his hazel eyes that tended toward green. It was disquieting.

"You don't have practice today," she said.

"I know." He stuck a raspberry onto the tip of his thumb and nibbled at it. "But I want to show Augustus and Poppy my uniform."

Alice couldn't get over the names Augustus and Poppy. Her older sister had always been a snob, but this was even worse than the transatlantic accent she had acquired since moving to London more than a decade ago.

As she packed a cooler with Gatorade, she called down the hall for Finn to get ready.

When she turned around, she found Kyle walking into the kitchen, cleaning bike grease off his hands with a rag. "Are we sleeping at the Folly?" he asked.

James popped another raspberry into his mouth. "Yes! Can we?"

Alice shot Kyle a look. She hadn't told the boys about her mother's request that they stay, mainly because she was deciding if she could stand that much time with Cait.

"We'll see," Alice said.

"I'm fine with it," Kyle said.

James jumped up on the stool, pressed his hands together in prayer, and cocked his head like a puppy.

Finn appeared at the kitchen entrance. Since starting eighth grade, he had grown and was now officially taller than Alice.

"There you are," she said.

Finn pressed the jersey to his nose. "My shirt stinks. Did you wash it?"

"Your mother is not your maid," Kyle said. "You can do your own laundry."

So can you, Alice thought.

"Sorry, Mother." Finn kissed her cheek. "You're coming to the game, right?"

"Oh, Finny, I can't. I'm so sorry."

There was no question that Finn liked things better when she wasn't working. He was stuck bumming rides from his buddies after practice and watching his little brother until she got home. To try to make it up to him, she'd slipped notes into his lunchbox at the beginning of the school year—

things like *Have an awesome day!* and *Love you!*—but he had recently told her that he was too old for that sort of thing.

Finn made a sad face but then walked by James and punched his arm.

"Ow!" James cried. He tried to swing back, but Finn jumped away.

"What was that for?" Alice said, restraining James.

"Stop messing with my stuff," Finn said.

"I didn't!"

James squirmed out of Alice's hold and charged Finn. Both boys rolled around on the kitchen floor until Kyle finally told Finn to get his sneakers. They jumped up and bounded down the hallway, pushing each other against the walls.

"Hey!" Kyle thundered.

The house immediately quieted as the boys hurried to their room. Kyle had grown up as an army brat and later became an Eagle Scout, president of his Catholic Studies Club at Seton Hall, and a National Guard soldier before getting hired as the principal at Saint Mary's. He'd perfected his "Hey!" so that it spoke for itself. Even Alice obeyed.

Kyle picked at the browning bananas in James's bowl. "We don't have to stay at your parents' if you don't want to," he said.

"No," she said. "We can. It'll make my mom happy."

Kyle nodded. His parents lived with his sister in New Jersey. Nothing was expected of him. In many ways, this was a relief. Alice's father-in-law had Alzheimer's, and Kyle's sister had the means to hire a caregiver. But Alice also knew Kyle got off easy because he was the son, not the daughter.

Kyle grabbed his jacket. She was trying something new lately—seeing what would happen if she didn't initiate the goodbye or welcome-home kiss.

"Mukesh wants to know what time he should come tomorrow," Kyle said as he tossed the fruit bowl in the dishwasher.

Mukesh was one of Kyle's buddies from the Guard. He was moving to London after the New Year to start work at a law firm, and Kyle had some grand plan to play matchmaker with Cait.

"Two o'clock," Alice said. "But I think she's too mean for him."

"That's what he likes," Kyle said, and winked. Then he called down the hall, "Finn, I'm leaving."

No kiss.

In her room, Alice slumped onto the unmade bed. She needed to put together a decent outfit for her meeting with David and leave soon, but exhaustion overtook her. She closed her eyes for a minute of relief, only to wake up to James yelling from the other room about missing his green karate belt.

"You can wear your uniform without the belt!" she shouted back. She rose from the bed even more depleted than before. How much time had passed?

"But then they won't know I'm a green belt," James said, walking into the room.

"You can tell them."

The phone rang. Her mother again. She looked at James. "Don't answer it."

She quickly changed, packed a bag of clothes for Kyle and herself, then went into the boys' room to get their stuff ready for the weekend.

When she walked in, she found James leaning against his bed holding a magazine. It took her a second to realize that it was a *Hustler*, the cover featuring a woman teasingly peeling off her bikini top.

"James!" she said.

He threw the magazine across the room and held up his hands.

Alice picked it up. "Where'd you get this?"

"It was in my duffel bag!"

Alice stuffed the magazine back in the bag. "Is this why Finn was upset with you earlier?" she asked. "Did he use your bag?"

James thought for a moment. "No, but Daddy used it yesterday for Finn's sneakers. He said they were too stinky for the car." He began crying. "Is he in trouble?"

Alice kissed his wet cheek. "No," she said. "Go put on your shoes."

James scampered off, and Alice eyed the magazine again. *Good God.* She was mostly confused. Kyle had always insisted porn was against their faith. She remembered a conversation with her sisters years ago where she had mentioned this, and Cait had laughed, making Alice feel like a total idiot in that way only her older sister knew how to do. Was she? With their sex life what it was these days, was this what he'd resorted to? Regardless, she was pissed he'd hidden it in James's bag of all places.

On her way out to the garage, Alice switched off the lights in the kitchen and asked James to grab the cooler Finn had forgotten, as she didn't have a spare hand. In a rush, she flung all their bags, including the duffel with the magazine, onto the passenger seat and headed to her parents' house. The snow was now sticking to the ground.

At the Folly, she pulled into the circular driveway behind the caterer's truck and handed James some bags to take into the house, instructing him not to tell his grandparents about the magazine. As she unpacked the rest of the car—everything but the duffel, which she left on the front seat—she noticed once again the rotting shingles along the north side of the house.

She could never get a straight answer from her father about what remained of the mortgage they'd taken out to settle the Larkins' lawsuit. All she knew was that they were still paying it off, and despite Cait's occasional financial contributions, her parents struggled to maintain the property. She'd tried to bring up selling the house, but her parents wouldn't hear it and her sisters were clueless about what it took to keep a hundred-year-old Victorian up and running. Anyway, she thought now, where would her parents even go? Beach cottages in Port Haven these days fetched millions before they even hit the market.

Inside, she found her father snacking on banana bread at the kitchen island. He was dressed in his beloved argyle sweater vest, probably to make a good impression on Isabel, whom he would meet that afternoon. A roaring fire made the room warmer than usual. Alice unzipped her jacket, poured herself a glass of cold water, and gulped it down. Then she turned to her father and said, "You need to call someone to fix the shingles."

Robert cut James a slice from the loaf and handed it to him on a paper towel. "Don't worry about the shingles," he said. "They're fine."

"They're not fine. And it's going to start impacting the integrity of the house."

Her father ignored her and turned to James. "Guess what arrived today!"

"What?" James asked as he took an enormous bite of the banana bread.

"The new Ferris wheel for the amusement park."

"I want to see it," James said, and off they went to the basement to play with trains.

Alice made her way to the living room, where she heard her mother laughing. "I'm here," she singsonged.

"There you are now," Nora said. She introduced her to Beth, the caterer, who stood nearby with a clipboard.

Alice noted that her mother still limped slightly, despite the new sneakers they'd recently bought her and all the physical therapy. At least she was using her cane. At just over five feet tall, Nora often felt doctors treated her like a child, and she could be defiant about their directions. Alice could relate. She had inherited her mother's small frame.

Alice checked her watch. "You've got me for ten minutes. What do you need?"

"Where should we set up the oyster bar for tomorrow?" Beth asked.

"Oyster bar?" Alice said.

"Your sister ordered three dozen Belons."

You must be kidding me.

Alice glanced at her mother.

Nora shrugged. "It's just a bit of fun."

"It's ostentatious." Alice turned to Beth. "Sorry."

Beth held up her hands. "You're good. I just need to tell the gals where to put it all." She passed Alice the clipboard. "And for you to approve the invoice."

Alice put on her glasses. Aside from the turkey, Cait had ordered an additional set of dairy-free sides. Apparently the evening also required not just two waiters but a bartender, too. The bill was nearly five thousand dollars. The number made Alice slightly nauseated, and she leaned on the arm of the leather sofa.

"This costs more than a weekend at Disney World," she said.

She knew this because it was James's dream to go to Space Mountain, and she was saving to make that happen. She had about as much money as the raw bar cost.

"What can I say?" Beth said. "Your sister has good taste."

Nora beamed. "Oh, she does, she does."

"It's Thanksgiving, not New Year's Eve," Alice said. She turned to Beth. "What about the pies? I don't see them here."

"You're baking the pies," Nora said. "Didn't Cait talk to you about making sure at least one is dairy free? Maybe the apple pie with shortening instead of butter?"

"*I'm* making the pies?"

"You make them every year."

"Do I have to shuck the oysters, too?"

Nora tsked. "Don't be cheeky."

Alice handed the clipboard back to Beth. "I guess it's approved," she said. "You can set everything up by the bay window in the living room."

Beth nodded. "That's what your mother suggested."

Alice followed Nora into her painting studio. After Topher died, her mother had stopped painting for years. They never talked about it, but Alice suspected it was a form of penance. Instead, her mother served as a sacristan for Father Kelly at Saint Mary's and delivered the Eucharist to the sick and homebound. Then one day, Alice sensed a new energy at the Folly and discovered her mother painting again. Something shifted in Alice, too. As Finn grew into a toddler, she missed working and socializing with adults beyond the other mothers she met at the park. There was a gnawing in her to do something more, and she enrolled in a design class at the local art center.

Alice stood now in the doorway and watched her mother clean her paintbrushes. She checked her watch again. She had five minutes to get to the Hickeys', but she couldn't leave without mentioning Maggie's text from earlier that morning about bringing Isabel home.

"It's wonderful," Alice said, and when her mother didn't respond, she added, "Isn't it?"

Nora set a brush on the rag to dry. "I'm not sure I know. I haven't met her yet."

Alice cocked her head and followed her mother into the kitchen. "And that's the point. You'll get to know her."

"I suppose I will."

Alice held her mother by the shoulders. "This is important to Maggie," she said. "You need to make Isabel feel welcome."

Nora frowned. "I would never make her feel unwelcome."

"Good." Alice snatched her keys off the counter. "I'm holding you to that."

Alice stepped outside and took a breath of fresh air. The snow felt good against her face, which was sweaty from the fire inside, but almost immediately she was hit with the smell of something—ammonia? Sulfur? Looking down, she spotted the trail of greenish-brown droppings along the path to the garden. *Damn it.* She'd meant to clean the goose poop yesterday but had forgotten.

She was on her way to the Hickeys' when the smell returned, stirring a disgust in her so intense she gagged and had to pull over. She opened the car door and tapped the bottom of her boots on the side to scrape off any droppings. Her body broke out in a cold sweat as she called Georgia to say she'd be a few minutes late.

"David just got here," Georgia said. "He's in a rush."

Alice tried to swallow, but her mouth was dry and sticky. "I'm on my way," she finally managed.

"Super. We'll see you soon."

When Alice arrived at the bungalow, she found Georgia waving for her at the end of her driveway. She lowered her window.

"David wants to meet on Monday," Georgia said. "He had to get home to cook." She looked at Alice and tilted her head to the side. "You look a little—" She scrunched her face in that way she did when Alice showed her a fabric she didn't like.

Alice glanced in the rearview mirror. She was pale, her eyes sunken. Had she seriously not put on lipstick? She must be coming down with something.

"You're sure?"

"I'm sure. You go take care of yourself, and happy Thanksgiving!"

Alice pulled away, and the nausea settled enough to allow her to grab the groceries for the pies in town.

At a stoplight on her way back, she eyed the magazine peeking out from James's bag. Maybe Kyle had confiscated it from a student? She thought of Kyle not kissing her that afternoon when he left the house—or ever, it seemed lately—and a surge of anger shot through her.

She turned the car toward Saint Mary's. At the school, she parked in the bus lane and snatched the cooler and the duffel with the magazine. In the gymnasium, it was halftime of Finn's game. His team, the Jayhawks, was up against the Golden Eagles from a neighboring town.

Finn waved to her from the court, where he was practicing shots. She waved back and gestured to the cooler, then sat on the bleachers and hoped she wouldn't run into anyone she knew. Kyle stood at the far corner of the court wearing a turkey hat, adjusting the padding on the basketball pole. When they moved to Port Haven and he became principal, she felt like they were two kids pretending to be adults. But he was so good at the job that even Father Kelly soon deferred to him on matters beyond his administrative duties. Parents and students alike adored him.

Alice tried to remember the last time they'd had sex. A few weeks ago. Halloween. She'd made lasagna, and her belly was full from that and the Kit Kats she'd snuck from James's pumpkin bucket. But when Kyle placed his hand on her breast, she slid her body beneath his, because it was so rare for him to initiate anything intimate these days. She'd missed him. It was over within minutes, clothes mostly on. Had they even kissed?

After the Jayhawks won the second-half tip-off, Alice walked over to Kyle and tapped him on the shoulder. "Oh, hey," he said, turning around. "I didn't think you were coming."

"You forgot Finn's cooler."

"We have drink boxes."

"And . . ." She scanned the room to make sure no one was nearby, then opened the bag an inch or so to let Kyle see the magazine.

He reached inside. "What is it?"

Alice yanked the bag away but quickly flashed him the magazine. "James said you were the last to use the bag."

Kyle frowned. "That's not mine."

Finn stood at the three-point line watching them, an expression of dread on his face. She and Kyle turned to each other at the same time.

Alice's stomach lurched, and the vomit burst forth so quickly and violently that she barely had time to aim for the bag.

4.

MAGGIE

"This is where you live?" Isabel asked as Maggie pulled past the SLOW GEESE CROSSING sign at one entrance of the Folly's driveway.

"No, I live in a one-bedroom faculty apartment next door to you," Maggie said. "This is where I grew up."

"At East Egg?"

Maggie laughed as she parked her Jeep next to the guest cottage. Just as the chair by the fireplace had always been her designated seat at family meals, this was her spot, inherited from Topher, on the pebbled circular driveway. She pressed Isabel's hand to her mouth.

"Listen," she said, "I've decided that if my mom's a jerk, we're just going to leave."

Isabel craned her neck to peek out the window, then turned to Maggie. "I have a cousin in Brooklyn," she said. "We can always go there." She grabbed the sunflowers they'd bought in town from the back seat and opened the door. "But let's go find out."

James burst forth from the front door in his karate uniform and snow boots as Maggie gathered their bags. "Aunt Maggie's here!" he screamed from the wraparound porch, and ran back into the house.

Isabel hooked a finger through one of Maggie's belt loops, pulled her closer, and kissed her hard on each cheek.

"I saw two girls kissing today," James said, reappearing at the door. "In a magazine."

Maggie pulled away from Isabel's hold. "Did you?"

"But I'm not supposed to tell Grammy."

Maggie looked at Isabel and raised her arms in a *don't ask me* gesture.

Inside, the house was eerily quiet, and Maggie was surprised it did not smell as she'd expected: like her mother and Alice had been cooking for the past two days. James kicked off his boots by the coatrack, and Maggie dropped their bags in the foyer at the base of the stairs. They were headed to the kitchen when her mother called from the dining room.

"Mairéad," she said, using Maggie's full name, as she often did in front of guests.

They walked down the long hallway, and Maggie caught her reflection in a mirror, quickly undoing her shaggy ponytail to please her mother, who preferred her hair down. It had been years since she'd brought a friend back to the Folly, and now she beheld the house through Isabel's eyes: the worn needlepoint rugs covering the herringbone floors, the pressed-glass chandeliers that had been in the family for decades, and her mother's landscapes crowding the walls.

They found her mother at the head of the dining room table, folding linen napkins around silverware. Maggie was relieved to see her social graces on full display when she looked up.

"Hello, hello." She stood with the help of her cane.

Maggie hadn't visited since the summer, before her mother fell gardening and hurt her knee, and she hadn't realized Nora was still using her cane. She was thinner, too, if possible, lost in a periwinkle shawl that brought out the blue in her perpetually wet eyes. Her silver hair was pulled back in a tight bun, and her reddish eyebrows arched in a look of nervous anticipation when Maggie introduced her to Isabel.

"Thank you so much for having me," Isabel said, and handed her the sunflowers.

"Oh, splendid," Nora said. "Perfect for the table tomorrow."

Nora glanced out the bay window. A flock of geese were making their way up the snowy hill from the beach. At first, Maggie couldn't make out what was different, but then she saw just beyond the garden that nearly half the fence leading to the beach had collapsed.

"I'm worried about Cait with this weather," her mother said. "Your father's tracking her flight and they've just landed, but we haven't heard from them yet." She turned back to Maggie and Isabel. "It's grand all the same. You're here now, and that's what's important. Can I make you tea?"

Maggie took the flowers so her mother could use her cane, and they walked into the kitchen to get a vase.

"What's all this?" Maggie asked of the dozen empty food platters and Bunsen burners covering the center island.

"Cait hired caterers." Her mother flipped on the electric kettle.

Maggie placed the flowers in a large Ball jar glass. "Why?"

"It's a big crew this year—"

"Who's coming?"

Her mother retrieved a sparkling crystal vase from the cabinet. "All of us, plus Kyle invited his friend Mukesh." She removed the flowers from the vase Maggie had chosen and plopped them into the new one. "And Father Kelly, of course," she added. Maggie simply nodded. "Which makes thirteen. Cait thought it would be easier with my knee and all. They're high-end caterers and have a beautiful meal planned."

"That's nice," Maggie said, though she found the idea of eating catered food on Thanksgiving slightly depressing.

Her mother prepared three cups of Barry's tea with extra milk and sugar as James entered the kitchen. He stood in front of Isabel and held up his fists. "I'm a green belt," he declared. "But my mom lost my belt."

"Show me some of your moves," Isabel said.

While James exploded in a swirl of "hi-yas" and kicks and punches, Maggie's father emerged from the basement and gave Isabel a big hug, putting Maggie at ease. Then he turned to Maggie and said, "You're behaving yourself?"

"Trying," Maggie said.

"Well, don't try too hard. There's no fun in that."

"And you?"

"Oh, I'm behaving myself," he said. "It gets easier when you're old. Too many people watching." He tilted his head toward her mother.

"Go on," her mother said, but laughed.

There in the kitchen with her parents, Maggie could admit how much she wanted them not just to accept Isabel but to actually like her. Everyone seemed to be getting along, and she felt a hint of cautious relief at having pushed through her doubts earlier that morning. She could almost imagine a future where coming home didn't make her feel so unbearably lonely.

"I'll show Isabel around," she said once her father and James went back downstairs to the trains.

Her mother opened her mouth, seemingly to say something else, but then stopped and turned to admire the flowers. "They really are stunning. Full of joy."

Maggie considered asking her what was on her mind but decided against it. If Nora had something to say, she'd say it eventually. Besides, there was a good chance Maggie wouldn't want to hear it.

Maggie closed the door to her bedroom, placed their teas on the desk, and scooped Isabel into her arms as they tumbled onto the bed.

"That went well," Isabel said, kissing her forehead.

"It did," Maggie admitted. She kicked off her sneakers.

Isabel stood and walked around the bedroom. "It's like a museum of your childhood."

Nora was reluctant to throw anything away. Aside from removing

Maggie's Jeff Buckley and Ani DiFranco posters from the walls, Nora hadn't changed much in the room since Maggie's senior year of high school, when she'd last lived in the house.

"Ooh," Isabel said, stumbling upon Maggie's old mix CDs stacked next to her decades-old stereo and plastic gold track trophies. "I'll need to go through these at some point." Next, she studied the shelves covered in books—everything from the book of saints Maggie received on her First Communion to the Jeanette Winterson and Michelle Tea novels she'd buy on trips to the East Village with her high school friends and hide from her mother. Isabel pulled a beat-up copy of *Anna Karenina* from the bookcase. "This looks loved. A favorite?"

"Never read it, actually," Maggie admitted. "I bought it used on a field trip in ninth grade. Trying to impress my English teacher, Sister Maria. She was from Russia. Must have been, like, twenty-five years old. Definitely gay. I adored her but couldn't get past all the Russian names, so I read the CliffsNotes instead. Don't tell my students, though."

Isabel laughed and pointed the book at Maggie. "'Anything's better than lying and deceit,'" she quoted in an awful Russian accent.

Maggie laughed but thought, *Indeed*. Her mind drifted again to Sarah, and she shuddered as though that might help her physically purge the memory.

Isabel studied the portrait from Maggie's high school graduation. Though she was more of a tomboy then, Maggie's appearance had pretty much stayed the same. She still wore her brown hair long and parted in the middle, and she could use a round of braces for the slight snaggletooth that her dentist alleged she got from sucking her thumb as a kid but that Isabel claimed to adore and begged her not to correct.

"The lighthouse," Isabel said, looking out the window. She turned to Maggie. "Like your brother's drawing in your office."

Maggie walked to her. The small castle-like tower was nearly hidden in the falling snow.

"It must be hard," Isabel said. "To see that every time you come home."

The Irish Goodbye

Maggie rested her chin on Isabel's shoulder. "It used to be," she said. Then: "I guess sometimes it still is."

* * *

Maggie had known something was wrong when Topher didn't show up at the dentist's office, though she told herself she shouldn't be surprised. She was twenty and home from college, but when they were younger, and he had to pick her up from piano lessons, he'd always arrive well after the session finished.

But this time, as she sat in the waiting room after having three wisdom teeth extracted, she was in pain. There was a pulsing numbness in her mouth, and all she wanted to do was go home and crawl into bed and sleep off the anesthesia. Her parents were in New Jersey visiting a cousin, and Topher was supposed to have been there half an hour ago.

She asked the receptionist to call the house.

"Sorry, hon. Answering machine. I'll leave a message."

Maggie slumped back into her chair and flipped through a *Highlights* magazine that looked like it had been there since she was a kid. Everything about the office was familiar. She remembered coming there with all her siblings, and one by one, they'd go in to have their teeth cleaned while their mother chatted with the receptionist and the rest of them watched cartoons on the TV.

Now the TV was playing the news, talking about school shootings. Maggie was going into her junior year at Wellesley, and she'd recently started an internship at a summer school program at a local high school. She wanted to stop watching the terrible images on the screen but felt obligated not to turn away.

Finally, she asked the receptionist to call her a taxi.

The driver seemed vaguely familiar, but they didn't talk. He smelled like patchouli, only sweeter, and drove slow and steady, which held back the queasy sensation in Maggie's stomach.

Once home, she started to shout Topher's name but stopped. Her mouth felt like an open wound, and she was pretty sure that wasn't normal. The house was still. She stood in the kitchen. The answering machine blinked, probably with the message from the receptionist. Sliced tomatoes and a package of bologna were on the cutting board next to a half-filled glass of milk. Topher must have been home because his Jeep was in the driveway.

Or was the Jeep hers now?

That morning, while they were sipping coffee on the back porch, Maggie mentioned to him that she needed a car now that she had the internship. Out of nowhere, Topher said, "Take mine." He'd been talking about heading to South Korea to teach English for a year, and Maggie was happy for him. Their parents were thrilled, too. But Maggie wasn't sure she trusted his plans, let alone his offer. Her brother had had his Jeep for nearly ten years, and it was home to him, more than any person or place. Plus, he had a history of making promises then changing his mind or, worse, pretending he hadn't made them at all.

To settle the soreness in her gums, she grabbed a warm 7UP from the pantry—her mother's cure for everything, though she insisted it needed to be flat and always stirred it with a spoon to release the bubbles. Was Maggie supposed to drink through a straw or definitely *not* drink through a straw? She had the instructions somewhere in her backpack, but she settled on the latter and cracked open the can as she walked upstairs.

It wasn't the strangeness of the note itself. Nor was it the Palmer penmanship, which their mother had learned from the nuns at the orphanage and insisted they practice when they were kids. What caught Maggie's attention was the haphazard duct tape securing the note, like a silver gash across the wooden expanse of Topher's door.

She took a small sip and swallowed the warm, sweet soda.

Still groggy, it took her a second to grasp that the note didn't make sense as an apology for leaving her at the dentist.

Maggie, don't come in—call Father Kelly. I'm sorry.

The door was locked, which alarmed Maggie. "Topher," she yelled, and her mouth filled with blood. She grabbed extra gauze from her pocket and fumbled to open the packaging before stuffing the pad into the fleshy wound inside her cheek. She knocked and pressed her ear to the door to listen and called his name again. When that didn't work, she retrieved a butter knife from the kitchen to pick the lock.

The room was empty, but there was a smell that made her check the bottom of her sneakers. She opened the window and a breeze flapped the curtains and scattered the papers from the desk to the floor. She picked them up; ink drawings of the lighthouse. Topher was the only one who'd inherited their mother's artistic talents. He dabbled effortlessly and beautifully. Maggie had always assumed that this—more than Topher's being the only boy—was what made him their mother's favorite. She placed the drawings back on the desk, using a worn copy of a Korean translation book as a paperweight. Perhaps he was serious about going to South Korea after all.

She opened the window wider to see if he might be sitting on the roof, which he often did as a kid, despite their mother's warnings. He wasn't.

Maybe he's at the beach. Or he went for a bike ride. Does he even have a bike anymore?

She started to leave the room when she noticed something. There was a tiny den off Topher's room that her parents used to store holiday decorations and winter clothes. Maggie had never seen the door open, but now it was slightly ajar. When she saw the tip of a sneaker jutting out from the opening, she couldn't make sense of its height or angle.

Until, suddenly, she could.

He was too heavy to hold. The extension cord was tied in an impossible sailor's knot she wouldn't be able to undo even if her hands weren't violently shaking. *Oh, God. Oh, God.* She couldn't move him and was not strong enough to lift him. She could hear her own breath, hurried and shallow, and her voice screaming Topher's name.

She kicked the stool he must have used out of the way but couldn't get past the boxes of ornaments to loosen the knot gripping his bruised neck.

She grabbed the stool again but wasn't tall enough to reach the high beam on the ceiling from which the cord hung. *Goddamn it! You just ate lunch! You didn't even clean the fucking dishes! What about South Korea?*

A gust from the window slammed the door into her back, knocking her off the stool. Her mouth gushed more blood, and she spit the gauze onto the floor. The lighthouse foghorn sounded, and all at once, she was back in her body with the startlingly clear understanding that she could not save him.

Back in the kitchen, Maggie's hands shook so much that she could barely press 911 into the phone.

The operator answered. "What's your emergency?"

Maggie's mouth tasted like copper, and she could feel her heart beating in her tender gums as she answered. "I think my brother's dead," she said. "You have to help him. He's dead."

She returned to Topher's room, sat on the edge of his bed, and stared out the window at the lighthouse. She didn't want to leave him alone.

Before she heard the front door open, footsteps pounded up the stairs, and an EMT rushed into the room and escorted her out. Someone took her blood pressure. She was the only patient there who needed attending.

"Do you wish you had listened?" the school counselor asked when Maggie returned to Wellesley. "To his note. His warning?"

Maggie answered yes because she could not stop seeing the dazed look in Topher's eyes and the cord digging into his swollen neck. The smell of his soiled pants. She had nightmares about frantically trying to untangle knots. As she sat in class or tried to fall asleep, his face would appear out of nowhere.

The school counselor told her to write down all the ways she'd supported Topher over the years. She'd been convinced that she must have missed something the morning they spent together before her dentist appointment—something that could have let her see that he needed help. *His body's still warm*, she'd heard an EMT call out when they first arrived.

The Irish Goodbye

She would later learn that meant Topher hadn't been dead very long. If only she hadn't wasted time in that stupid waiting room. She could barely remember the list now, though it comforted her knowing that she'd been one of the few people who hadn't given him a hard time for not having his life figured out. She was almost a decade younger, and it had never been her place to question him. Sure, it upset them all when he disappeared for months, but he was a grown man and free to lead his own life. Or, as it turned out, not.

Still, why had he made it so that she was the one who found him? She must have been picked for some reason, but she had no idea what that was.

* * *

Thirteen years had passed since then. The disturbing images no longer leapt out at her unexpectedly. Therapy and time had helped, even if she still flinched when her students casually said, "I'd rather kill myself than do that," or when Isabel drew the Hanged Man card from her tarot deck. Now, days could pass without her even thinking about Topher, but when she was home, the memories were always there, roiling beneath the surface. She didn't want her brother's life replaced by the nightmare of his death, but that took effort.

She turned from the window and sat on the bed. "Cait wanted my parents to sell the house," she said. Isabel lay down and snuggled against her. "I think that's why she took the job in London right after he died. She said it was to be with Bram, but I didn't believe her. She couldn't stand being here. She rarely comes back."

"Did your parents consider selling it?"

Maggie shook her head. "Too much history, for better or worse."

For years, Maggie wondered what it would be like to open Topher's bedroom door again. These days, though, she mostly worried about what would happen with all his stuff after her parents were gone. She remembered when Nora had to clean out the attic after the roof leaked in high school. They'd found some cool stuff, like her grandfather's old waders and clam rake, as well as the original plan for the Folly, but it took forever because there were four generations' worth of clutter that her mother had to sort through. Nora promised Maggie and her sisters she wouldn't leave them with the same burden, but while the attic was now a TV room for the grandkids, Topher's room remained untouched.

There was a knock at the door and Isabel sat up.

"Come in," Maggie said.

Her mother opened the door a crack and peeked her head through. "Oh," she said, stepping into the room and noting Maggie and Isabel's luggage by the desk. "I wanted to let you know we prepared the cottage for Isabel."

Neither Maggie nor Isabel said a word.

Finally, Maggie said, "Okay."

Her mother nodded and left.

And there it was. Maggie knew her mother had something to say earlier in the kitchen. Even though there was a bed in the cottage, it was pretty much used as a storage space these days. The single-paned windows allowed a draft that made it chilly even in the summer.

"Fuck that," she said to Isabel. "You don't have to sleep in there."

"Well, it's her house," Isabel said. "I'm not going to go against her wishes. Why don't you try talking to her?"

"I'm too pissed right now," Maggie said. "I need to calm down."

She felt a buzz in her back pocket, and when Isabel stood to remove her boots, she checked her phone. She expected the text to be from one of her sisters, but it wasn't. It was from Sarah.

I'm sorry about Friday night. Can we talk?

Maggie wrote her back quickly and discreetly. Though the timing was abysmal, she needed to know if Sarah's apology had anything to do with her getting called into Headmaster Cunningham's office on Monday morning.

Give me a minute. I'll call you.

5.

ALICE

In the gas station restroom, Alice lined the toilet-seat rim with paper towels, sat, and ripped open the pregnancy test. She held the stick in the palm of her hand and thought about the tests she'd taken for her pregnancies with Finn and James. In her own bathroom, with Kyle there. Always, they'd been excited. How different from now.

It can't be. It absolutely cannot be.

After she threw up at the basketball game, Finn ran off the court to see if she was okay. The assistant coach handed her a towel, and within seconds the janitor wheeled over a mop inside a bucket of gray sludgy water, which nearly made her sick again.

"I'm all right," she'd assured Finn, and Kyle instructed him to get back in the game as he escorted her out of the gymnasium. He wanted to take her to the nurse, but she insisted it was the stress of everything—maybe it was?—and that she was feeling better already. Kyle carried the duffel bag gingerly by the handle, zipping it up to hide the magazine before tossing it into the dumpster outside. He cradled her elbow as he walked her to the car.

"You parked in the bus lane," he said when they got to her minivan.

She held on to his hands. "I don't want this to ruin the weekend," she said. "Try to find out what happened, but we can have a bigger conversation with Finn after Thanksgiving."

Kyle nodded and opened her door. He hugged her, but then someone at the far end of the parking lot called out, "Hi, Principal Williams!" and he pulled away and kissed her dryly on the forehead.

"I think the milk in my cereal this morning was off," she said, and climbed into the car. "Or maybe it was all the goose poop at my parents'?"

"The goose poop?"

"Can you clean the walkway tonight?"

He brushed snow off her window. "I'll more likely be shoveling if this keeps up."

She looked up at the snow pouring from the gray sky. "Oh, right."

"Try some Pepto. That'll help."

Alice drove to the pharmacy in the town over, where instead of purchasing Pepto-Bismol, she bought the pregnancy test, which she planned to take in the bathroom there until she opened the door and found shit smeared across the stall walls. Instead, hands shaking, she drove to the well-maintained gas station she'd used when she was pregnant with James and constantly had to pee.

She had spent the last half hour eager to take the test and get the results over with, but now she sat on the edge of the toilet seat, elbows on her knees, chin resting in her upturned palm, nervous to go through with it.

Finally, she released her bladder, then placed the stick on the sink counter, buttoning her jeans as she watched the unmistakable pink lines—had tests always been this fast?—emerge to tell her what she already knew.

What had she done?

This was all her fault. The one—the one!—pill she'd missed when her prescription ran out the month before. Kyle hadn't been keen on her going on birth control in the first place. They'd had to pay for the prescriptions themselves because their health insurance through Saint Mary's didn't cover the cost of contraception. He'd agreed only after James was born, and Alice's preeclampsia was so serious that the doctor said she could have had a stroke.

Alice assumed missing the pill didn't matter, considering they hadn't had sex in so long anyway. Then, Halloween. Her belly full of lasagna and candy and all that. Kyle had looked adorable in the Eeyore costume he'd had to wear after losing a bet with the boys. She still couldn't remember if they'd kissed.

She cradled the test in her hands, dumbfounded.

I don't want this.

She closed her eyes and tried to calm her breathing. She couldn't believe what she was thinking—what she was *feeling*—in such a knee-jerk way.

I don't want this.

Okay, okay, okay, she told herself. Slow down.

She splashed cold water onto her face and neck, then sat back on the toilet and lowered her head between her knees. Blood pulsed in her temples.

Just as she was on the brink of a new life. Just as the boys were getting older and more independent. She would be consumed. No, not consumed. Obliterated.

She wasn't sure how long she'd been sitting there when she heard a knock.

"Sorry," she said to the door. She stood in front of the mirror. The light in the bathroom was brutal. Or was it? Her auburn hair looked like a halo of frizz. She kneaded the red spot on her chin and felt a hard lump she knew would be a full-on cystic pimple by evening.

There was no garbage can in the bathroom, so she stuffed the test back into the box and then into her bag. "Sorry," she said again to an older man in a mechanic's jumper as she opened the door and rushed back to her car.

On the dashboard, she found a Post-it note from Kyle that she hadn't noticed before, reminding her to pick up the dry cleaning. His handwriting was atrocious, and she sometimes wondered if that was intentional, to hide all his misspelled words. She tossed the Post-it onto the passenger seat and thought about how, when they first started dating, he used to leave love notes in her coat pocket.

Kyle had been Alice's first serious boyfriend. They were introduced by mutual friends when she was just out of college, working in marketing for a textile company and living in a two-bedroom apartment with three roommates in Brooklyn Heights. He was in his first year of graduate school. On their first date, he explained that he was studying education, because, as a kid, his undiagnosed dyslexia had made school miserable. This was where he knew he could make a difference.

From the beginning, she admired his discipline. He woke at the same time every morning, even on the weekends, to run. He was close to his family, but not so close that it took over their lives. She'd stopped attending mass regularly in college, but he went every Friday night, and almost immediately after they met, she started to join him. For Kyle, it was about faith, but for her it was about the rituals. The collective worship. The sense of belonging. Even the smell of frankincense. Mass once again became part of the rhythm of her life, and it was comforting. Afterward, they'd go out for sushi or ramen on Montague Street and then back to his studio apartment in Red Hook to watch a movie. While her roommates drank Cosmopolitans they couldn't afford at bars in Tribeca, hoping to meet a guy in finance, Alice couldn't have been happier with her and Kyle's quiet life. It was what she'd always wanted.

At twenty-five, she knew everyone thought she was marrying too young, but she didn't care. She loved him. She hadn't expected to get pregnant so quickly, but that didn't bother her either. Her parents had met and married in their early thirties, and Nora was in her mid-forties by the time Maggie came around. In the early days of her marriage, Alice had been excited to throw herself into the role of mother and wife, but that was not how she felt now. A third child as she neared forty had not been part of the plan.

The Irish Goodbye

It wasn't until she arrived back at the Folly that she could calm herself down. She applied lipstick in the rearview mirror, combed her hair, and snuck around to the side of the house to stuff the pharmacy bag and the test deep into the garbage bin. She swore she spotted the raccoon her father had been going on about all week scurrying away as she approached.

When she walked through the front door, James was there to greet her in hysterics because Finn had informed him that one of his most valuable Pokémon cards was in fact a fake. Her father followed after James with the question, "What's for dinner tonight?"

"Pizza?" she said.

"That'll do!"

"And your feral friend is out by the garbage again," Alice said.

Her father groaned. "That's it." He reached for his jacket on the coatrack. "I knew the hot sauce and Epsom salt weren't going to work."

"What are you going to do?" Alice asked, but by then, her father was heading out the front door, James had returned to get her opinion on the counterfeit card, and her mother was calling for her from the kitchen.

6.

CAIT

Hours after they landed at JFK, picked up the car rental, and devoured a round of McDonald's fries and chocolate milkshakes, Cait and the twins arrived at the Folly. As soon as they pulled into the driveway, the twins erupted into an argument over who could say hello to their grandparents first.

"You can say hello together," Cait shouted as she parked the car. The twins quieted. They'd been traveling for fourteen hours, and her head throbbed from drinking on the plane. She wished she could bypass the greetings that awaited, collapse onto her childhood bed, and—for the love of God—sleep.

It was just after five but already dark and snowy, the house lit up from within. The stairs to the wraparound porch were decorated with snow-covered pumpkins and bright yellow mums. Despite everything that had happened there, the house was still more home to her than any place she'd ever lived. Her father had always assumed the property would be passed down to one of the four, but after Topher died and Cait moved to London, that possibility became less of a reality. Maggie had no use for a five-bedroom house on the Long Island shore, and although Alice might have made the most sense, she and Kyle couldn't afford the taxes and upkeep. What would happen to the house after her parents passed wasn't a question anyone discussed, but Cait couldn't bear it leaving the family. The land was probably worth more than the house itself, and she knew that whoever bought it would tear it down to build one of those awful McMansions going up around the village.

She shuddered at the thought, switched off the car, and checked her phone for the hundredth time since they'd landed—still dead.

"Is that Papa?" Poppy asked, pointing toward the house.

Augustus pressed his face to the window. "He's holding a gun!"

Cait looked up, but because the window was fogged, all she saw was a blur. She squinted. "No, he's holding a—"

"It is a gun!"

"Is it real?"

Cait rolled down the window. "What the hell is he doing?"

"Mummy!" the twins yelled, forever united in their willingness to call her out on any minor language transgression.

"Stay here." Cait opened the door and closed it to the sound of the twins' protest. She walked around the car, and her father emerged from the garden on the south side of the house with his old 12-gauge hunting shotgun broken open and slung over his shoulder. "Dad?" she said. "What's with the shotgun?"

"There's a gaze of rabid raccoons. Alice just spotted one in the trash."

"So call animal control."

"What are they going to do that I can't do myself?" He let out a hearty laugh. He was a few months away from eighty but looked nearly a decade younger. He always said his excellent health came from spending so much time outdoors, which he certainly did.

She was about to tell him to put the shotgun away, when Poppy figured out how to undo the lock and flung open her door. She and Augustus charged out of the car.

"There they are!" her father said.

"Wait!" Cait grabbed their hands, wrenching them back, and turned to her father. "Put that away."

He removed the shotgun from his shoulder, showed her the empty chambers, and snapped it shut. As a kid, Cait was the only one of her siblings willing to join their father on winter weekends to hunt ducks in the marshlands near Freeport. When they'd do the spring turkey hunting season, she was known for mimicking the best gobbles to lure the turkeys to the clearings for the hunters. He used to store the shotgun on pegs over the fireplace in the kitchen, but he hadn't been hunting in years, as far as she knew, and the last time she'd seen the gun, it was on the top shelf of the cottage coat closet next to a rotted box of shells.

"All safe now," he said, and rested the shotgun against the lattice under the porch as though it were a piece of firewood.

Cait released the twins' hands, and they hugged their grandfather.

"Let me guess who is who," he said, playing the game that delighted them to no end.

Poppy hopped on her tippy toes. "I'm—"

"Augustus!"

"No, *I'm* Augustus."

Her father snapped his fingers. "Wrong every time!"

Inside the house, Cait breathed in the familiar combination of piney turpentine from her mother's painting studio and the lingering hint of tobacco from her grandfather's pipe that had defined her childhood. Her last visit, six years ago, was in the spring, and she and Bram fought so incessantly that she'd wanted to leave almost as soon as they'd arrived. Pretending her marriage wasn't falling apart—especially while pregnant with twins—was even more exhausting with an audience. Here now, she realized maybe she'd stayed away for too long. And for what?

It was on that last trip that Cait first consciously noted the ease with which her parents interacted with each other. The way her father brought her mother a cup of tea or her mother fussed over whether he'd be warm enough when he left to go fishing. After decades together, they still cared for each other like newlyweds. The observation was bittersweet—the only reason she'd noticed it was because her own marriage was so very different. "He's my best friend, your father," Nora used to say to Cait and her siblings when they were younger. For years, Cait would roll her eyes at this, but she'd learned that she was wrong. Friendship was probably the most important thing.

In the kitchen, she found her mother and Alice sitting at the wooden island, snacking on Tayto Cheese and Onion crisps. Every time Father Kelly went to Ireland, he'd fill a bag with treats to bring home to Nora—Irish brown bread, sausages, and rashers. She had a special cabinet where she kept all her favorite biscuits that she couldn't get in the States—Mikado, Coconut Creams, and Custard Creams.

Cait had seen her parents in October when they'd joined her and the twins in the Cotswolds, but she hadn't seen Alice since her last visit home, and she was struck by how her sister seemed so—well, maybe she was just tired. Alice looked more like their mother in every way. Petite stature, coppery hair, and freckled skin. By the time she pulled up a stool, Cait was recounting the story of Poppy nearly flushing her phone down the toilet on the airplane, somehow managing to turn it into a funny anecdote.

"You're not mad anymore?" Poppy asked her.

"No, sweetheart," Cait said. "Of course not." Though, of course, she *was*. She wouldn't be able to buy a replacement phone until Friday when the stores were open again, with hordes of people searching for Black Friday sales. She tapped Poppy on the nose. "Go find your brother."

As her father reported details about tracking the raccoon, Cait poured a glass of pinot noir; she had to stop herself from wincing at its sour taste. She was about to ask about Maggie when James swung open the door to the back porch, and her youngest sister appeared with someone Cait didn't recognize. The woman's cheeks were rosy, and her bright smile made it seem like she'd been laughing. She was pretty. Cait determined this swiftly, maybe even competitively. So this must be Isabel, the woman

Maggie had told her about months ago. Kind of dykey in her Patagonia fleece, but Cait supposed that was a good thing—certainly better than a closeted Boston Brahmin decked out in Brooks Brothers. Cait had never met Sarah, but she'd seen enough pictures to get the vibe.

James ran up to the twins. "I'm four years older than you," he declared, then grabbed their hands, and they all ran downstairs to check out their grandfather's trains.

Maggie whispered into Cait's ear as they hugged. "You haven't answered any of my texts or calls."

"I'm sorry," Cait said. "It's been a crazy few weeks."

"Why?"

"Later," Cait said, and turned to introduce herself to Isabel.

They all gathered around the island again. Cait grabbed her glass of wine and sat on a stool. She was morbidly curious to see how her mother would respond to Isabel and felt bad that she hadn't responded to Maggie's texts.

"Isabel's a new teacher at Grove," her mother explained.

"I'm there to finish my play," Isabel said. "I'm teaching one workshop for now, but hopefully, it'll become more permanent."

Isabel glanced at Maggie when she said this, but Maggie was scrolling through her phone like a teenager.

"A play," her father said. "What's it about?"

"Eleanor Roosevelt."

"She was Irish, you know," Nora said.

"I do," Isabel said. "My grandmother was a seamstress at the White House and worked for her. The play is about one afternoon when she read her tarot."

Cait hip-checked Maggie, and Maggie quickly stuffed her phone into her back pocket.

"What did the reading reveal?" Alice asked.

"Well, the cards help you learn more about your past, present, and future. You ask the deck a question, and the reader interprets whatever card's drawn. In the play, Eleanor asks the deck whether her husband is having an affair with Lucy Mercer Rutherfurd."

"Oh," Nora said.

"It's funny," Maggie said hurriedly. She turned to Isabel. "Don't you think?"

Isabel considered this. "I'm not sure *funny* is the word I'd use, but I guess there are some funny parts?"

Cait was about to ask more about the story, but her father interrupted her. He clapped his hands. "Who's getting the pizza?"

Cait understood he was trying to prevent the conversation from going too far into the pagan practice of tarot readings and upsetting her mother, but it was rude. "I'd love to hear more later," she said to Isabel.

"Sure," Isabel said.

As the conversation turned to arranging the pizza order, Cait snuck into her father's office, hoping to check Luke's email, but when her plan was derailed by Finn, who was using the computer to play *Minecraft*, she had a better idea.

"I'll get the pizzas," she said, returning to the kitchen. "And more wine, too."

"You've been traveling all day," her mother said.

"And I already bought plenty of wine," Alice said.

Cait pointed to the bottle she'd been drinking. "Like this one?"

"You don't like it?"

"It tastes like the sacramental wine at Saint Mary's."

Alice picked up Cait's glass. "You don't seem to mind too much."

"You try it," Cait said.

Alice hesitated, then swirled the wine in the glass and took a small taste. "It's fine," she said. "I know you have your wine hand-imported from the Italian Alps—"

"Loire Valley."

Alice rolled her eyes and grabbed a notebook to take everyone's requests for the pizza toppings.

"Are we going to have to feed that thing dinner, too?" Cait asked, pointing to the zit on Alice's chin.

Alice flashed Cait a quick middle finger behind Nora's back. "I assume you need a pie with that cashew goop they call vegan cheese?"

"I feel so seen," Cait said, clutching her chest.

While Alice placed the order, Cait rushed to her bedroom to refresh her makeup, rinse with mouthwash, and slip into the blush La Perla bra and silk thong she'd recently bought at Harvey Nichols. You never knew. She hoped Luke was actually home and didn't have company. She changed into her favorite jeans, a black low-cut silk blouse, and her cashmere camel jacket, and was halfway out the front door when Maggie appeared and said she would join her.

"You don't have to," Cait said.

Maggie buttoned her peacoat. "I know I don't have to," she said. She studied her more closely. "Why'd you get changed?"

"Seriously," Cait said, jangling her keys. "I could use a minute to myself after this day."

Maggie took her by the arm and led her outside into the cold, snowy night. "I need your advice on something." She closed the door and hopped off the front steps.

"Where's Isabel?" Cait remained on the porch, refusing to concede to the change of plans. "Go show off your sexy Scrabble skills."

"We'll play when I get back," Maggie said. "She's getting her nails painted by James."

"She is?"

Maggie shrugged.

"I want to catch up," Cait said. "I want to hear all about Isabel, but I just need—"

The door flung open, and Cait turned to find Poppy.

"Papa said I can come with you."

Cait swallowed down a scream. "Darling," she said. "Mummy's going to be right back. Why don't you have James paint your nails!"

Her father appeared in the foyer. "Ah, good," he said. "You haven't left." He raised Poppy's hands to slip her arms into her jacket.

Cait could cry. She unzipped Poppy's jacket. "She's going to stay here."

Poppy jerked away. "I want to come with you," she said. She tried to zip her jacket again, and when she couldn't, Cait's father knelt to help her.

"And your mother wants a house salad," he said to Cait.

Cait reached for Poppy's hand. "Got it."

"Dressing on the side."

"Yup," Cait said. "They always drown it."

He snapped his fingers. "Exactly." He blew a kiss to Poppy, then closed the door.

Cait tossed the keys to Maggie. "You drive. I'm all turned around, and I'll end up on the wrong side of the road."

As Maggie crossed the causeway and entered town, Cait's bitterness about her thwarted plans to pop over to Luke's house turned to an unexpected nostalgia. Christmas lights were already strung around the firehouse, and wreaths hung from the traffic lights along Main Street. Kids smoked cigarettes outside O'Reilly's, the bar they used to pack on the Wednesday night everyone returned home from college for Thanksgiving break. The town was so small and yet a world wholly unto itself.

Cait pointed out different landmarks to Poppy—the park where she broke her arm in kindergarten, the diner where she had her first job as a waitress, Saint Mary's school and church. She had not been to Saint Mary's since Topher's funeral service, but she did not say this now to Poppy. The twins knew she had a brother who'd died—*he's in heaven*—but they didn't know anything about the circumstances. Someday, she supposed.

The nostalgia turned, and Cait said, "I don't know how Alice stayed here."

Maggie stopped at a red light and leaned on the steering wheel. "Eh," she said. "It's kind of sweet." Then she said, "And I don't think she felt she had much choice."

"Everyone has a choice," Cait said, though she wasn't sure she believed that herself. What if Alice hadn't moved back to Port Haven after Topher died? Would Cait really have felt like she could move to another country? She thought back to her parents at that time. Her father with his vacant stare and her mother always sleeping and unable to eat. What a relief it had been to have not only one but two reasons to run away to London—Bram! A job that promised to pay off her law school loans and much more! All the same, she couldn't stand how Alice held this over her even now, as if Port Haven wasn't exactly where Alice wanted to be.

After grabbing a case from the wine store, Maggie gave Poppy a handful of quarters to play Golden Tee at the pizzeria while she and Cait split a beer at a booth and waited for their number to be called. Cait half followed Maggie's story of how things had started with Isabel but was distracted by trying to figure out how to get in touch with Luke.

". . . And then she kissed me, or I kissed her, and we've been pretty much inseparable since."

Cait looked up at her sister. "Well, she seems great to me. Smart. Hot. And"—she played a little drumroll with her pointer fingers on the tabletop—"gay!"

Maggie laughed. "She is—all of those things." Then something seemed to shift. "Hey, do you know anything about employment law?"

"Why? What's up?"

Maggie took a sip and handed the beer back to Cait. "Nothing," she said. "I had a question about my contract, but what's been going on with you these last few weeks? Why haven't you returned any of my calls?"

Cait flicked her wrist. "Just busy," she said.

She toyed with the idea of confiding in Maggie about reconnecting with Luke but decided against it. The last thing she wanted was to have to defend herself. Besides, who knew what would happen when she and Luke met up this weekend, assuming she could even get in touch with him.

"With work?" Maggie pushed. "How's the partner thing?"

"That's a whole other story," Cait began, relieved when Poppy interrupted from across the room.

The Irish Goodbye

"Come watch me play," Poppy said.

"I can see from here, darling." Cait turned to Maggie. "Do you remember when you were a kid and thought adults wanted to watch every last thing you did?"

Maggie considered this. "I don't think I've ever felt that way in my life."

Cait questioned whether this was true but let it go. "How's Mom being with Isabel?"

Maggie stuck out her tongue.

"That good?"

"Well, she's expecting her to sleep in the cottage, if that tells you anything."

"She made Bram do that when he visited before we were married," Cait said. "And we were living together at that point."

"Right," Maggie said, smiling. "Once we get married, it'll all be okay."

Cait laughed.

"I need more coins," Poppy called out.

Maggie searched her wallet for quarters, but then the teenager behind the counter called, "Order up for Alice Williams." It had been almost fifteen years since her sister had changed her name in marriage, but Cait still couldn't get used to it. Alice was still "Alice Ryan" in Cait's phone and always would be. It took only one time for Kyle to mistakenly introduce Cait using Bram's last name to learn that she, unlike her sister, was still very much a Ryan.

Cait stood and handed Maggie her Amex. "You pay," she said. "I'm going to the bathroom." Then she stopped. "Can I borrow your phone for a second?"

Maggie hesitated.

"Relax," Cait said. "I'm not going to read your sexts to Isabel. I just need to check something."

Maggie handed Cait her phone, and Cait snuck into the bathroom, where she was finally able to read the email from Luke.

call me when you're settled. i may head into the city for thanksgiving with a friend. let me know your plans. i don't want to make things awkward with your family, so you lead the way.

Heading to the city?

She didn't have his cell phone number memorized, but miraculously—that's how she felt, like it was a freaking miracle—she remembered the Larkins' home number.

She tried twice, hanging up each time his mother's voice boomed from the answering machine, giving her the chills. She finally conceded defeat and met Maggie and Poppy back in the car, but as they passed the road leading to the Larkins' house, she told Maggie to take a left.

"Where are we going?"

"The long way."

"But I'm hungry," Poppy said.

The pizza did smell outrageously delicious. "It'll just be a minute," Cait said, quickly dabbing gloss on her lips. When they got to the house, she told Maggie to pull over, and then she honked the horn.

"What are you doing?" Maggie asked.

The lights were on, but the house looked empty. Her mother had assumed Mrs. Larkin would move out after the lawsuit was settled, but she'd stayed until the very end. Maybe she'd expected the Ryans to leave Port Haven. Cait had once thought her parents should do exactly that. Why would they want to stay when they were grist for the small town's rumor mill—not only after Daniel's accident and the lawsuit, but when Topher died? But they, too, stayed, and she supposed now the town had moved on from both tragedies.

Cait leaned over and honked again.

Maggie jerked her hand away. "Stop it," she said. "I'm going."

Before Cait could respond, the garage door lifted, and Luke appeared. Cait lowered the window and waved. He smiled and waved back as he headed down the driveway. In rolled-up chinos, a plaid flannel shirt, and untied snow boots, he was even more gorgeous than she remembered him being in London.

"This is a surprise—" he said, then stopped when he spotted Maggie.

Maggie angled toward the passenger-side window. "Hi, Luke," she said.

Poppy poked her head between the two front seats.

"Hey, sweetie," he said.

His voice sounded sugary and contrived, and Cait cringed.

"How's it going?" she asked. *Why are you going to the city when I just got into town?!*

Luke glanced back at the house. "Uh, well. It's awful."

Awful. Right. Packing up his childhood home. What was she thinking? My God, he was even more beautiful when sad. How could she be upset with him? Of course he didn't want to be there alone on Thanksgiving! She wished she could send Poppy back to her parents with Maggie and spend the weekend with him.

"I'm so sorry about your mom," Maggie said.

Luke lowered his face to the window. Cait could smell the booze on his breath. "Thanks," he said. "I'd invite you guys in, but—"

Cait cut him off. "It's okay. We have to get going anyway. We just stopped by to see if you're around to join us for dinner tomorrow." She felt Maggie tense beside her, but she continued. "We're having it catered. Oyster bar and all. Father Kelly will be there and I'm sure he'd love to see you."

"Sure," Luke said, without seeming to give it a second thought. "Yeah, I'd love to. I was supposed to see a friend, but—"

"The more, the merrier."

"We need to get going," Maggie said. She was trying to be polite, but her voice was tight.

Luke straightened. "Right," he said, then paused. Cait worried he'd back out, but then he said, "I'll bring a Hammerschlagen game. There are some extra tree logs out back."

Maggie shifted the car into drive.

"Sounds great," Cait said. "Swing by around two."

They said goodbye, and Maggie drove off.

"What the actual fuck?" Maggie said as soon as Cait rolled up her window.

From the back seat, Poppy gasped. "You said—"

"Don't you dare!" Cait said, knowing Poppy would be thrilled to use this as an opportunity to repeat the word herself.

Poppy pouted and slumped back into her seat.

"Sorry," Maggie said, glancing at Poppy in the rearview mirror. She turned to Cait. "What just happened there?"

"You saw how upset he was," Cait said. "What were we supposed to do?"

"No, no," Maggie said. "Don't make this about *we*. That was all you." Then she said, "I didn't even know you two were in touch."

Cait winked at Poppy, but Poppy, still indignant, stuck out her bottom lip and held her chin high. Cait raised the volume on the radio, then leaned across the console, and in a voice low enough that she hoped Poppy couldn't hear, she said, "I met up with him in London in September and we've been talking ever since."

Maggie stopped the car in the middle of the road. "What?"

"Why'd we stop?" Poppy asked.

"What do you mean *talking*?"

Cait hesitated. "I'm not sure, actually."

Maggie looked back at Poppy again. "Fine," she said to Cait, taking her foot off the brake. "But you need to give me the scoop later." Then she said, "It's never not going to be weird to see him."

Cait knew this was true but hated hearing it.

"And what's a Hammerschlagen game?" Maggie asked.

"I have no idea," Cait said distractedly. She was remembering the last time she was at the Larkins' house when she was seventeen. It didn't feel nearly as long ago as she would have imagined.

* * *

The Irish Goodbye

Cait and her friends were huddled around a bonfire at the beach club when a rainstorm moved in. Everyone called it a night, but Cait and Luke hunkered down in a cabana with Topher and his new sidekick, Marcus, a local dealer who sold them sketchy weed and claimed to be on his way to the marines. Cait couldn't stand Marcus, but Topher hung out with him more and more lately. They were always getting into some kind of trouble. Topher had skipped so much school his senior year, he almost didn't graduate, and she'd heard rumors he was messing around with more serious drugs like coke, which he'd only halfheartedly denied.

When Topher asked if they wanted a ride home, Luke peeked his head out from the cabana's cabinet, where he was searching for snacks, and said, "Don't go yet."

At first, Cait thought he was talking to Topher, but then he pulled a bag of weed from his back pocket and pointed it at her. "Smoke a joint with me, then I'll walk you back home."

When Topher and Marcus left, the rain turned to a mist, and Cait sat on the picnic table under the cabana's covered deck to watch Luke roll the joint, paying close attention, because his were always tight and hers were always coming loose.

He lit the joint, and they passed it as they talked about his plans to leave for Boston College in two days. Cait would be a senior that September at Saint Mary's and was already looking at schools. She was considering Boston herself but didn't mention this because she didn't want him to know that he was part of the reason.

Luke had moved from Connecticut to Port Haven three years earlier, when his parents divorced and yanked him out of Deerfield Academy. He lived in a small house with his mom and brother now, a few streets away from the Folly. Cait didn't know much about his dad, except that he lived in Arizona with a woman who was only eight years older than Luke. He spoiled Luke and Daniel with fancy gifts—most recently, a Boston Whaler for Luke's eighteenth birthday—and took them on exotic trips to places like the Galápagos Islands. When Luke first moved to Port Haven, Cait barely noticed him. He was always fly fishing on the seawall behind their house with Topher, but beyond the boarding-school allure, there was nothing particularly special about him. Then, last summer, he did an Outward Bound trip in the Pacific Northwest, and when he returned, he'd chopped off his shaggy hair so you could see his blue eyes and gotten into shape. Overnight, he became the hottest senior at the school, and Cait told her friends he would be her boyfriend by the end of the year.

Her plan hadn't exactly worked out, but they'd hooked up a few times, mostly at parties when Topher wasn't around. Each time, Luke would find Cait at school or the beach club the next day and stumble through an apology, saying he'd made a mistake. They should just be friends. Or—and this was the one that annoyed her the most—it was too weird with Topher being his best friend. And each time, she'd laugh and say she'd been drunk anyway, then spend weeks afterward sick to her stomach with a longing that brought her almost as much pleasure as it did misery. In that longing, everything felt more real. More alive. Plus, she knew that in a few weeks they'd make eye contact at some party, and he'd pull her into another room, and they'd be right back at it again.

The high from the joint came on gently, and they watched the small black waves roll onto the shore. Cait was thinking about how much next year would suck, with Topher and Luke away at school, when Luke leaned over and his lips found hers. His mouth tasted like weed and Bazooka gum. There was a sweetness about the kiss, a lingering that hadn't been there before, and his breath tickled her ear as he whispered, "Do you want to come over?"

It was after ten, and her curfew wasn't until midnight, but she wasn't exactly sure what he was asking. To hook up? To watch a movie? She'd be thrilled to do either, though the only times they'd been together were at other people's houses or the beach—drunken make-outs that usually ended shortly after they started. This felt like something different.

"What about your mom?" she asked.

The Irish Goodbye

"She goes to bed early." He played with the Saint Jude pendant around her neck, then looked up at her with half-cast eyes and smiled.

When they entered the house, Luke took her hand and led them through the dark foyer. She'd been to the Larkins' only a few times, to watch old horror movies in the finished basement with Topher and their other friends.

She stopped halfway up the stairs. "Are you sure your mom isn't going to wake up?"

Luke pressed his finger to her lips. He'd gone clamming with Topher earlier that afternoon, and she could smell the brine on his skin. "We don't have to if you don't want to," he said quietly.

Even in the darkness of the stairway, she could see the scar on his lip, his hair wet and messy from the rain. *He's leaving for college in two days*, she thought, *where he'll meet tons of girls and forget all about you.*

"I want to," she said.

He reached for her hand again as they tiptoed up the stairs. The hallway was even darker, except for a band of light under Daniel's door. She worried Mrs. Larkin might wake up and find them but was relieved to see Luke's room was over the garage, away from the rest of the house.

He closed the door behind him and gestured across the room as if to say, *Here it is.* Like Topher, most of his stuff was packed in boxes for college, but several Joy Division posters covered the walls, and his desk was filled with ribbons from the high school debate team. His bed looked like it hadn't been made in weeks, and when she sat down, his gingham sheets smelled musty, like scalp. She wasn't sure if she liked it. He slipped a CD into the stereo, and a familiar song came on that might have been the Rolling Stones or the Who, then he sat next to her.

When he kissed her again, his lips tasted like the barbecue chips they'd stolen from the cabana to eat on the walk to his house. It wasn't either of those bands, she thought as they lay down. It was Pink Floyd, though she didn't know the song. She tried to focus on Luke. She shouldn't have smoked as much as she had. She went back and forth, trying to decide whether to tell him that this was her first time. She'd almost lost her virginity to her boyfriend last year, but she hadn't wanted to, and then he'd broken up with her to date a girl from another town.

As Luke kissed her neck, desire swelled between her legs, and in that moment she decided she wouldn't tell him it was her first time. She didn't want to give him any reason to stop. When his mouth made its way back to hers, she kissed him harder, and he hiked up her T-shirt dress to take off her panties.

She was higher than she'd thought. He watched as she unbuckled his belt. Then, to fight off the wooziness, she grabbed him by his shirt and slid her tongue deeper into his mouth, and before she was ready, he pushed into her. She gasped at the stab of pain. She had expected it to hurt but was shocked.

"Are you okay?" he asked, and when she nodded, he closed his eyes and pressed his hips into hers.

Something smelled weird. At first she thought it was the sheets, but then she realized it was the ragged sailor's bracelet on his wrist. She turned away from it, but that set off a sudden vertigo, and she had to cling to his shoulders to steady herself. She struggled to follow the rhythm of his body, but just when she had it, he reared and pulled out of her—a soft moan as he came on the sheets—then collapsed against her chest. She pressed her palm against the wall to stop the room from spinning and stared at the faded glow-in-the-dark stars covering the ceiling.

"That was awesome," he said.

Was it? Was she supposed to have had an orgasm? The wetness between her legs embarrassed her. She knew that was supposed to be normal, but it seemed excessive and sticky, and kind of gross.

"Thanks," she said, and immediately felt lame.

Luke slid off her body, and because she could breathe easier now, this helped with the vertigo. He bunched up his pillow and rested his head on his forearm. He started to say something, but then the CD switched and suddenly the title track from the *Footloose* album started playing.

He jumped off the bed, pulling on his shorts as he rushed over to the stereo.

Cait laughed as she reached for her panties. "My sisters and I used to belt out 'Let's Hear It for the Boy' with our hairbrushes."

But Luke wasn't embarrassed. Rather than changing the album, he turned the stereo up. "This was my jam," he said, and pulled her into the middle of the room, laughing. She wasn't a good dancer, and on any other day, the idea of dancing in front of Luke would have mortified her, but the lights were dim, and his moves were a goofy imitation of Kevin Bacon's, so when he grabbed her hand and spun her around, she went with it.

When the song ended, they collapsed onto the floor and laughed. Then Cait saw on the alarm clock that it was minutes after midnight. "Shit," she said. "I have to go."

Luke's playfulness settled on the walk home along the oak-lined streets, and he was now mostly quiet. Cait filled the silence by asking him questions about college, her chest tight as she waited for him to say once again that this had all been a mistake. But maybe it hadn't been a mistake? She didn't want to get her hopes up. She could already feel how much harder it would be when he let her down this time.

When they reached the top of the Folly's driveway, Luke suddenly looked confused.

"Where's Topher?" he asked, noting the empty space where Topher's Jeep was usually parked.

Cait shrugged. "He blows off his curfew so much, my parents stopped trying." Then she laughed. "Don't worry about him. He doesn't care about us."

Luke shook his head, but his expression was serious. "That's not it."

Of course that's not "it," Cait thought, embarrassed by her assumption. *That's not "it" because there is no "us."*

"I just don't like him hanging out with Marcus," Luke said.

"Oh," Cait said. "Yeah. I don't get that either."

Luke looked at her. "You know he's Topher's supplier, right?"

Cait laughed again. Her brother managed to get himself into plenty of trouble, but there was no way he was doing anything that stupid.

But then Luke said, "How do you think he bought his boat?"

Now Cait believed him. When Topher had bought his boat that spring, Cait had asked him where he'd gotten the money. He said from his pizza-delivery tips, but he only worked two shifts a week, and she knew where that money had gone: to beer, weed, and tickets to Dead and Phish shows. How clueless could she have been? She wasn't sure when things had taken a turn for her brother, but lately, it seemed like there was always something. Broken curfews. Getting kicked off the lacrosse team for missing too many practices. Another notice from the school. What annoyed Cait most was how he always managed to get caught, then fought with their parents rather than just apologizing and promising to do better. Still, when their parents interpreted his saving for and buying the boat as a sign that he was growing up, Cait had thought they might be right.

"What's he dealing?" she asked.

"I don't know," Luke said. "Dodgy weed. Maybe more? He won't tell me. You should say something to him, though."

"Like what?"

"To be careful."

Cait turned to face the dark windows of her house. She hoped her mother wasn't awake to see her and Luke standing there. The crickets and cicadas sang in the wooded shrubs across the street. Everything smelled ripe and earthy from the rainstorm earlier that night. The road. The wet soil. Her father's rosebushes by the porch. Her own body.

The bathroom light flicked on in her parents' room.

"I have to go," she said. "I'll see you tomorrow?" Their friends were throwing a boat party by the lighthouse for Luke's send-off before he left for Boston the next day.

Luke nodded. "I'm taking Danny fishing in the morning, so you guys can meet us there." Then he shuffled backward, gave a half wave, and turned to make his way down the street again.

*   *   *

By the time they got back to the house, the pizza had cooled, and Alice was annoyed at them for running late.

"We invited someone to dinner!" Poppy announced.

Cait caught Poppy watching her when she said this, as though her daughter knew this information gave her power.

"Who?" Alice asked.

Cait reached for the salad bowl on the counter. "We ran into Luke Larkin," she said. She sensed the energy in the room shift as soon as she said his name, and everyone seemed to stop what they were doing. To avoid eye contact, she tossed the salad in the bowl and picked out a piece of wilted lettuce as she continued. "He's in town cleaning out his mom's house. He was a mess—" She turned to Maggie. "Right? I mean, a mess. Anyway, he mentioned he didn't have plans for tomorrow, so we thought it would be nice to, you know, invite him."

No one spoke. Cait hoped they didn't suspect she'd exaggerated the story to defend the invitation.

"Wait," Alice said as she spun off the stool and stood. "You invited Luke Larkin to dinner?"

"Yes," Cait said.

"Here?"

"Yes."

"Tomorrow?"

"Yes!"

Cait turned to her mother. "I can cancel," she said, though she'd never do that. Now that she'd asked him and he'd agreed, she needed to see him. To be near him.

Her mother sat on a stool by the island. "That won't be necessary," she said. "This is unexpected, but we can—"

"You have to be kidding me," Alice said. "Like, is this a sick joke or something?"

Oh, stop it! Cait wanted to tell her sister, but she didn't want to upset her mother more or give Alice reason to maintain her gripe. Instead, she said, "His mom just died and he's all alone on Thanksgiving. Have some compassion, for God's sake."

"Girls," their father said, as though they were still girls and not grown women. He wrapped his arm around Nora. "It'll be fine."

Cait found some comfort in her father's optimism, but she couldn't ignore how the announcement deflated her mother. "I know it might be uncomfortable at first," she conceded, "but I think we can all be together for an evening."

Alice plated the pizza. "You're unbelievable."

Cait no longer had an appetite, and instead of eating a slice of the vegan pie, she poured herself a full glass of wine from a new bottle and tried to remember when her parents must have last seen Luke. At the beach club the afternoon Daniel died? The Larkins explicitly requested the Ryans not attend Daniel's funeral. On that day, the Folly was filled with a silence even nine-year-old Maggie knew not to disturb. Cait and her sisters stayed in their respective rooms, while their father holed up in the basement with his train set, and their mother painted the lavender blooms out in the garden. Where was Topher? Cait didn't know. He never spoke to her about her part in the accident, and she certainly wasn't going to say anything. Even now, she looked back on the day with shame—how, amid the horror of Daniel's death, she couldn't stop thinking about losing her virginity to Luke the night before. She knew it was the last thing that could or maybe even should happen, but she was consumed with her longing to touch Luke again. She spent hours in bed replaying every detail of the night before, masturbating and crying, a continuous loop of desire and remorse. Her guilt over Daniel and her ache for Luke were inextricably linked, no matter how desperate she was to separate them. When Luke left for college a few weeks later, she waited for him to reach out, but he never did.

The twins refused to eat their dinner because the crust was cold and the cheese was burnt, and Cait gave in and let them each have a bowl of cereal and a banana, which they barely ate anyway. When Poppy cried at how Cait cut the banana slices, Nora chimed in to say maybe they just weren't hungry. Then she recounted the same story she always told about how the nuns at the orphanage forced her to eat all her food, disgusting gray sludge they called porridge, bread fried in lard and topped with baked beans, and meat with the gristle. When Poppy wouldn't settle, Cait downed the rest of her wine and scooped the twins into both arms.

"Bedtime," she said, grateful for an excuse to head upstairs.

The twins tried to wrestle free as she brought them into the bathroom but quieted once Cait got them into the tub. She thought of her father returning home from work when she and Topher were young and Alice was a toddler. Her mother was always understandably overwhelmed. Her father would come in smelling like the outside world and take over. He'd put Alice to bed, make boxed macaroni and cheese, plop Cait and Topher into the bath, and feed them their dinner there.

Cait dimmed the lights and read to the twins while they played in the tub with a plastic tugboat and a small rod that caught wide-mouthed fish with a magnet. Then Augustus got upset at Poppy for taking an extra turn and smashed the rod over Poppy's head. As Poppy started to stand, she slipped and banged her eyebrow against the faucet. Both stopped yelling as soon as they saw the blood, then broke into a simultaneous wail, making Cait want to cry herself, because this would delay bedtime.

"It's *just* a boo-boo," Cait said, kissing Poppy's wet forehead, where a small egg was already blooming on her eyebrow.

She lifted them out of the bath and gave Poppy a cold wash towel to hold against her eye while she dried them off and then dabbed ointment across the gash, igniting another wail from Poppy, before applying a Band-Aid. "All better now!" She ushered the twins across the hall to the bunk room, and when they heard James laughing downstairs, they insisted on joining their cousins.

"Everyone's going to bed," Cait said.

"They're not!" Augustus said.

"I'm hungry," Poppy said.

"Me too."

"And I want to show Grammy my boo-boo."

"Will you read us one more book?"

"And sleep in here? I'm scared."

"Me too!"

Cait stuffed their limbs into their pajamas and grabbed a book from the bookcase. She was relieved to dodge the family drama caused by her earlier announcement and figured everyone downstairs was probably talking about her. She didn't want to hear what they had to say anyway. Luke was coming tomorrow. She was still pinching herself that she'd invited him, let alone that he had accepted.

She flopped onto the bottom bunk and tapped the space on either side of her. "Come," she said, and the twins piled onto the bed.

"You'll stay?" Poppy asked again.

"Yes, shh."

A creak from the ceiling fan drowned out the voices from the kitchen below, and before Cait was halfway through the book, the twins' bodies settled. Hers followed. Even though she was upset about her broken phone, she couldn't help but notice how present she was with the twins without it in her back pocket. Now that she'd connected with Luke, she could allow herself to relax. She lowered herself so that her face nestled between their faces, their sweet breath on either cheek, their wet hair dampening the pillowcases. She kissed Poppy gently on her Band-Aid and ran her fingertips along the insides of their wrists, as they liked.

The Irish Goodbye

This was the only time of the day, as they were falling into sleep, when she felt capable of being the kind of mother she had imagined she would be, before she became the mother she apparently was—the kind that liked her children best when they were behaving well and didn't need anything from her.

7.

ALICE

Alice had already baked the pumpkin and apple pies, which were cooling on the kitchen table, and was now onto the pecan pie.

"Something's off," her mother said from where she sat at the table.

Alice froze, thumb pressed in the dough stretched along the rim of the ceramic dish. *Can she really tell I'm—what? A week?—pregnant?* But when she looked up, Nora was inspecting the crust of the apple pie with a butter knife.

"The crust's crumbly," Nora said. "Is this the dairy-free one you made Cait? Without the butter?"

"Oh, for God's sake." Alice returned to the counter and poured the sticky pecan mixture into the crust. "I forgot about that."

Her mother followed her. "Well, it's not God's fault."

No, it never was. God was the only one to ever get a pass.

"Cait's just so particular about what she eats," her mother said. She scooped a bite onto her pinky finger to taste. "It's delicious. Do we have more pecans? Maybe we can make another one of these using the shortening?" She thought for a moment. "Although, does Cait eat pecans?"

It was already nine in the evening. Alice was used to her mother bending over backward for beautiful, successful Cait, but her sister's stunt earlier had sapped Alice's patience. Trying to keep the peace, she offered, "I'll tell Kyle to get some apples and shortening in the morning so I can make a new pie."

Nora wrapped her arms around Alice's shoulders and planted a kiss on her cheek. "Nothing to worry yourself about."

But they both knew Alice would worry about it and make the dairy-free apple pie. Just as they both knew Cait wouldn't eat it—she'd make a show of cutting a slice, and it would sit, untouched, on the table in front of her while she drank another Moscow . . . or whatever the caterers were serving as the ridiculously expensive signature cocktail.

Upstairs, she heard Kyle yelling at the boys to get back into the bunk room, and though she didn't care about Cait needing to sleep off the jet lag, she wouldn't wish the waking of the twins on anyone, so she called up through the back stairway in a loud whisper for them all to quiet down. Then she put on the electric kettle and slid the pie into the refrigerator to bake tomorrow. She was too tired to wait for it tonight. *Because you're pregnant.* The truth of this reverberated in her head as it had all evening.

She brought a cup of tea to her mother, who was back at the table writing out the place cards. The name LUKE sat at the top of the pile.

They hadn't discussed Cait's unexpected dinner guest yet, and Alice wasn't in the mood now. She was incensed and wanted to stay that way; her mother would defend Cait no matter how absurd it was for her to invite Luke to Thanksgiving. Compassion? Please. And at the same time Maggie was introducing Isabel to the family. Cait needing to add more drama to the weekend was no surprise, but Alice couldn't have predicted she'd go this far.

Alice remembered being a kid and hiding on the backstairs landing with Maggie—where was Cait then?—while they listened to their parents talk to Mr. Powers, the family lawyer, about the Larkins' wrongful death lawsuit, accusing Topher of negligence. It was only a few months after the accident. Father Kelly had set up a memorial at the school's library with a photo of Daniel from confirmation the year before and an open notebook for students to write letters to his family. She was tempted to look through the notebook but wouldn't dare risk anyone catching her. Her brother was the reason Daniel was dead, or so everyone believed, and she didn't want to be associated with it in any way. All she knew was that the police investigation had revealed Topher's jerry-rigging of the steering wheel hadn't contributed to the crash, and the toxicity report showed that Daniel's blood alcohol was twice the legal limit. But as the suit claimed, Topher had allowed Daniel, a minor, to drive his boat while drunk.

Her parents had already agreed to an out-of-court settlement payment. They wouldn't reveal the exact sum, but Alice had heard her father on the phone with the bank discussing how to mortgage the house. Mr. Powers was there to let them know that in addition to the monetary settlement, the Larkins had added a new nonmonetary demand.

"The defendant must accept legal responsibility for the negligence as a continuation of the release," Mr. Powers said. "Topher will not face criminal charges, but the Larkins do not just want a check. They want it in writing that he accepts responsibility for Daniel's death."

There was a long moment of silence. Then Nora said, "I won't do it. I won't ask that of him. Of course he feels responsible, but Daniel was also drinking. It is not just Topher's fault, and for them to ask him to state that is cruel. He's just a boy himself. We can say no, can't we?"

Alice sensed the anger, or fear, in her mother's voice, but she pretended everything was all right, so Maggie wouldn't get upset. The wooden floor beneath them was cold and hard, but they sat still and waited for the response. Topher was at college in Rhode Island, and Alice knew her parents wanted to shield him from everything as much as possible so that he could focus on his studies. She missed him at home but was relieved he wasn't there to hear what they were saying.

"If this goes to court, it will be an expensive, public, and drawn-out trial," Mr. Powers said. "And because Daniel did not die immediately and was still responsive when they brought him to the hospital, the court can infer that he suffered and—"

"We will do it," Alice's father said, cutting him off. "Topher will admit negligence if that's what's necessary for all of this to be over. Because that's what we need: for it to be over."

Nora laughed. She often said a good laugh and a long sleep could cure almost anything, but it didn't seem to Alice that either was happening in the house those days. Most nights, she would wake to find her mother downstairs cleaning or reorganizing her painting studio. Laughter felt like a betrayal. This was a hard laugh anyway, and it startled Alice.

"Over?" Nora said finally. "Oh, no. It will never be over."

Standing there now and staring at Luke's name on the place card filled Alice with even more anger toward Cait. In many ways, her mother had been right. Settling the lawsuit hadn't meant it was over. Alice wasn't sure the suit was to blame for the downward spiral that led to Topher ending his own life, like Nora believed, but she supposed that watching their parents suffer the financial stress of the settlement and having to admit legal negligence had not helped her brother's crushing sense of guilt about Daniel's death.

She lifted the card. "Are you sure you're okay with this?" she asked her mother.

Nora sighed. "What can I do?"

"You can tell Cait to call it off. The whole thing. I don't get it."

Nora blew her nose into a hankie. "I don't either," she said.

"I'm going to talk to Cait."

Nora reached for her arm. "Don't," she said, then stopped and looked behind Alice's shoulder.

"James is waiting for you to come say good night," Finn said.

Alice turned. "Where's Dad?"

Finn shrugged.

"Okay, I'll be up in a few minutes."

She hadn't planned on going up in a few minutes. She'd planned on Kyle getting the boys settled. She could tell that Finn was still upset about what had happened at the game that afternoon, though she wasn't sure what he was upset about most. That his team lost? That she'd embarrassed him by getting sick? That he was in trouble for the magazine?

She tossed the place card back onto the pile and noticed her mother staring at her. "What's wrong?" she asked.

"Nothing," Nora said. "You're feeling better, then?"

A knot formed at the base of Alice's stomach. "I'm fine." She quickly gathered the teacups. "I told you, it was just food poisoning or a stomach bug."

Her mother tapped her pen on the table. "You're sure it's not something else?"

In her head, Alice screamed, *I'm pregnant and don't want to be and don't know what to do about it!* But she did not say this. Instead, she squeezed her mother's shoulder and assured her: "It's not something else." Then she loaded the cups into the dishwasher, said good night, and dashed upstairs before her mother could press her any further.

The lights were out in the kids' bunk room, but the boys were hunched over their iPads and barely noticed Alice when she walked in to say good night. Cait and the twins stirred in the bottom bed of the second bunk.

"Let's go," Alice whispered to Finn and James. She was annoyed Kyle hadn't completed the job. He was probably filling out staff evaluations or reviewing curriculum or whatever he did that was of such great import.

Finn glanced up from his screen, his face covered in blue light, and said, "Okay," as he turned over. Alice stood momentarily stunned before it dawned on her that he was only so agreeable out of fear about the magazine. Still, she counted it as a win for the day. And because Finn so readily obliged, James followed, asking if he could have back tickles, his body twitching as he slipped into sleep almost as soon as she placed her hand on the small of his back.

Finn bent over the railing of the top bunk.

"Am I in trouble?" he whispered.

Alice stood. "I haven't even talked to Dad yet."

Finn laid back and covered his face with his arm.

Though she hadn't heard from Kyle about their conversation, she hoped there was an explanation for the magazine. She felt bad Finn was under extra scrutiny as the principal's son. And now his mother had thrown up at his game in front of his friends. He deserved his own school, where so much wasn't expected of him. She worried about the pressure. He seemed to be handling it all, but she imagined there was plenty she didn't know about his life. The older he got, the less time they spent together. She knew this was a normal part of growing up, but she couldn't help but feel alarmed whenever he was upset about—school? Basketball? Friends? A girl? A boy? He rarely ever told her. If she asked, he'd mumble something under his breath and hide out in his room. Hours later, he'd reemerge as though nothing had happened. Sometimes she'd wait outside his door and listen. For what, she wasn't even sure. Would she be this protective—no, suspicious—had her brother not done the unthinkable? Finn knew Topher had taken his life, but they'd never discussed the details. This was her fault. She didn't want him to know the details. But she loathed how this reminded her of her mother, who avoided the word *suicide* at all costs.

"It's nothing to lose sleep over," Alice said to Finn. "We'll talk after this weekend."

Then came the tears. "I feel bad you got sick," he said.

"Sweetheart, that didn't—*you* didn't make me sick."

"Dad said I did."

She rose up on her toes to kiss his wet cheek. "I haven't been feeling well all day," she said. "It's probably a stomach bug."

"Okay." He rested his head on the pillow and she kissed him again, the smell of his skin sweet and familiar.

In the bedroom, Kyle sat in his boxers, clipping his toenails on the rocking chair that Alice's grandfather had made for her when she was born.

"I didn't say *he* made you sick," he said. "I told him you were upset, which you were. You brought it into my school."

And that's when she realized why he'd been so absent, even a bit cold, ever since he'd returned home from the game. He was upset with her. She'd assumed she was the one avoiding him—or, more specifically, avoiding having to tell him about the pregnancy test. She knew she should, but she was not ready.

"I thought the magazine was yours," she said, rifling through her bag for pajamas.

Kyle looked up from examining his big toe. "And that would make it *better*?"

She hadn't thought about it that way. Mostly she just wanted to hear about Finn. "Did you talk to him? What'd he say?"

"He said it was Leo's."

"Okay, so it's not his. I guess that's good?"

"He stole it from their house last weekend."

"Oh."

Kyle gathered his nail clippings and tossed them into the wicker trash can, which Alice would empty on Monday after everyone left and life resumed its mad dash, and when she would certainly have to tell Kyle about the pregnancy.

"Two weeks is a suitable grounding," he continued. "No after-school stuff except basketball and no weekends with his friends."

"We can't just punish him," Alice said. "He probably took it because he's curious. That's natural. He's getting to that age. You need to talk to him."

"I will," Kyle said, but then added, "He also needs to learn consequences. You're too easy on him."

The Irish Goodbye

This again. *Yes, sir, Principal Williams!* A stirring of annoyance moved through her. "He does have a consequence," she said. "He's upset. He couldn't fall asleep—not that you noticed."

"He should be upset."

"Okay." Alice hoped to prevent a fight or a lecture. "I'm tired."

She turned away from him as she changed.

Kyle climbed into bed. "You have to understand what that could have meant for me. You marching in like that and—"

"I know," she said, and then couldn't help herself: "You're a very important person."

Kyle looked at her.

"I'm sorry."

He nodded, then kept at it. "It would have been deeply embarrassing for my son to be caught with—It could have undermined my authority, you know, with the students and the faculty."

"You're right," she said to end it.

As they settled into sleep, she turned back to him. "I need you to pick up shortening tomorrow morning," she said. "And more apples."

Kyle adjusted his pillow. "For Cait's pie?"

"Yes."

"You didn't get any at the grocery store?"

"I need more," she said into the darkness.

"Okey dokey." He rubbed his bare feet against hers, a jagged toenail scraping her heel.

She turned to the wall and closed her eyes. When she imagined how Kyle would respond to the pregnancy, resentment surfaced for how little his life would change with the arrival of a new baby. It would be her dreams that would go unfulfilled.

8.

MAGGIE

"'Strange'?" Maggie asked. "Strange, how?"

"You ignored me all night." Isabel perched on the bed's corner and pressed her hands to her knees. "And that's when you were here—as opposed to when you left to get pizza without even telling me."

Maggie leaned her hip against the dresser. She slipped off her bracelets and placed them on the delicate pale blue Wedgwood tray that once held her baby teeth for the tooth fairy.

Isabel was right. After Maggie answered Sarah's text, she'd snuck into the cottage bathroom to call her, but Sarah didn't answer. She wanted to ask whether Sarah's husband, Frank, had told Headmaster Cunningham about their affair. More specifically: Was Maggie's job at stake? She'd sent Sarah another text that said, When can we talk? Then she deleted the entire thread between them in a futile attempt to undo the past. A yearlong documentation of their doomed relationship from start to finish, gone with the press of a button. Sarah still hadn't responded.

In the meantime, Maggie knew she was distracted and unsettled, even if it was hard to be called out by Isabel. "I'm sorry," she said.

Isabel relaxed a little. "I appreciate that, but it doesn't explain what's going on with you."

Maggie looked down. Over the past few months, they hadn't had any arguments, nothing serious anyway, but Isabel was upset. And unlike Sarah, who would turn sulky and withdraw anytime Maggie annoyed her, it was clear that Isabel would not let her off the hook.

"It's stressful introducing someone new to your family," Isabel said. "I get that. And I know things are hard with your mom—" She stopped, then said, "You were just so chill about the whole thing when you invited me, I thought—I don't know. Are we moving too fast here?"

"We're not. That's not what's going on."

"Then why don't you try telling me what *is* going on." Isabel watched her. "So I don't have to guess."

Maggie buried her face in her hands, then looked up. She had to offer something. "Maybe it is the stress of introducing you to my family," she said, taking the easy option. "And now with Luke coming here tomorrow." Not entirely untrue.

Isabel pulled her knees to her chest. "Why did you invite me?"

"Because I like you," Maggie said. She couldn't stop her legs from shaking, so she sat crisscross on the bed. "And I want us to be together."

"Wanting that and living that are two different things."

Maggie could hear people in the hallway, but she wasn't sure if it was her sisters or her mother. "Can you lower your voice?" she asked Isabel.

Isabel raised her eyebrows and said, "I'm not even slightly elevating my voice."

"Well, the walls are thin," Maggie whispered, to make a point. "And I don't want to share this conversation with my entire family."

Isabel fell back onto a pillow and crossed her arms over her face. After a moment, she said, "Maybe I should go to my cousin's tomorrow."

"What?" Maggie's heart pounded so fast it made her feel sick. "Why would you do that to me?"

Isabel sat up. "I don't want to do anything *to* you, but it doesn't seem like you even want me here. I feel like I'm in the way or—"

Maggie stood. "Fine. If you don't want to be here—"

"I never said I don't want to be here! And where are *you* going?"

"To take a bath." Maggie closed the door behind her.

Inside the bathroom, she threw off her clothes and lowered herself into the tub, which she filled with water that went from ice cold to scalding hot within seconds. She watched the storm swirling outside the window. How had she gotten herself into this mess?

When Sarah had called her last Friday night in Boston to say Frank had taken the kids to the Cape and the house was all hers, Maggie told herself this would be a proper goodbye—she deserved at least that after the way Sarah had ended things so abruptly. But she knew Sarah had other intentions as soon as she opened the door to her Beacon Hill brownstone. She knew when she hugged Maggie and said, "You look gorgeous." And she knew when Sarah held up a bottle of Riesling and said, "I saved it!" The bottle was from a vineyard they'd visited on the North Fork last summer, when Sarah snuck away from her family vacation for an afternoon.

Sarah hadn't offered a tour of the brownstone, but as they sat in what she called the parlor, Maggie took in all the ways their lives could not be more different—from Sarah's manicured nails to Frank's golf clubs in the entryway to the kids' boots lined up in size order at the foot of the stairs. Halfway through the Riesling, Sarah pulled out a joint, loosening things up even more. And here was the thing Maggie couldn't deny: though she'd pulled away when Sarah finally kissed her, she did not do so immediately. She froze. Was it a second? Several? It didn't matter.

Maggie turned off the water and used her big toe to stop the faucet's incessant leak. She was still trying to calm down when she realized that she'd left her phone on the bedside table. Sarah could be texting back at any moment with God knows what kind of response. She pulled out the stopper, and the water gurgled down the drain as she dried off, shivering from the cold.

When she returned to the room, Isabel wasn't there but had left a note on the desk: *In the cottage.*

Maggie imagined Isabel walking past her mother in the kitchen on her way to the cottage. Well, at least someone had gotten what they wanted tonight.

She checked her phone—nothing—and turned it off. Standing in the middle of the room, her eyes adjusted to the darkness, and she gazed out the window at the fresh white landscape and the collapsed fence leading to the beach. Kyle and Finn helped out at the house as much as possible, but when would it all be too much for her parents and Alice to maintain the property?

She debated whether to go to the cottage. She wanted to say good night, at least, but she did not want to deal with her mother in the kitchen or, worse, Isabel grilling her more about why she was acting so strangely.

She was supposed to be rereading *Wuthering Heights* to prep for her class's midterms next week, but instead, she grabbed the copy of *Anna Karenina* Isabel had left on the desk, flipped on the bedside lamp, and stayed awake for a long time reading. This many years later, she could somehow keep track of all the names, and the story provided the distraction she craved until she eventually allowed herself to fall asleep, listening to the house do the same.

It was snowing harder when she woke to the honks and barks of the geese. Dawn emerged, blushing the gray sky. The branches on the oak tree outside her bedroom window were suspended in white, and snow blew across the bay, where the geese hovered over the rolling, white-capped waves. The house was quiet.

Maggie turned her phone back on—still nothing from Sarah—then wrapped a throw blanket around her shoulders and snuck out of her room and down the back staircase leading to the cottage door. She crawled into the bed next to Isabel and closed the terrible space between them. Isabel turned and nestled into the crook of her shoulder, and Maggie breathed in all her mingling scents, endearingly sharpened from sleep. They held each other, dozing on and off, until the sun broke through the only window in the cottage and Isabel placed her hand on Maggie's chest and said something Maggie hadn't expected.

"I wish you'd let me in," she said. "I was looking forward to getting to know you more by being here, but it's like the opposite is happening."

Maggie felt so relieved to be back in Isabel's arms. She wanted to stay there and not talk about any of it, but she had to repair some of the damage she'd done. "What do you want to know?" she asked.

Isabel draped her leg across Maggie's. "What do you want to tell me?"

Oh, so much. The thought of it made Maggie lightheaded. She wanted to tell Isabel about that stupid night in Boston. How she wished it had never happened and yet, at the same time, how it had taught her something she'd needed to learn: she was done with Sarah, truly done. She would have to explain it all eventually, but she did not want to do so here and now. She did not. It would ruin everything. Maybe it already had.

Maggie looked around the room. When she and her siblings were teenagers, they'd used the cottage to hang out with friends or watch movies. Though Alice had turned it into a guest room, Maggie swore she could still smell hints of stale popcorn and cheap beer.

"Here's something," she said now to Isabel. "My mom discovered I was gay when she caught me on this bed with Julia Graham junior year of high school."

"I thought you came out in college?"

"Well, before that, my mom walked into the cottage one day after school and found Julia and me making out while pretending to work on our zine."

"That sounds both horrifying and kind of hot?"

"Hot, then horrifying."

Her mother hadn't actually caught them making out, but they were lying in bed with their arms wrapped around each other. Moments earlier, they'd kissed for the first time, after months of what Maggie had been telling herself was just an exciting new friendship, but what she soon realized was a force beyond anything she'd ever known.

Unlike kissing Will and Matt, the only boys she'd ever dated, this kiss was perfect. Finally, she understood the poems she'd read in her English classes, all those sappy love scenes in movies, and why her friends obsessed over guys. For years, she'd only pretended to understand. It was as revelatory as it was terrifying. She was both sick to her stomach with shame and soaring from the discovery of her body and heart and all the beautiful things that had once eluded her.

"What'd she do?" Isabel asked. "After she found you?"

"When she opened the door, we jumped up, but I guess she'd seen enough," Maggie said. "After Julia left, I tried to tell my mom that we were just taking a nap or something, but she knew. Probably even before then."

"That sucks you had to lie."

"I guess. But I was right to at least try. Everything went downhill from there. My mom called Julia's parents and told them—"

"She didn't!"

"She sure did. Julia and I weren't allowed to see each other, and my parents removed the private phone line in my bedroom. They figured out that our zine was for fans of Jeanette Winterson—"

"Yikes."

"Yeah, so they put an end to that, too. And I guess the final insult was my mom sending me to talk to Father Kelly to—"

"Ungay you?"

Maggie laughed. "I think the term they used was *spiritual counseling*." Then: "Though the point was definitely to guide me back to the flock."

Isabel held her closer and pressed her lips to her forehead. "I'm glad it didn't work," she said.

"I am, too."

* * *

When Maggie's mother picked her up from school that day, Maggie knew something was different, but it wasn't until they rounded the corner and pulled into the parking lot of Saint Mary's rectory that she realized what was happening.

Nora clutched the station wagon steering wheel and kept her eyes straight ahead. "I'll wait here," she said.

Maggie sank into the seat. "I'm not going in," she said. As natural as it had felt to kiss Julia, it felt equally unnatural to disobey her mother. It was futile anyway. Nora's power of persuasion had never been in a raised voice or threat of punishment. It was in her sadness, her disappointment.

Nora didn't say anything, and they sat in the car for several minutes, until Maggie couldn't take the silence anymore. She opened the door and slammed it closed behind her.

The smell of incense and coffee followed her as she and Father Kelly made their way through the quiet rectory hallways and into the kitchen, where he arranged a plate of Nilla wafers and poured her a glass of milk as though she were in kindergarten. He gestured for her to sit, sit. When she did, she expected him to launch into one of his stories, but instead he sat across from her and got straight to the point.

"You understand your mother's concern, yes?"

Maggie nodded and stared at a basket of palm branches waiting to be braided into crosses. She did not dare say a word. Silence was the only way to contain the tears. Besides, what could she possibly say?

"You know," he continued, "you are a very bright girl and you have a lot of curiosity about the world."

And that's when she noticed it. His delicate hands and soft voice. The way he crossed his legs. She'd known Father Kelly her whole life. He'd baptized her and all her siblings, had taught her religion class the past year, and was at nearly all her family holidays. And yet, she'd never detected. Or—that wasn't it. She *had* detected. She'd just never had a word to explain it all. Now she did. The same unspoken word—she hadn't even said it to Julia—that applied to her as well. But instead of connecting her to Father Kelly, a sort of kinship, she felt the opposite. The hypocrite. How dare he?

"The sin is in the act, but before we act, we think." He tapped his forehead as though she didn't know where one had thoughts. "Right?"

Something within Maggie collapsed. She wished she could talk to someone honestly. To tell them what was happening. To get advice that was actually helpful. To hear that it was all going to be okay. She did not want to upset her parents, but the moment she'd kissed Julia, she'd understood that this need, this drive, was an essential part of herself that would never go away. Even if she wanted it to.

She watched two finches fight for a spot on a bird feeder hanging from a bare tree outside the window. All she wanted was for the conversation to end. To leave and go to her room to be alone.

Father Kelly sat back in his chair and placed his hands behind his head. "Perhaps you're being called to fulfill God's will," he said.

This caught Maggie's attention—mostly because she didn't know what he was talking about—and she looked up at him. As a kid, she would pray every Sunday that she got the piece of communion broken from Father Kelly's host. She'd adored him. Maybe he did have something to offer her now.

"In facing difficulties," he continued, "we are given a chance to reevaluate the role faith plays in our lives and in determining our life choices." He sat up and leaned forward. "That is the point. Not desire."

Fuck off, Maggie thought. *Desire is the point! Desire makes everything clear.* She was too angry to cry, and when Father Kelly reached his hands across the table, she just looked at him.

"You are a child of God and you have His mercy," he said.

He had it all wrong. It wasn't the grace of God she had lost; it was her mother's. She was no longer the precocious little girl in her communion dress, white patent-leather shoes, and lace-frilled socks.

On her way out, Father Kelly said, "Sure, with everything your parents have been through the last few years, I know you won't be giving them any more grief." He came from the same area of West Cork as her mother, and they shared the same gentle lilt that made *won't* sound like *want*.

How's that fair? Maggie thought. *Because my brother was involved in an accident that killed a boy and nearly bankrupted my parents, I can't live my own life?* Like her parents had a finite amount of forgiveness and empathy to offer, and Topher had cleaned them out? Maybe he had.

Maggie slumped back into the car. She strapped the seat belt across her chest and stared out the window. She wanted to tell her mother what she'd discovered about Father Kelly. Nora had met him shortly after moving to Port Haven, and, as she told it, he soon became her "spiritual father." *Well,* Maggie thought, *your spiritual father is a first-class homo.*

But she didn't say this, because she didn't want to hurt her mother, and because as much as she had lost all respect for Father Kelly, she now knew what it meant to be yanked out of the closet against her will. She didn't want to be the one to do that to anybody else.

After a moment, her mother, clutching her rosary beads, said, "I trust that was helpful."

It was not a question, but Maggie didn't want to give her mother the impression there was anything remotely helpful in the conversation. To offer that felt like a complete denial of herself. A denial her mother would insist upon. It hadn't always been this way between them, but so much had changed in the past few days, it was disorienting.

"Sure," she said, and her mother started the engine.

* * *

Maggie lay her head on Isabel's belly. "The crazy thing is that when I finally came out in college, my mom acted shocked. It wasn't a big deal for anyone else, but for her—I mean, she definitely believes my soul is at risk."

"How did you tell her?" Isabel asked.

"I sent a letter apologizing," Maggie said. "I regret doing that, apologizing."

"Why did you?"

"Because I really was sorry."

Isabel played with Maggie's hair. "You shouldn't have been," she said.

"I guess."

"You guess?"

It was hard for Maggie to explain it all, but she tried. "Topher died a few months after," she said. "The church had always been a life raft for my mom, but at that point it became everything."

"Have you guys talked about it since?"

"Not really. In our last conversation, she told me, 'If I don't have my beliefs, what do I have?' And I was like, 'Um, *me*? You have me!'"

Even in the most chaotic times of her mother's childhood, Nora had always found order and safety in her faith. It was the one thing, Maggie understood, that her mother could rely on. How could she ever compete with that?

Isabel was quiet for a long moment, then said, "Maybe she's changed? I'm here, after all. She's welcomed me. That must be a good sign."

"You are here." Maggie held Isabel's hand and studied the surprisingly decent manicure James had given her the night before with the neon-green nail polish from his Shrek Halloween costume. She loved that Isabel hadn't removed it. "And I don't want you to sleep in the cottage," she said.

Isabel lifted Maggie's face to hers. "I'm sorry about last night," she said.

"Don't be," Maggie said. Isabel's contrition only made her feel worse.

Outside the cottage door, a flurry of footsteps and squeals emerged from the driveway; then they heard Augustus yell, "The raccoon got the garbage! Mummy!"

Maggie turned her attention back to Isabel. "So you won't go to your cousin's?"

Isabel sat up on her elbow. Her braid was messy from sleep, her olive skin dark against her white V-neck. Maggie was sure she was the most beautiful woman she'd ever known and would ever know, and she had to stop herself from pulling her closer and begging her to stay.

Isabel stretched and yawned. "I don't think I could leave even if I wanted to," she said, and faced the window. "It's like we're in a snow globe." Then she turned back, and her brown eyes glowed as she lowered her face to kiss Maggie on the lips and said the thing Maggie was waiting for her to say. "But, anyway, I want to be here. I want to be with you."

"Same," Maggie said.

"And I'm glad you shared all that with me," Isabel said. "It helps me understand more. I wish you'd told me earlier."

A queasiness surfaced in Maggie's stomach when she thought of everything she still had not shared with Isabel. About Sarah. The impending meeting with Cunningham. At least they were back on solid ground, she told herself. At least there was that. She hoped the snow globe would hold, and that she hadn't already cracked the glass.

9.
CAIT

Cait had been awake since dawn with the twins and was desperate to sneak in a morning nap on the sofa in the sitting room, but the door to the back porch swung open and roused her.

"The raccoon got the garbage!" Augustus yelled from the doorway.

Cait sat up. "You're not wearing snow clothes."

Augustus looked down at his flannel pajamas and sneakers, both soaking wet, and shrugged. "Finn said Papa's going to shoot the raccoon," he said.

"He'll do no such thing."

Cait turned toward the doorway and said, "Morning, Mom," then looked back to Augustus. "The raccoon's not out there now, is it?"

Augustus shook his head. "James and Finn are tracking him in the woods."

"Go tell Auntie Alice." Cait pulled the blanket around her shoulders. "And come inside. It's freezing out there. You can cuddle with me and take a nap."

Augustus scrunched his face at her as though she'd lost her mind, then hopped back outside and closed the door behind him. From the window, Cait followed the top of his head as he ran to the side of the house.

"He'll freeze," her mother said, and headed to the kitchen.

Cait grumbled and stood. As she put on her shoes, she heard Alice coming down the back stairs—Cait considered it a talent, her ability to identify every person in the family just by the sound of their footsteps—and quickly hid. When Alice reached the bottom step, Cait leapt out from the corner and yelled, "Boo!"

Alice screamed and tossed the handful of dish towels she was holding at Cait.

Cait couldn't remember when she'd laughed so hard. She used to jump-scare Alice all the time when they were kids, but it was even more fun as an adult.

"You need to grow up," Alice said, picking up the towels.

Cait bowed. "Why, thank you," she said. "I agree that was one of my better ones."

Outside, Cait found Augustus and his cousins standing with sticks along the edge of the woods separating the Folly from the Callahans' property, where Cait and Topher used to hide their beer in high school.

"Hey," she yelled. "Get away from there. Where's Papa? You guys can't catch the raccoon yourselves. They're dangerous."

The three boys skulked away from the wooded area, and Cait pointed to the garbage scattered across the driveway.

"Let's grab some bags to clean up," she said. Then she looked at Augustus. "And you need some snow clothes."

The boys dragged their sticks across the snow as they made their way back into the house and changed, Augustus borrowing one of James's old snowsuits. Bundled and back outside, Cait monitored their cleanup from the front porch. Finn wasn't happy about the chore, but Augustus and James made it a competition, and even though Cait was cold and tired, she couldn't help but smile watching them all play together. She hadn't necessarily worried about them getting along, but she was glad at how quickly they'd bonded, especially Augustus and James. Augustus seemed more relaxed than he'd been in months. He'd taken the divorce harder than Poppy and had asked Cait just last week if his father would be joining them on the trip to New York. Cait and Bram had rarely visited the Folly, but when they did, he was always bored, and she had to entertain him as though he were a child. She was glad they had never been there together with the twins. Now she and the twins had a fresh slate to make their own memories.

Finn was the self-proclaimed judge of the Best Garbage Collector competition, so naturally, Augustus won. James did his best to protest, and he was right, but he let it go once Finn suggested another game.

"You guys can stay out here," Cait said. "But if you see a raccoon, you have to come let us know. And avoid the geese. They're not nice either."

"We know," Finn said, which was what he seemed to say about most things.

"I'll shoot them with my laser." Augustus held up a small plastic stick. "Pow, pow!"

"What is that?" Cait asked. From where she stood on the porch, it looked like a pregnancy test.

Augustus shrugged. "It was in the garbage."

"Let me see."

Cait glanced at it quickly—two positive lines—and tossed it into the garbage bag. "This isn't for you to play with," she said to Augustus.

"What is it?" he asked.

"Nothing," Cait said. "Come with me to wash your hands."

After washing Augustus's hands and her own, she let him back outside and closed the front door.

It must be Alice's, she figured. There was no one else. Though why would Alice have taken the test there and not at her own house? And was she even allowed to be pregnant after the crazy high blood pressure that had nearly killed her before James was born? Cait thought back to her conversation with Maggie at the pizzeria last night. Was this possibly *her* test? She and Isabel weren't trying to have a baby already, were they?

Just then, Alice and their mother walked by from the kitchen.

"I'm helping Mom pick out an outfit for today," Alice said as she headed up the stairs, dodging Cait's eyes. She was clearly still annoyed about Luke coming for dinner.

"Fantastic," Cait said enthusiastically, to annoy Alice. She kissed her mother on the cheek. "I'm sure you'll look beautiful."

From halfway up the stairs, Alice peered down at Cait and rolled her eyes, then kept on going.

Cait waved her off and headed to her father's office to see if she could sneak in another attempt to call Luke. She wanted to make sure he was still coming and to explain what had happened to her phone in case he tried to get in touch. She could tell that he'd been drinking last night when he accepted the invitation and wouldn't be surprised if he backed out now. When there was no answer, she slumped into the leather chair and placed her feet on the desk.

Framed photos of the family covered the wall. The last one of Topher was from a boat he worked on in Maine the winter before he died. In the picture, he was leaning against a bunch of stacked crates and banding the claws of an enormous blue lobster, the churning sea behind him. Nora had hated him working on the boat, fearing it was too dangerous, but Cait understood why she'd put up the picture. Topher's ruggedly handsome smile made him look almost wholesome, and that was the memory their mother was determined to preserve.

Cait never understood why people lionized the dead. All their flaws vanished, and suddenly they emerged as an idealized version of themselves. For her, though, that didn't happen with Topher. What she remembered most about her brother was his decline. Maggie once asked if she ever sensed Topher's presence, and she said no because it was true, but the idea scared the hell out of her. She didn't hold on to much from her

Catholic upbringing, but one thing she felt sure of was that the dead do not become angels.

Above her, she could hear her mother and Alice shuffling around in her parents' room. She should have gone upstairs with her mother instead of Alice. Maybe she was asking for too much today.

There was no sense dwelling on it now. *What's done is done.* And if she and Luke were going to keep talking like they had been over the past few months, she'd eventually have to tell her family anyway.

She knew what Alice was thinking. *How could you invite this person who elicits so many painful memories to dinner?*

What else was new? She felt Alice's judgment every time she returned home. There was always something. She didn't visit enough. She'd left too soon after Topher died. Beyond writing the occasional check to keep the Folly afloat, she didn't help out with their parents. The list went on and on.

But it wasn't Alice's judgment that haunted Cait the most. She could admit that. It was her own. It had always been her own.

She judged herself not only for Daniel's accident, but for what happened years later when Topher showed up at her apartment the night before her bar exam. She'd never told anyone about their fight, and when she was in London, it was almost easy to forget it had even happened.

Here, not so much.

* * *

Cait woke to the knocking on her apartment door and listened for a groggy moment. A drunk neighbor? The alarm clock next to the bed read two minutes after midnight. Her bladder was full, and her throat throbbed from a cold she hoped to hold off until after her test that day. As she calculated how much sleep she'd still manage to get, she sat up, and her monstrous BARBRI US Bar Review book slid off her chest and slammed onto the wooden floor.

There was another loud knock.

"Cait?"

Through the peephole, she could see her brother standing in the hallway, laughing. She undid the chain and opened the door.

"What the fuck?"

"Good to see you, too, kid."

The smell of booze lingered as he walked past her and into the apartment. He tossed his backpack, tattered and covered in patches, next to the desk and turned to her with red cheeks. Their mother had hoped, when he dropped out of college, he would find his way and not drift aimlessly. Cait wasn't as confident, and every time she saw him, she'd think, without pleasure, *I was right.*

"How'd you get into the building?"

"A delivery guy held the door for me."

"That's comforting."

"I told him not to." He smiled. *"No creo que hablase inglés."*

"You're drunk." She was annoyed but also worried. He'd never just shown up like this, and she wasn't sure what he wanted.

He chuckled as he collapsed onto the paisley upholstered chair from their grandmother's old bedroom.

She remained standing, watching as he rubbed his swollen, cracked hands against the armrests. The only window in the apartment framed him. Rain fell lightly on Bleecker Street.

"Seriously, Topher. No word from you in—what? A year? And you show up here now? Like this?"

"Hey!" He raised his hands in defense. "I sent postcards. Did you get the one from—"

"Mom can't even keep track of you."

The last time Cait spoke to their mother about Topher was when they'd learned he was going to Maine to work on the lobster boat in the middle of winter. Over lunch at Captain's Diner in Port Haven, Nora cried and told Cait she was worried that he'd taken a turn for the worse. Cait wasn't sure why—Topher was always making stupid decisions—but she suggested her mother tell him that. Nora didn't, of course. She never said anything to Topher that might be taken as criticism. Not when he dropped out of college and pretended to still be enrolled for months until the official withdrawal notice arrived and he couldn't deny it anymore. Or rode a motorcycle through rural South America without a map. Or applied to become a helicopter firefighter in Montana and lied on his medical form about his asthma. This had always been the case with Topher. Sometimes Cait was jealous of his free pass, and other times she saw how it just gave him permission to be an asshole.

Topher smiled and raised his hands in an *aw shucks* kind of way. "Well, here I am," he said. "Tracked."

"You reek." More than the booze, it was layers of tobacco and sweat and weed, the hint of something briny and decayed. Maybe even gasoline.

"I'm sure I do. I came straight off the boat—"

"Why?"

"Just got into town for Alice's wedding." He crossed his legs and entwined his hands on his lap.

Alice's wedding was a week away, but last Cait heard, Topher hadn't responded to their mother's panicked inquiries about whether he'd be attending. Cait wasn't sure she believed him anyway. He could have ditched the boat for any reason. He got fired. He quit. He was off to Siberia. It had been years since she'd understood him in any real way. Every time she saw him, he was less recognizable to her, less accessible. He even looked different. Born eleven months before her, they were Irish twins, but standing there now, he seemed much older, his hair thinning in the front, face puffy, shoulders hunched.

"What is she doing getting married anyway?" he continued. "Who is this guy?"

"Kyle's all right."

Cait liked Kyle, even if he was a bit rigid.

"She's too young," Topher said.

The idea of Topher judging anyone for how they lived their life floored

Cait, but she also agreed with him, and so she didn't say anything as he scanned her one-room studio, nodding at the books stacked near the radiator and the plants covering the windowsill.

"Your timing is shit," she said. "I'm taking the bar in the morning."

"Dude." He slapped his forehead. "I'm so sorry."

He shook off his Carhartt jacket, and beneath his flannel, the Saint Christopher cross their mother had given him for confirmation hung around his neck. It surprised her that he still wore it, and she found herself softening.

"It's fine," she said.

He picked up the textbook from the floor and flicked through the pages. "Why are you doing this?" He asked it like they'd had the conversation before. "What good do lawyers do?"

Whatever small amount of sympathy she'd had for him was waning. She understood where his disapproval of lawyers stemmed from, but what right did he have to barge into her apartment in the middle of the night and interrogate her like this? More irritating was the younger-sibling part of her that still wanted to impress him, even longed for his approval.

"I don't know," she said. "Little things like advocating for equal rights and making sure people are treated justly."

Topher tossed the book onto her bed and leaned forward, elbows on his knees. "And that's the kind of lawyer you're going to be?"

She smirked. "I'm going into corporate law."

"True justice indeed." His laugh had an edge. "But you still haven't explained why."

Cait bristled. She knew he was waiting for her to say it was for the money, so he could give her one of his anti-capitalist rants, but she refused.

"I happen to find it interesting," she said. "And challenging, intellectually. Remember that?"

For a moment he seemed to actually be remembering something. Then he said, "Sure," and his half shrug infuriated her. He had always been the smart one. The one who didn't need to study to get the best grades and the highest test scores. The one their mother assumed would become a doctor, though Cait never once heard him talk about medicine.

"Well," she said, "maybe it's not as rewarding as being a deckhand on a lobster boat—"

"Sternman." He winked.

"But not anymore?"

"We'll see," he said. "Think I might head to South Korea to teach English."

"That almost sounds civilized."

"I also have a buddy with a logging outfit in Durango, so—"

Cait snorted. He always "had a buddy."

Topher watched her. "Anyway," he said after a moment. "Can I crash for the night? I haven't slept in over a day, and I'm beat. I can sleep on the floor. I'll get out of here first thing in the morning."

"Where will you go?"

"Home," he said.

"Is Mom expecting you?"

He whistled. "What are you? Her gatekeeper?"

Cait didn't want him there. He stank. She'd had a whole plan for her morning—a run, coffee, shower, then off to her test. But he was her brother, and she loved him and worried about him, so she said, "You can stay one night."

Topher pressed his palms together in prayer, a gesture he'd acquired after living on a communal farm in India a few years ago when he was still in his early twenties. Then he lowered his head in a slight bow, annoying Cait to no end—this former altar boy acting all holy—and said, "Thanks, kid."

Cait stepped into her slippers. "I need to grab the blow-up mattress from the basement. I'll be back in five."

Downstairs, she flipped on the lights and clapped her hands to scare away the mice as she walked toward her locker. The only time she'd ever been down there was three years ago when she first moved in, and her landlord showed her the storage space. The basement was spooky and cold, and she was grateful she remembered the code for the lock. She grabbed the bag and ran upstairs two steps at a time, but when she made it back to her apartment, the door, which locked automatically, wouldn't open. She knocked.

"Topher," she whispered loudly.

She pounded harder.

"Topher!" she yelled. "Open the fucking door!"

After a few minutes, she slid down and collapsed onto the blow-up mattress bag, her back against the door. The hallway was freezing, her throat raw, and she still hadn't gone to the bathroom. Now and then she pummeled the door, no longer caring if she woke her landlord—at least she could use their bathroom—but Topher didn't hear a thing, because he was passed out on their grandmother's old chair, where Cait had left him in her warm apartment.

When he opened the door hours later, dawn flooding the hallway where Cait dozed, he was mostly sober and spouting apologies and rubbing his bloodshot eyes.

"How long were you—"

"Just shut up!" She leapt to her feet. She was so furious she wanted to hit him, but she desperately needed to relieve her bladder before anything else. When she emerged from the bathroom, her fingers stiff with cold, she found him drinking a glass of water in her tiny kitchen nook. It was cloudy outside, but in the early morning light, he looked even worse than he had last night, the bags under his eyes swollen, as though he was the one who'd slept in the hallway.

She opened the window to let in fresh air and get rid of the day-old smell of his booze and sweat. Bleecker Street was quiet, nearly empty aside from a man walking his dog. The sidewalks and trees were all drenched from rain.

He placed the glass in the sink with a shaky hand and turned to her. "I don't totally remember what happened," he said, his voice gravelly.

The Irish Goodbye

Cait stormed past him, grabbed his backpack, and thrust it at him. "You have to leave."

He blinked. "You're pissed. I get it."

Cait handed him his jacket. "No, you don't get it," she said. "If you got it, you'd grow the fuck up."

She'd never spoken to her brother like that—she'd followed along with their mother and pretended like all was fine and normal even when it wasn't. Topher stared at her hard, but she refused to be the one to break eye contact.

Finally, he nodded and said, "Okay," then put on his jacket and tossed the backpack over his shoulder.

But his composure enraged her more. She'd buried it for years—the horror of his pain, his lostness a constant reminder of her gnawing guilt—and now she couldn't contain herself.

"And I'm not Mom's *gatekeeper*, but I am so tired of her having to worry about you all the fucking time. Do you know what that's done to her? To all of us? I don't give a shit anymore. Mom's right. All you're doing is trying to kill yourself on these stupid jobs, and now—what?—you're going to go climb hundred-foot trees? I'm done trying to stop you."

These were not the last words she'd said to her brother, but they might as well have been, for the way she would regret them. For years and years, they would settle within her like rot.

10.

ALICE

Alice held up the houndstooth blazer, which her mother liked because Cait had sent it from Milan, and apparently, it was quite expensive.

"How about this?" she asked.

"I don't have shoes to match."

Alice grabbed a pair of black loafers off the side door. "Wear these."

"I won't look like an old lady?"

"Never," Alice said.

Nora laughed. "I'll wear it with a black turtleneck, then. And maybe a scarf."

Alice lay a pair of trousers and a black turtleneck on the bed next to the blazer. "I know today's going to be tough," she said. "As much as I don't understand why Cait invited Luke, it's nice of you to try."

Her mother sat on the bed and picked at the pilling on the blazer's elbow. "It's important to Cait, so it's important."

Alice sat next to her. "You're a good mom."

The Irish Goodbye

Nora smiled weakly. "It's hard to be a mother when you never had one yourself."

"It's hard to be a mother full stop." Alice stood and walked to the closet. She did not want to linger on the subject. It brought up her doubts about the pregnancy, and she worried Nora would notice again. "Where are your scarves?"

Nora pointed to the top shelf. "Somewhere in all that mess."

Standing on a step stool, Alice rummaged through the boxes. "I'm going to clean out your closet next weekend," she said over her shoulder. "One of these could fall on you and—"

"Leave that one be!" Nora stood up from the bed.

Alice inspected the shoebox in her hands. It was worn along the edges and wrapped tightly in a yellowed ribbon. "Why?"

Nora held on to the bed rail and sat again. "Just put it back." She motioned at the box. "I don't want to see it."

Alice turned to the shelf, now even more disheveled, then back to her mother. "What's in here?" She gave the box a slight shake. Had her parents saved some of Topher's ashes?

"I told you. Please—just put it back where you found it."

"Okay," Alice said. As much as she wanted to know what was in the box, she had no interest in upsetting her mother any more, and after discovering the *Hustler* in James's duffel yesterday, she figured maybe it was best to leave well enough alone. Anyway, her mother was entitled to her privacy. She stuffed the box on top of a plastic bin that was labeled HANDBAGS but looked like it held yarn, and grabbed the basket of scarves, which she placed on the bed.

"I'm sorry," Nora said as Alice laid different scarf options against the blazer. "I didn't mean to shout at you."

Alice noticed her mother's hands were shaking and reached for them. "What's going on?" she asked. "What's in there?"

"It's the condolence cards," Nora said after a moment. "For Topher."

Alice sat on the bed and stared at the box in the closet. Then, thinking about Luke's imminent arrival, she said, "I still can't believe Mrs. Larkin never reached out after Topher died. I know there was so much history and everything, but some kind of—"

"She did," Nora said. "She sent a card."

Alice was confused. She had been the one to respond to all the cards on behalf of the family, and she was sure she'd have remembered one from Mrs. Larkin. "When?"

"Oh, it must have been nearly a year after—"

"Why didn't you ever tell me? What did it say?"

"I don't know."

"You don't know why you never told me, or you don't know what it said?"

"I never read it."

Her mother's eyes watered, but Alice couldn't let this go without some kind of explanation. "Did you keep it?" she pressed. "Is it still in the box with the others?"

"They're all in there," Nora said. She shook her head. "Every day I look up at that box, and I wish it wasn't there."

"We can put it somewhere else," Alice said. "There's no need for you to suffer like that."

"I tried, but I can't make myself do it," Nora said. "But I'm glad you know now. You can do with it what you want."

"Me? What should I do with it?"

Instead of answering, her mother stood and picked up the red silk scarf Alice had draped across the jacket. "I like this one," she said. "It's cheery, don't you think?"

Alice nodded, then turned back to the closet. The knowledge that Mrs. Larkin's unopened card was in there—and that her mother did not want anything to do with it—was another burden she could have done without that day.

11.

MAGGIE

While Isabel showered, Maggie returned to her room, eager to check her phone to see if Sarah had responded. Still nothing. This was so typical of Sarah that Maggie felt at once relieved to be out of the clutches of the relationship—how many holidays had she spent waiting for Sarah to sneak away from Frank to call her for a quick "I love you"?—and full of renewed regret that she'd put herself in this position in the first place.

As she made her bed, her thoughts turned to Isabel's question from earlier that morning about whether her mother had changed. Maggie was sure she hadn't. For years she'd had to work hard to keep her expectations low. It was the only way she'd managed to have a relationship with her mother at all. Why open old wounds?

And yet, with Isabel there, at the house, how could she not wonder what it would be like if things were different? How could she not want that?

In the kitchen, she found her father dressing Poppy in James's old winter clothes.

"Kyle got bagels." He pointed to the spread on the island. He finished tying Poppy's boots and ushered her out the side door. "Snowman time!"

"Have fun," Maggie said. She thought of snow days when they'd wake up and discover that school was canceled, and their father would take them snowshoeing along the beach. She wished Cait lived closer so her parents could spend more time with the twins.

As soon as her father closed the door, Cait peeked into the kitchen. "They're gone?"

"You're safe."

Cait poured a cup of coffee and took a sip. "I hate playing."

Maggie looked out the window at Kyle making the kids snow cones with maple syrup. "Isn't that the fun part of being a parent?" she asked. "Playing in the snow and stuff?"

"Only someone without children would think that," Cait said. "No offense."

"None taken."

Suddenly Cait regarded her with narrowed eyes. "You don't have anything to tell me, do you? You mentioned work last night."

Maggie froze. She had wanted to talk to Cait last night about everything with Sarah but had dropped it when Poppy joined them to pick up the pizza, and there was no way she was going to get into it all now with everyone running around the house. "I'll tell you later." Then, to change the subject, she said, "And we need to talk about Luke—"

Cait grabbed the newspaper by the sink. "Not now we don't. I've been up with the twins since the crack of dawn, and I just want to drink my coffee and read the paper in silence."

"Understood." Maggie was still dismayed by Cait's invitation to Luke, but her sister was in no mood to get into it, and she knew that pushing would only annoy her more.

Maggie threw on her father's decades-old Barbour coat and headed outside, where she found her mother on the front porch, wrapped in a wool blanket and watching the kids play.

The Irish Goodbye

"Morning, love," she said when Maggie opened the door. Despite any anxiety her mother might have had about Luke joining them for dinner or unease around Isabel being there, Maggie knew she relished having the whole family together.

"It's cold out here." Maggie buried her hands inside the jacket pockets and was alarmed to find two shotgun shells.

Nora tightened the blanket around her shoulders. "It is cold," she agreed. Then she said, "Alice was looking for you earlier. She has a to-do list she needs help with."

"I'm sure she'll find me," Maggie said.

Poppy handed Nora a snow cone, then collapsed onto the driveway with Augustus to make snow angels.

Watching her mother laugh with the twins stirred an unexpected tenderness. "They must bring up a lot of memories from when we were kids," Maggie said.

Her mother turned to her and half smiled. "It snowed so hard the winter after you were born, we couldn't get the station wagon out of the driveway for a week. You had colic, poor thing, and your brother would spend hours playing in the snow just to get away from all your hollering."

Maggie remembered a home video of that winter. Topher, Cait, and Alice outside playing, her screams echoing in the background.

"He'd come back inside," her mother continued, "teeth all chattering." She laughed. "Ah, but we get on with it. Don't we?"

"I guess we do," Maggie said. It wasn't like her mother to evoke a memory of Topher so casually, and she wondered if it had anything to do with Luke coming for dinner. "How are you feeling about today?"

Maggie didn't know Luke that well. Like her brother, he was nine years older than her, and he and Topher had pretty much stopped being friends after Daniel died. She'd always liked the alliteration in his name—Luke Larkin—and had foggy memories of him from the beach club, but that was about it. He and Cait had had some sort of fling back in high school, though she wasn't sure what her sister meant when she said they'd been back in touch over the past few months. Cait had conspicuously omitted that detail when talking to the family last night.

"You know about Mrs. Larkin passing," her mother said. "Cait's right. It's the kind thing to do."

"I guess," Maggie said. She kept her questions about why Luke would want to come to dinner with them in the first place to herself.

Nora took a bite from her snow cone, then met Maggie's eyes. "I just wish—" She stopped.

"What?" Maggie asked, with a flicker of hope that her mother might say something about Isabel or maybe about wanting to repair their relationship.

But then her mother said, "Has Cait mentioned seeing anyone new lately?"

Of course.

"I don't think so," Maggie said flatly. She was not only disappointed but wasn't sure if her mother was asking something about Cait and Luke.

"Well, it'll be nice for her to meet Mukesh, then."

"Is Kyle trying to set them up?"

"Mukesh is moving to London," Nora said, as if that answered the question.

"Does Cait know that's Kyle's intention?"

"No, no."

Does anyone in this family talk to one another?

Her mother continued. "I still don't know what was so awful about Bram."

Maggie had been more upset when Cait said she was marrying Bram and moving to London than when she announced her divorce a decade later. Before Cait's wedding, Maggie had met Bram only once, on a visit to Brighton. Over curry and beers, Bram spent the night talking about himself, scolded the server for forgetting the biryani, and, at the end of the meal, quietly slid the check across the table to Cait while he pontificated about his prized sneaker collection. Maggie had tried to give him the benefit of the doubt, but that first impression turned out to be generous. After the divorce, Bram returned to Amsterdam and settled for quarterly visits with the twins and a month in the summer.

"She didn't love him," Maggie said. "I don't think she ever did." She wasn't sure why she said the last part and if it was even true.

Her mother watched the kids make a snowman in the garden. "Yes," she said.

The small concession impressed Maggie. Her mother had been understandably upset by the divorce, but she'd mostly blamed it on the stress of the twins and Cait working such long hours.

Returning now to Isabel's advice, Maggie found herself saying, "So, do you like her?"

Her mother turned.

"Isabel," Maggie said impatiently. "Here we are talking about Cait, but you haven't mentioned anything about Isabel. What do you think of her?"

"Well, I'm getting to know her as such . . ."

Nora turned back to the kids, and Maggie waited to see if she might finish her sentence. Was that seriously all she had to say? When several moments passed, and her mother didn't offer more, a swell of familiar loneliness engulfed Maggie. She shouldn't have tried.

Nora held her hand over her forehead and squinted as she pointed to a pair of blue jays in the cherry tree at the center of the circular driveway. "Did you know they're not actually blue?" she said. "Their feathers don't contain any blue pigment. It's the way they reflect the light. They're brown."

Maggie watched the birds.

"It's some trick of nature or perspective," her mother continued, then closed her eyes and lifted her face to the sky. Snowflakes landed on her silver hair and dissolved.

Maggie marveled at the power of such a tiny woman to make her so frustrated and full of longing for acceptance that she could scream. She turned to the birds. Bright blue against the white snow, they fluttered from branch to bare branch. "'We don't see things as they are,'" she said. "'We see them as we are.'"

Her mother blinked.

"Anaïs Nin," Maggie said, and headed back inside where it was warm.

Maggie and Isabel made more coffee as Poppy marched into the kitchen, tracking snow and complaining that it was cold and the boys were playing too roughly. She kicked off her boots and wiggled out of the snowsuit, all of which were too big for her and, once removed, revealed plaid pajamas. She hopped onto a stool by the island and announced that she was "very starving."

Isabel pulled up a stool next to Poppy. "I'm very starving, too," she said. "What's for breakfast?"

Maggie prepared a plain buttered bagel for Poppy and everything bagels with vegetable cream cheese for herself and Isabel.

"Sliced tomato?"

Isabel shook her head no.

"You say that funny," Poppy said. She brushed her curly locks away from her face.

"Say what?"

"To-may-to," Poppy said.

Maggie planted her elbows on the island. "Do I?" she said in a mock British accent.

Poppy looked up, confused.

"Just kidding," Maggie said, and kissed the back of her hand.

Poppy inspected the bagel with a frown. "Can you cut it up for me?"

"Girl, you don't cut up a bagel!" Maggie said. "You eat it with your hands like this."

Poppy watched her but then tossed her bagel back onto the plate and grabbed her red crayon again.

"You're a good artist," Isabel said.

Poppy bit her lower lip and studied her picture the same way she'd done her bagel, but this time, she said, "I don't color things properly."

"That's impossible," Isabel said. "It's art! There's no 'proper' way to do it."

Poppy slapped her hands onto the counter and closed her book. "I'm going to tell my mummy that!" she said, and tucked the book under her arm as she stomped off.

"What about your breakfast?" Maggie asked.

"I'm not hungry anymore."

Maggie grabbed the empty stool next to Isabel and kissed her, her breath a mixture of minty toothpaste, coffee, and garlic from the bagel.

"That's better," Isabel said. She cupped the side of Maggie's face the way she did when she wanted her to pay attention. "I'm glad we talked this morning."

"I am, too," Maggie said. She was glad. But when she kissed the inside of Isabel's palm, she didn't taste the vetiver perfume on her skin that she loved so much—she tasted Sarah's lips, and her whole body flushed with the fear that this one mistake would cost her Isabel.

Isabel took a bite of her bagel and smiled as she chewed. "This is delicious."

"It's all in the water," Maggie said.

She tried to imagine what it would have been like to bring Sarah home to meet her family. She'd introduced her to Alice once in Vermont, but it wasn't until they broke up that Alice admitted she'd found Sarah standoffish, and Cait said, "My God, finally. Even from here, I could see it was a mistake." It was almost impossible to imagine Sarah sitting there now eating a bagel, as easy and affectionate as Isabel taking the extra slice of tomato off Maggie's plate and leaning in to kiss her again. She would have insisted on staying at a hotel, and Maggie would have obliged.

"Did you talk to your mom?" Isabel asked.

Maggie pushed her plate away. "I think I just have to accept that she tolerates it—or me, I don't know. She's never going to change. She's never going to—"

Alice strode in from the dining room, trailing the vacuum behind her.

"There you are!" Maggie said. "I've been looking all over for you."

"Sure you have," Alice said. "I need you to tackle the basement den."

Maggie jumped off the stool. "Aye, aye," she said, and blew Isabel a kiss.

In the basement, she found her father straddling the same worn leather stool he'd sat on throughout her childhood. Augustus and James stood next to him, looking at something in a tin box.

She plugged in the vacuum and walked to the table, which was covered in tracks, mountains, and clay villages with tiny figures she used to secretly play with when her father wasn't home. When they were younger, Topher attended the Train Collectors Association's national convention every year with their father, but he stopped after Daniel died. He was headed to college anyway—not that he stayed for even a whole year—but Maggie felt bad when her father left for the convention alone. The following year, she said she'd like to join him, and they traveled to Pittsburgh together by train. Once there, Maggie got food poisoning at a private collection tour and spent the rest of the weekend holed up in their hotel room. Though her father still volunteered for the association, she wasn't sure when he last went to a conference. Her parents' world shrank after Topher died. Her mother retreated to the church and Irish charities, and aside from work, her father spent most of his free time alone with his trains and on short backpacking trips. Neither had agreed to therapy, though Maggie and her sisters had tried to insist, but she supposed there were worse ways to grieve. It was nice to see him at the table with Augustus and James.

"Papa's giving us his Lionel Standard trains!" Augustus said.

Maggie turned to her father. "The ones you store behind the glass in the—" She gestured toward the cabinet, now empty. "Why are you doing that?"

Her father shrugged. "They asked me," he said.

Sitting on the floor, James smashed his tank car into Augustus's.

The Irish Goodbye

"Hey," Augustus said. He cradled his train in the palm of his hand like a baby bird, then kissed its nose.

"Dad," Maggie said, "those are probably covered with lead."

"You kids played with them and never had a problem."

"You wouldn't let us touch them!"

"No kissing the trains," her father said to the boys. "Got it?" He turned back to Maggie. "Better?"

Now she felt like the odd one. "Those are valuable antiques. Maybe give them to Cait and Alice to hold on to? So they don't lose or scratch them?"

He laughed away her concern. Maggie was incredulous. When she was a kid and would sneak into the basement to play with the figurines on the table, she'd make painstaking efforts to remember precisely where to return each one before her father came home from work. He would notice every detail. Once, she put a milking cow on the wrong side of the red barn, and that evening he went around the table and asked each of the kids if they'd moved her—and though they all knew that it was Maggie, each one gave an emphatic no. "Maybe there's a ghost in the house," Topher had said, then mooed like a haunted cow, and everyone laughed, and their father huffed and gave up on the interrogation.

Maggie grabbed the vacuum, but instead of turning it on, she watched her father, his hand shaking slightly as he adjusted something on his new Ferris wheel in the center of the carnival. She thought of Topher again. She was in college, and he was handing her the keys to his Jeep and telling her it was all hers in what she mistook as the greatest gift she'd ever received, but which she would come to know was just her brother preparing to die. She gripped the table and lowered herself onto the floor, where James and Augustus used lines on the carpet as imaginary train tracks.

"You're lucky," she said, and they both nodded indifferently. She grabbed the green caboose, which had always been her favorite. "This one's mine."

"Hey—" James said, but then seemed to think better of it and stopped.

Maggie stuffed the caboose into her pocket and stood. "Okay," she said. "Skedaddle. I have to vacuum."

No one acknowledged her except when she needed to get around the table. Even then, the three just patiently waited for her to finish, which she did hastily, because when her phone buzzed in her back pocket, she knew before checking that it must be Sarah.

12.

ALICE

After getting herself and the boys showered and ready, Alice snuck off to the sunroom. She hoped for a minute to herself before the guests arrived, but when she opened the door, she found Isabel sitting cross-legged on the hanging rattan, arranging a set of cards on her lap.

"I'm sorry," Alice said. "I didn't know anyone was back here."

Isabel quickly gathered the cards. "No, you're fine," she said, and smiled as she took off her horn-rimmed glasses.

She looked different from yesterday. Her skin was glowy, her lips red, and the unexpected but charming combination of her dark denim shirt and golden velvet blazer made Alice feel frumpy and conventional in her black leggings and white blouse. "Part of the waitstaff, are we?" Cait had quipped when they passed each other in the kitchen.

"Are those the tarot cards you were talking about last night?" Alice asked Isabel.

Isabel shuffled the deck. "They are. I do daily check-ins where I pull a single card for a reading. It gives me guidance or insight for the day."

"Like a psalm."

"Exactly."

From somewhere on the other side of the house, James screamed, "I'm it!"—a rallying cry for a game of hide-and-seek.

Alice reached for the handles on the glass-paneled doors. "I'll close these behind me," she said as she turned to leave, "so the kids don't bother you."

"They're no bother," Isabel said. "This room is beautiful, by the way. Maggie said you recently fixed it up."

Alice looked around the room. She hadn't done much. Just snagged the barely used rattan chair and some pillows that Georgia no longer wanted and bought a new light fixture from Target, but the small changes had transformed the space into a cozy nook. She was proud of how it had turned out, and it was nice of Isabel to notice—neither of her sisters had mentioned it.

"Thanks," she said.

Isabel smiled. "How long have you been—you're an interior designer?"

Alice wavered. "Yes, well, sort of. I was never formally trained, so—" She stopped, cringing at herself for blabbering on. She knew she needed to just embrace the title of interior designer, but she felt like a fraud every time she used it. When Georgia hired her to revamp her beach bungalow, Alice contemplated turning down the job to save herself the humiliation of failing. In the end, she agreed because Finn needed braces, and part of her—small but there—thought, *Maybe I can do this.* The first time she went to the D&D Building in the city, she expected to be called out and promptly ejected. But that's not what happened. She put together a fabric blend for the bungalow's living room that impressed the designer standing next to her.

"Fabulous," he'd said. "Mind if I borrow it for a villa in the Maldives? No one will ever know." Did she mind? She wanted to hug him! The story didn't translate later that night when she shared it with Kyle.

"He stole it?" he said.

The Irish Goodbye

"It wasn't like that," she told him. "I was flattered."

Kyle was skeptical. "If only flattery paid the bills," he said.

Alice shrugged him off. How could she care about that when an entire world was opening before her? A world filled with possibility and colors and textures and shapes. A world that had nothing to do with the PTA or basketball courts or the parish or the endless cycle of laundry and grocery lists and her parents' doctor appointments.

Since birth, she'd been under the shadows of her overachieving siblings, with their academic distinctions and all-American titles. Even years after Topher dropped out of college and they barely knew where he was living, their mother would talk about how he was wasting his brilliance. Alice hadn't the brilliance to waste in the first place. The only thing she'd ever felt capable of was taking care of other people—her parents, Kyle, the boys. The dutiful daughter, then wife, then mother. And she was good at it. Very good. In those roles, she was able to hide. She was safe. But she no longer wanted to hide. And as Isabel now waited for her to answer this seemingly simple question, she considered again how having another child would end it all.

"I suppose I am an interior designer," she said finally. "I'm applying to a program at Parsons." She had never stated that out loud, and it was thrilling.

Isabel nodded. Neither the pause nor the mention of going back to school seemed to make a big impression on her either way. She shifted her attention to the framed photos on the coffee table and picked up one of Nora as a child. "Who is this?" she asked.

"My mom," Alice said. "It's from outside her family's house in Cork. Those are her sisters and two brothers with her. We don't know the exact date, but it was sometime before her father sent the younger ones to the orphanage."

"Why did her father do that if he was alive?"

"My mom's mother died shortly after she was born," Alice said. "They were destitute. She was the youngest of six. The older girls stayed at the house, but my grandfather couldn't manage a toddler, so the nuns basically raised her, and then she would spend summers back at her family's house."

Alice examined the photo. She hadn't seen her aunts in decades. After Daniel's accident, her parents stopped paying for the whole family to visit them in Cork, as they had every summer since Alice was young. Instead, Nora went alone to spend time with her sisters. She rarely talked about her childhood. It was terrible. Maybe that was all Alice would ever know. When she was younger, Alice and her sisters would imagine they were in an orphanage. Cait would play the nun, and Alice and Maggie would be the kids who had to beg for toys and eat foul food. They knew enough to play out of earshot of their mother, but one time she overheard them and came into the room. "We didn't ask for toys," she corrected them emphatically. "We were to be 'seen and not heard.' We didn't dare ask for a thing."

The glass door behind Alice creaked open, and Poppy peeked her head in. "Can I hide in here?" she whispered.

Alice was about to say no, but then Isabel said, "Sure," so Poppy grabbed a green pillow off the lounge and put it on top of her head as she crouched in the corner behind the potted fig tree. "Do *not* tell them I'm here," she commanded.

Isabel made the gesture of zipping her lips.

Before Alice left, she said, "Your cards. Do they help?"

"Some days more than others," Isabel said, "but that's life, I guess. I usually ask the deck what I need to know at that moment and then try to interpret whatever card I pick." She held up the card on top of her pile. "This is the one for today. The Moon. In reverse."

"What does that mean?"

"I'm sort of new to all this myself," Isabel said. "My grandma tried to teach me when I was a kid, but of course I didn't pay any attention." She continued: "The Moon represents things that can't be seen or are, you know, hidden beneath the surface. Illusions. Secrets. That sort of thing. But this one was in reverse, so I'm guessing it means the opposite. The truth will be revealed."

Alice's skin felt clammy. She shivered.

"Do you want me to do a reading for you?" Isabel asked.

"Oh," Alice said. "Sure." She sat on the stool.

"Think about your question." Isabel shuffled the cards. "Or something you need help with."

"Do I have to say it out loud?"

"Not at all."

Alice closed her eyes. *Do I have to have this baby?*

Isabel fanned the deck out in front of her. "Pick one."

Alice picked a card and flipped it over.

"Interesting," Isabel said, and looked up.

"What are you doing?" Poppy asked from behind the pillow.

The question felt like the universe jabbing its finger directly at Alice. *How could you have asked that question?* What *was* she doing? She stood. "You know what? You don't have to read it," she said to Isabel.

Isabel placed the card back on top of the deck. "I'm sorry. I didn't mean to upset you."

"No, no, you didn't," Alice assured her. "I just—"

In the corner, Poppy threw the pillow off her head and stood. "They're not even trying to find me," she said.

"Maybe your hiding spot is *too* good," Isabel said.

Poppy stuck out her bottom lip. *My God*, Alice thought, *the apple does not fall far from the tree*. "I'm going to tell them I won, then." She stormed out of the room. A moment later, they heard her scream, "No tag backs!"

Isabel held the deck in her hand. "One thing," she said to Alice.

Alice turned. "Yes?"

"What's a word you would use to describe yourself? Don't think too hard. Whatever comes to mind first."

Though she'd been instructed otherwise, Alice found herself quickly trying to find a word to impress Isabel. She went with the first one to stick. "*Reliable*," she said.

"Reliable," Isabel repeated.

Alice glanced at the cherry blossoms on one of the green pillows, and another word popped into her mind. "I take that back," she said. "*Blooming.* That's my word."

Isabel brightened. "Lovely," she said. "An active verb."

Alice smiled, pleased with herself. "Does that have anything to do with the card I picked?"

"No, it's just a game I like to play," Isabel said. "Let's you get straight to the heart of things."

"I like that," Alice said, and she did.

On her way back upstairs, Alice returned to the question she'd posed to herself earlier.

Do I have to have this baby?

She held on to the banister.

Of course you do!

She wasn't sure how long she'd been standing there when she heard the faint call of "Mom!" There's a word. Then she heard it again, and Finn appeared in the foyer, his new khakis already too short and hovering above his suede oxfords, which were wet from the snow. He pressed his hands together in prayer. "I know you'll say no," he began, "but the guys are going to Leo's to play the new *Madden* after dinner tonight." He bounced on his wet toes and pouted his lips in that way he knew she struggled to resist. "Can I please?"

"Finn, no," Alice said. "Please don't ask that of me today of all days."

"But it's so close," he said, pointing out the window. "I can walk there and be back in like an hour."

"There's no way your father will approve, and it's not just about spending the day with your family." She looked at him. "Do I have to bring up what happened yesterday?"

Finn flushed. "But I told Dad it was Leo's."

"And you stole it from him, which makes it even worse—"

"I didn't steal it," Finn squeaked. "Leo told me to keep it so his mom wouldn't find it!"

"That's not what your dad told me—"

"Because he never listens to anything I say!"

Alice wasn't sure what to believe. She liked to think of Finn as honest, but lately, she'd caught him in a bunch of lies, and she was beginning to worry that Kyle was right about her blind faith in him. This frightened her. What else might she be missing?

"Either way, the answer is no."

"This is so unfair!"

Nora appeared around the corner. "What's unfair?" She was passing through the foyer on her way to the back room with the caterer, Beth, who was sporting a chef's hat—*Come on!*—and carrying a tray.

Alice composed herself and turned to Finn. "Go ahead, tell Grammy."

Finn huffed and stormed up the stairs.

"It's nothing," Alice said to her mother. "Don't worry." She turned to Beth. "Do you need me for anything?"

"We got it, love," Beth said. "But look—" Before she even lifted the tin foil from the tray to reveal the oysters, the smell of something like stranded shellfish on the beach hit Alice's nose and sent her stomach swirling.

Alice tried to maintain her calm. "Hmm, delicious. Yes, totally worth it. Cait always knows!" She swallowed down the nausea. "I'm going to find Finn."

Upstairs, she snuck past the bunk room, where the boys wrestled and laughed in a way that she knew would wrinkle their clothes and soon end in tears, and as she walked into the bathroom, Kyle emerged from her bedroom across the hall and joined her.

He closed the bathroom door behind them. "You're sick again?" he asked.

Alice sat on the covered toilet seat. Like the boys, Kyle wore the outfit she'd chosen for him. Tan cords and a navy cashmere sweater her mother had given him last Christmas. His freshly shaven face and neatly combed side part made him look like a preppy schoolboy.

"What can I do?" he asked.

What she wanted more than anything was for him to leave her alone, but if she asked for this, he would only be suspicious something else was going on. So instead she asked him to get her a cup of ice, and while he was gone, she dry heaved into the toilet.

He returned a minute later and sat on the tub's edge. He cupped her forehead. "You're warm," he said.

Alice slid off the toilet and onto the floor. She lowered the seat cover and rested her head on the side, grateful she'd cleaned the bathroom yesterday in preparation for her sisters' visit.

"I think I know what's wrong," Kyle said. She stared at him and popped a piece of ice into her mouth. "This isn't about bad milk or a stomach bug, is it?"

The nausea swirled again, and Alice lowered her head between her knees. "No," she said, "it's not."

She waited.

"You're stressed about Georgia's bungalow," Kyle said.

Alice squeezed her eyes closed. *Please stop*, she thought. *Please.*

Kyle slid onto the floor next to her. "Look," he said. "Maybe it's not the right time to go back to work. I know you're worried about money, but you don't have to do this for us."

"I love working," she said. "I'm doing it for me, not for you." She was surprised by the need she felt to hurt him.

Kyle moved back to sit on the edge of the tub, elbows resting on his spread knees. "All I'm trying to say is maybe you're taking on too much. I'm worried about you."

"I'm pregnant." She stared at the cracked tile beneath the clawfoot tub when she said it.

Kyle sat up. "What?"

When she didn't answer, he started to reach for her again, but she brushed him away.

"I'll be sick," she said.

"Right, sorry." He stopped and stood. "Okay, this is, well. Huh. This is—When did you—"

"I took a test yesterday."

"And you're just telling me now?"

She lowered her head into her hands. "I needed a second to process it all," she mumbled.

Kyle paced back and forth in the small room, then hovered over her. "And you're sure? Weren't we—I mean, you were on—"

"I missed one," she said. *It's my fault.*

"Don't cry. We can—There are precautions we can take, the doctor can take. James was—That was nine years ago. I'm sure things have changed. I mean, medically speaking. They must have. How many tests did you take?"

Alice looked down at herself, sitting on the bathroom floor, her face plastered to the toilet. "I think it's fairly obvious beyond the test." She pointed to the pimple, which had officially become a tender cyst on her chin. "Plus, this."

Kyle looked at her. "I had noticed that."

"Thanks."

"No," Kyle said. "Sorry, I meant, just that it's new. Or not new. I remember with the boys." He scratched his head, messing up the neat side part. "But okay, okay."

"Can you stop saying that?"

"Sorry. This is—No, this is great. It's a lot. It's unexpected. But great."

"Stop saying that, too." Hearing him try to pretend was only making things worse.

Finally, a moment of quiet.

Alice was twenty-five years old when she became pregnant with Finn. She and Kyle had been married for less than a year. The pregnancy wasn't planned, but she'd been excited. When James came along four years later, she'd secretly hoped for a girl but was happy for Finn to have a brother.

But none of that joy, excitement, or even curiosity was there for her now, and it wasn't for Kyle either, as much as he was trying. And this wasn't just about the fear of her developing preeclampsia again. They both knew that.

No one had to say it.

13.

MAGGIE

Maggie snuck into the butler's pantry, closed the door behind her, and pulled out her phone to read Sarah's text.

Can't talk—at Frank's parents'. Will call you on Sunday. xx

Throughout the affair, Sarah had always claimed she was the one who had "everything to lose" if they were caught, but they both knew that wasn't true. That had never been true. And now it was Maggie's job and relationship on the line. What was she doing, hiding away and texting Sarah? Even if she found out that Cunningham knew about the affair and he called her into his office on Monday to fire her, there was nothing she could do about it here.

She leaned against the copper sink and typed furiously into her phone.

Don't call me on Sunday.

Adrenaline shot through her body. She doubled down.

Don't call me ever again.

Enjoy the rest of your life.

I don't want any part of it.

She reread her texts, hands shaking. Part of her worried Frank was on the other end taking screenshots to send to Cunningham as evidence, and part of her was so enraged by it all that she didn't care. She needed to pull herself together for Thanksgiving dinner. She needed to talk to Isabel.

No, she thought.

Don't do that.

She stared at the sacred heart of Jesus plate hanging on the wall by the window.

Later, she promised him. *I'll tell her everything.*

* * *

Maggie had just pulled away from the kiss when they heard Frank walk into the house. Sarah bolted up, stunned, then leapt off the couch. Frank was supposed to be on his way to the Cape with the kids to visit his parents.

"Bunny?" he called from the foyer.

Sarah hid the half shell holding the nub of their joint under the marble coffee table, and Maggie frantically straightened her shirt. All the while, she thought, *Bunny. Huh. That's what he calls her.* Maggie had spent the year of their affair obsessing over Sarah and Frank's marriage. Sarah claimed they were no longer in love or slept together, and as much as Maggie wanted to believe this, wanted to believe Frank was as awful and controlling as Sarah made him out to be, she knew otherwise. Oliver's essays about his father-and-son fishing trips were sweet, and Sarah's anecdotes, which Maggie sometimes suspected were used to make her jealous—"Frank's pestering me for a date night" or "I'll buy it! Frank said I should treat myself"—were charming. Maggie used to feel sick to her stomach after Sarah left her and returned to him at the end of their weekends away, imagining the small, domestic details of their life. Reading in bed together before falling asleep. Cooking dinner. Date nights. These were the things she wanted—to entwine her life with another. Or she would imagine the opposite. Their fights. The tension. Sarah wishing she was falling asleep with Maggie instead of Frank. Either way, it was all an illusion. Here was their life. Their actual life. He called her *Bunny*. She could hear the casual affection and ease in Frank's voice. *This is my home. I'm greeting my wife.*

Maybe Sarah doesn't love him, Maggie thought, *but he loves her.*

Before Maggie turned around, she understood that one of the children must have been with Frank from the syrupy voice Sarah used when she said "Hi!" When Maggie turned, she recognized a three-year-old version of Sarah—blond hair and brown eyes and pouty lips—her arm wrapped around her father's leg as she sucked on the ear of a pink stuffed dog.

"What's going on?" Frank asked.

Maggie looked up at Frank and was surprised to find that he was not the refined, handsome, sophisticated surgeon she remembered from the first and only time she'd met him in person at a school fundraiser. Instead, he was slightly shorter than Maggie and a bit chubby, with a face that looked like it was probably kind when he wasn't standing in the living room with an unexpected guest smoking a joint with his wife and disheveled from—what?

"This is Maggie Ryan," Sarah crooned. Maggie recognized the cloying voice from when Sarah would call home on their weekends away—weekends when Sarah pretended to be at a yoga retreat or visiting a friend. It used to unsettle Maggie, but now it made her cringe. "Oh, you remember her! Oliver's English teacher from last year? His favorite teacher!"

Was I? Maggie's head was foggy from the joint, and her heart thundered in her ears.

Sarah turned to Maggie, and this—more than the kiss or Frank's unexpected arrival—took Maggie by surprise. Her calm. Whatever fear she'd expressed in that first moment of panic was replaced by a cool and unwavering confidence that made Maggie wonder with horror if she'd set this whole thing up on purpose. She watched as Sarah walked to the little girl—Hope was her name. "The baby that was supposed to save our marriage," Sarah once quipped, which Maggie had found egregious for many reasons. Sarah scooped Hope into her arms and gave her a loud, dramatic kiss on the cheek.

Frank regarded Maggie. "I'm not sure we've met." He walked across the room and held out his hand. "Frank Thompson."

"Nice to meet you." Maggie reached out her hand, and he gave it two hard pumps. She needed to get out of there as quickly as possible, but she wasn't sure how to do that inconspicuously, so she heard herself say, "I've read about your fishing trips." *Your fishing trips?!*

Frank gave her a confused look.

"I mean—" Maggie stuttered. "In Oliver's essays. For class."

Frank turned to Sarah. "I didn't know you were having company?"

"Maggie's in town to see Anne Carson read at the MFA." Sarah was talking to Frank but looking at Hope. "She just popped over for a quick hello."

That's right, Maggie thought. *That is what I'm supposed to be doing.*

"It smells yucky in here," Hope said.

"Oh," Sarah said. "That's Mommy's new candle!"

Hope held her nose. "I don't like it."

Frank observed the half-drunk bottle of wine on the coffee table and the makeshift ashtray beneath it with the joint, then turned back to Sarah, who smiled and swayed with Hope on her hip as though nothing was amiss.

"What are you doing back here?" Sarah asked. Again, speaking to Frank but looking at Hope. Again, that voice.

"We forgot Hope's scooter," Frank said, but it was clear he was distracted and trying to figure out what he'd walked into. "Oliver is in the car—" He stopped. Then slowly, brutally, Maggie watched his face turn as the knowledge, the recognition, entered him. He whipped his head around.

"I'm going to leave," Maggie said.

"I think that's best," Frank said.

Hope looked up from Sarah's shoulder and turned to Frank, then Maggie. Her bottom lip trembled. And if there was a moment when Maggie realized what a mistake she'd made, how selfish she'd been in this whole thing, it was here, as Hope, sensing the anger in her father's voice, burst into tears.

Maggie avoided all their eyes as she grabbed her bag and jacket and quickly decided to leave her scarf on the kitchen counter. "I'm sorry—" she began, but Frank placed his hand on her shoulder and gently but firmly guided her past Sarah, who was trying to comfort Hope and doing everything possible to avert her eyes, to the foyer.

Maggie didn't say anything to Frank as he opened the door and released her into the crisp fall evening. The city was alive with the hustle of rush hour. She listened to the door close behind her and held the wrought-iron railing as she hurried down the steps. She stood at the bottom of the stoop, high and dazed, her heart slamming into her chest, and tried to gather herself. If she never saw Sarah again, that would be fine. Preferable. But the damage was done—to their lives, and to her own. She wanted to call Isabel, but that would be a mistake. Any capacity she'd had to deny what she'd been doing with Sarah—from the first kiss to now the last—had been punctured.

As Maggie made her way down the block toward the Commons, someone called her name. When she turned, she spotted Oliver, his head sticking out of the back-seat window of an Audi SUV, a big smile on his face. He waved, cupped his hands around his mouth, and yelled, "What are you doing here?" Maggie waved back, then turned and continued walking.

The drive back to Vermont the next day was long. Maggie was sick with regret. All she wanted was to get home, melt into Isabel's arms, and beg for her forgiveness.

That night, Isabel made them bean tacos for dinner, and Maggie sat at the two-top table nursing a beer as she half listened to Isabel talk about a scene she'd struggled to write over the weekend.

"So," Isabel said. She popped a black olive into her mouth, took a sip of her beer, and then straddled Maggie rather than sitting in her own chair. "Your turn." She kissed Maggie's neck. "Tell me about your weekend."

Do it now, Maggie thought. *Do it now, do it now, do it now.*

"It was terrible," she said.

Isabel pulled away. "Was it? Why?"

Maggie pressed her head to Isabel's chest. "I just like it better here with you." She told herself that was as true an answer as anything. The other truth she would bury deep within and pray that's where it stayed.

* * *

Maggie nearly gave the caterers a heart attack when she darted out of the pantry and into the kitchen, but she was able to sprint up the back stairs and sneak into the shower before anyone in the family spotted her. She was working conditioner through her hair when someone opened the bathroom door, and, assuming it was one of her sisters, she yelled, "Get out!" The door closed, but after a moment, she realized that whoever had opened it was now in the bathroom with her.

"Why does Sarah want to talk to you on Sunday?" Isabel asked.

Maggie went numb. The conditioner ran into her eyes, blurring her vision, but she snapped to and ripped open the curtain.

Isabel sat on the toilet, legs crossed, Maggie's phone in her hand. "And why did you tell her to go have a nice life?"

Maggie kept the water running to drown out their voices but stepped out of the shower. "Let me just—" She wrapped a guest towel, the ones her mother never let them use, around her body and lowered herself onto her knees to face Isabel. The room fogged with steam. "This past weekend in Boston—" She stopped to wipe the conditioner and now tears off her face.

The Irish Goodbye

"What happened in Boston?"

"I ran into Sarah and—"

Before she could finish, Isabel cut her off. "You *ran into her*, or you made plans to see her? Is that why you went to Boston?"

"No," Maggie said. She felt dizzy. The towel kept slipping off her bare chest. "That's not why I went at all. But once I got into town, she sent me a text and invited me to her house."

"That's not 'running into her.' And she just happened to know you were in Boston?"

"Please. Let me finish." She placed her hands on Isabel's knees, but Isabel brushed them off. "Don't touch me," she said. "Finish!"

Maggie turned off the faucet in the shower. "Okay, Sarah is—Well, I never told you this part, but Sarah is Oliver Thompson's mom."

"What the hell?" Isabel shook her head. "I feel like I'm in the *Twilight Zone*. Your ex is the mother of my student? Of *your* student? How could you have not told me that?"

She hadn't told Isabel before because it all felt so icky, so scandalous, but now she regretted withholding that context. "I was going to but—"

There was a knock at the door.

"Just a sec," Maggie yelled.

"Hurry up," Cait said. "I need to shower, and Mom and Dad's is slow as piss."

Maggie turned back to Isabel. "Can we talk in my room?" she asked. This could not get any worse. There was no way she could make this better before all the guests started to arrive for dinner.

Cait pounded on the door again. "Maggie," she said. "Get your skinny ass out of there, or I'll break down the door."

"Give me a goddamn second," Maggie said. She started to turn on the faucet for more privacy, but Isabel snapped, "Leave it!"

Maggie stood. She held out her hand to help Isabel up, but Isabel stood on her own. She tucked Maggie's phone into her back pocket, wiped the tears off her face, and reached for the doorknob.

The door opened to reveal Cait, hands on her hips.

"Seriously?" Cait said. "Now's the time?"

Isabel strode past her, and when Maggie shot Cait a look, Cait raised her arms in defense. "Jesus," she said. "Take a joke." Then she said, "Sluts," and walked into the bathroom.

14.

CAIT

From behind the yellowed linen drapes, Cait watched the circular driveway. Her bedroom was the only one facing the front of the house rather than the bay on the back side. She'd traded rooms with Alice when they were teenagers to get a walk-in closet, and though she hadn't lived at the Folly in more than two decades, she still regretted giving up the water view.

She pulled closed the drapes. She was supposed to be getting dressed, but instead, still in her robe, she sipped the cranberry Moscow mule she'd snuck from the bar on her walk upstairs. Outside her door, the kids laughed as they ran down the hallway, and she held her breath, waiting for one of the twins, likely both, to barge into the room with some sort of demand. But then they were off again. She was confident Alice must be somewhere condemning her for not monitoring their every move. What did her nanny, Ruthie, call Cait? A free-range parent. Cait pictured a hen surrounded by dozens of baby chicks. She shuddered.

Opening her closet door, she resumed her debate between the black silk blouse and pencil skirt she'd bought last week at her favorite vintage boutique on Brompton Road, and the blush Chanel suit she'd treated herself to last year when the stress from the divorce helped return her to her prepregnancy weight. Flirty or sophisticated?

She heard a car door slam outside and checked for Luke again, only to find a random Honda parked at the top of the driveway. Probably a caterer.

All the longing from the last few weeks settled in her stomach. Standing in her childhood bedroom, she didn't feel like a woman with a Chanel suit, a mother of two, an associate at one of London's top legal firms (well, she wasn't that anymore, was she?). She felt like a horny, angsty, heartsick teenager.

She heard more tires on the pebbled driveway and looked outside. Father Kelly. He was nearly as diminutive as her mother, and Topher used to call him Father Leprechaun behind his back. Years ago, when Maggie enlightened her about Father Kelly most definitely being gay himself, Cait couldn't believe she'd missed all the signs.

Back in front of the mirror, she let her robe drop and studied herself. Now she felt like a mother. Or looked like one, at any rate. She may have been back to her prepregnancy weight, but she still wore the battle scars of carrying two six-pound babies to thirty-six weeks. Cupping her breasts and stretching her abs taut, she imagined Luke's hands on her and—

Where was he?

She heard James in the hallway and slipped on her robe, opening the door a crack.

"Hey," she whispered. "What are you guys up to?"

"They're teaching me how to say words in Dutch," James said.

Though at the beginning of their relationship, Bram had been sweet about Cait's spectacular inability to learn Dutch, he'd wielded the language difference like a weapon toward the end of their marriage and would refuse to talk to the kids in English when angry at her.

"*Dat is geweldig*," she said, one of the few things she'd managed to absorb.

The Irish Goodbye

"I haven't learned that yet," James said seriously.

Cait looked down the hallway and then back to James. "Do me a favor and go tell Auntie Maggie to come to my room for a quick second to help me pick out something to wear, okay?"

He nodded and ran off.

Back in her room, Cait returned to the window. An elegant man dressed in a wool blazer and wingtips, who she assumed was Kyle's friend Mukesh, exited the Honda and walked up the driveway holding orange chrysanthemums and a bottle of wine. She watched him stop and regard the house for a long moment, and without knowing exactly why, she opened the drapes and dropped her robe. She stood naked, shivering from the draft, waiting for him to notice. After some time, his eyes locked onto hers, and she jumped away from the window, laughing as she grabbed her robe. She was slightly horrified by herself, but there was a certain thrill in knowing that all night, this handsome stranger would be picturing her naked body.

By the time she finished her drink, Maggie still hadn't come, but at least the vodka was finally doing the trick to dull her anxiety over seeing Luke. She felt lighter, more optimistic. Flirty it was. She threw on the La Perla bra and lace undies she'd worn briefly the night before, stepped into the skirt, applied her makeup, and pulled on her boots. Behind her neck and under her knees, she dabbed the white musk perfume she hadn't worn since high school but had serendipitously discovered at Heathrow departure duty-free yesterday. She checked her breath and peeked out the window to see if Luke's car was there yet. It wasn't, and now she worried he might have canceled because of the snow or gone into the city after all. She decided to sneak past the guests to her father's office to call him again.

The smells of turkey roasting and pies baking filled the house. A child's yell emerged from somewhere, and Cait listened to make sure it wasn't one of the twins. James nearly ran her down as she reached the bottom step. He skidded to a stop and turned to her with a look of alarm.

Cait inspected her skirt. "What?" she asked.

He pinched his bottom lip nervously. "I forgot to tell you that Aunt Maggie's too busy to help you get dressed."

Cait tousled his red hair. "And yet," she said, "somehow I managed all by my lonesome."

"Come on," Poppy yelled, and grabbed James's hand. Her hair was already loose from the braids she'd fought against from the beginning, and her Mary Janes were nowhere to be found.

"Look who it is!"

Cait turned.

"Father Kelly," she said.

He kissed both of her cheeks. "Aren't you a lovely sight."

She squeezed his hands and smiled. She hadn't seen him in more than five years, but he looked the same—as compact as a jockey, with gentle blue eyes and hair far blonder than his seventy-plus years should allow, which made her wonder, with a certain kind of glee, whether he dyed it. Before he launched into one of his stories, she gestured toward the office and said, "I just need to make a quick call!"

"Right-o," Father Kelly said.

Cait dialed Luke's number, but no one picked up, and the answering machine was now disconnected. She tried once more, then slammed the phone onto the receiver.

Despite the roiling in her stomach, she glided through the crowd as if Luke were there watching her: her smile slight, her eyes warm, and her posture like a ballerina's at the barre. She paused in the slant of good lighting by the bay window, and as Kyle introduced her to Mukesh—was he blushing?—she caught a glimpse of Luke's head disappearing into the living room from the kitchen. Relief flooded her until she caught him again, approaching her mother.

Across the room, she observed their interaction while Kyle made Mukesh laugh with a story about one of their buddies from the National Guard. Luke hugged her mother—*a good sign*—and then, thank God,

The Irish Goodbye

Father Kelly appeared, and a server walked by to offer a plate of stuffed mushrooms. Cait excused herself from Kyle and Mukesh to join their circle, but as she was walking over, someone yanked her arm.

She spun around. "What the—"

"I need your help," Maggie said. She pulled Cait into the hallway and away from the party.

Cait eyed her sister. "You certainly do," she said. Maggie was a mess. Dressed in the same clothes as yesterday, her hair was wet—greasy?—and streaks of black mascara circled both her eyes. "What happened?"

Maggie hurried Cait into their father's office and closed the door behind her. She turned around.

"Isabel wants to leave," Maggie said, biting her nails and staring at the floor.

"Why?"

Maggie wiped tears away with the corner of her sleeve. "I saw Sarah in Boston last weekend," she said.

"And . . . ?"

"And she kissed me," Maggie said. "I mean, kind of. For like a *second*. It wasn't even what I wanted, and then Frank showed up—"

"Oh, man."

"Isabel found texts from Sarah on my phone, and now she wants to leave. I don't blame her, but I'm so sorry, and I don't even know why I did it."

Cait leaned against the desk. "Jesus, Maggie. What were you thinking?"

"That doesn't help me!"

"I know, but Isabel is so perfect for you. And Sarah? Really?"

"Here's the thing," Maggie said. "I'd gone there hoping to have, I don't know, an actual face-to-face conversation about how our relationship ended, but when she went to kiss me, I was like, Holy shit, what am I doing here? But it was too late. Part of me wanted to explain it all to Isabel right when it happened, but I didn't, and that's just made it worse."

Cait felt terrible for her sister. She knew it was a big deal for her to bring Isabel home, and now this. But she was also worried about Luke and her mother talking and was eager to get back to the party and check on them.

Maggie slid down the wall. "This is all my fault," she said, burying her face in her knees.

"Where's she going?" Cait asked.

"Her cousin's in Brooklyn."

Cait nodded. "I was looking forward to seeing her at the table with Father Kelly," she said, and nudged Maggie's shoulder.

Maggie frowned. "You and nobody else."

"Maybe she just needs some time," Cait said.

Maggie looked up. "What do I tell Mom?"

"I don't know. The truth?"

Though Maggie wiped more tears from her face, they both laughed at that one.

"I'll tell everyone for you," Cait said.

"No," Maggie said, standing. "I can do it."

As Maggie trudged upstairs to deal with Isabel, Cait returned to the living room, where her excitement at seeing Luke turned into confusion when she spotted him standing beside a petite brunette who looked vaguely familiar.

Luke noticed Cait looking his way and gave her a casual wave. *You asshole.* She gestured to the hallway, hoping to talk to him privately, but his expression turned serious, and he pointed toward something at her feet.

"Mummy!"

Cait felt a pull on her skirt. Like a silent movie, she looked down and watched Augustus's mouth open and close until finally, as though someone had turned on the sound, she could hear the panicked "Mummy, Mummy, Mummy, Mummy."

"Darling," she said, grateful for the distraction and a moment to reorient herself. "What's wrong?" She was keenly aware that Luke was still watching her as Augustus explained that Poppy was upset because Papa said he would kill the raccoon.

"He's just teasing," Cait assured him, but Augustus grabbed her hand and walked her to where Poppy sat at the bottom of the stairs.

Cait scooted next to Poppy and wrapped her arms around her shoulders, pulling her in close. Sure, she was performing a bit for Luke, but who wasn't putting on a show in this room?

"Papa's not going to hurt the raccoon," she swore to Poppy, and made a note to pass along that promise to her father.

Poppy stopped chewing on the end of her braid and jumped to her feet. "He said he'll shoot her because she's rapid!"

"*Rabid*," Cait corrected.

"Who's going to shoot who?"

Cait looked up at Luke, standing before them and smiling that stupid, exquisite smile. The nearness of his body, the crinkles in the corners of his squinting blue eyes, hair full and thick but also silvered—oh, it all enraged her. She turned toward the fireplace and Father Kelly, who was talking to the brunette—why was she so familiar?—then back to Luke.

She tried to wipe away the cookie crumbs she now saw Augustus had gotten all over her skirt as she introduced Luke to the twins. Augustus shook Luke's hand and Poppy huffed, then slumped onto the bottom step, spread eagle.

"She's sad because my dad's trying to get rid of a raccoon," Cait explained. Sweat prickled along her forehead and upper lip. She wished she could pinch Poppy to let her know she should behave, but that would only make things worse.

Luke kneeled next to Poppy. "A raccoon, huh? They're pretty tough to be friends with, you know? They're mean."

"No, they're not!" Poppy said. "They're lovely!"

Thanks, Luke.

Cait steeled herself—rattled by Luke's date and humiliated by her inability to calm her own child. Poppy was headed toward one of her full-on tantrums, which she somehow always seemed to time perfectly to humiliate Cait.

Luke apologized to Poppy and stood.

Cait followed. She straightened her skirt and kissed him quickly on the cheek. "When did you get here?" she asked.

Luke went to answer, but Poppy grabbed hold of Cait's leg.

Cait's cheeks flared as she looked down at Poppy. "Mommy's trying to have a conversation," she said. She turned back and indicated for Luke to continue, but Poppy shrilled.

"Do you need to, uh—" Luke said.

When Cait looked down again, Poppy's face was red, and tears poured from her eyes. Cait reached for her hand to pull her up, but she resisted.

"You're hurting me!" Poppy yelled, and then Augustus joined.

"I'm going to bring her upstairs for a nap," Cait said to Luke, who looked on with a mixture of concern and—Cait could *feel* it!—judgment.

"I'm not taking a nap!" Poppy sobbed. "I'm not tired!"

Alice appeared from around the corner. "Is everything all right?" she asked.

"She just gets this way when she's tired," Cait said through gritted teeth.

Cait dragged Poppy up the stairs. Inside the bedroom, she did her best to contain her anger and embarrassment, because if she let loose on Poppy, she would never get back downstairs. She brushed Poppy's hair, matted to her sweaty forehead, to the side, and said, "Come on, darling, let's lie down together on the bed." When Poppy protested, Cait could no longer contain herself, and she scooped her up and brought her to the bed. She held on as Poppy thrashed and yelled about how she wasn't tired and raccoons were lovely and she wanted to play with her cousins and she missed Juju and didn't like her Furby because it made scary noises.

Then Cait remembered something.

In the bathroom, she dug out the Children's Benadryl from the twins' toiletry case. She read the instructions, skimming the part about *not* using the medicine to make your child sleepy. To assuage her guilt, she only gave Poppy half the recommended dosage—after bribing her with one of Nora's licorice allsorts—and finally got her to lie back down in the bed by letting her cuddle with an old, discolored teddy bear that had sat on the armchair by the window since Cait was a kid. She rubbed Poppy's back and answered her endless questions about the teddy bear—What's his name? Where'd you get him? Can he be mine?—until she dozed off. Cait climbed off the bed cautiously, fixed her hair, and refreshed her lipstick. She kissed Poppy on her sweaty forehead, assuring herself Poppy would not slip into a coma, then headed back downstairs to find out what the hell was going on with Luke.

But Luke was nowhere to be found. Cait spotted his friend—date?—at the raw bar talking to Mukesh and Kyle. A server approached and offered Cait a cranberry brie bite, but she said no and walked to the group, straightening her back and holding in her stomach. She wrapped her arms around Mukesh's and Kyle's shoulders. The brunette was asking how exactly one eats an oyster.

"With your mouth mostly," Cait said. She reached for a half shell and inspected its pearly meat. "Swallow it whole," she said, "or, if you're a barbarian, you can chew it a little." She placed the shell to her mouth and did just that before introducing herself.

The woman giggled—she was pretty enough, Cait could now see, but mousy and skittish, and this realization emboldened Cait—and said, "I know who you are!" She held her hand to her chest. "Nicole. We ran track together at Saint Mary's."

Nicole Shirley. Of course. She was younger by two or three years—maybe Alice's grade? Cait remembered Nicole used to cry when she lost a meet, which, Cait thought as they shook hands, happened frequently enough that it didn't seem to warrant tears.

"Ah," Cait said, flipping her hair back. "The good ol' Flying Hawks." She prepared another oyster. "Let me help you. For your first one, try it like this—" She topped the oyster with a few drops of vodka and lemon and handed it to Nicole.

Nicole held up her hands as though Cait was offering her poison. "I'm good," she cackled.

Cait winked at her, then shot the oyster down herself. She scanned the room for Luke, but instead Alice approached, as stressed as ever.

"Can you—" Alice began.

"No," Cait interrupted her, excusing herself from the circle and heading toward the bar. There was no more ginger beer for the Moscow mules, so she ordered a Hendrick's and tonic instead. As she squeezed in an extra lime, Alice appeared at her side.

"You need to step it up," she whispered into Cait's ear.

Cait pulled back. "Excuse me?"

"Do you know how much I do around here to help our parents?" Alice spat. "All the cleaning and grocery shopping? Guess how many doctor appointments I took them to last week."

"They can drive."

"Mom's finally driving again now that her knee's slightly better, but have you driven with Dad lately? He's turning eighty in—"

"Thanks, I know our father's birthday."

"You return home and make your grand entrance, acting like everything's perfect, all *Don't mind me for dropping by every five years*, and the one time I need your help—"

"Did I not arrange for this entire day to be catered?" Cait said. She was so tired of Alice making her feel inadequate when it came to taking care of their parents, like nothing was ever enough.

"You footed the bill," Alice said. "And it's absurd, by the way."

"I was trying to help!"

"This?" Alice shot back. "You think *this* is what they need help with? Or first-class tickets to visit you in the Cotswolds? They can't afford long-term care insurance. Have you seen the roof? It's rotting! And don't even get me started on the taxes for this place. I actually don't know how much longer they'll be able to stay here, but you want congratulations for—"

"Wait, slow down."

The Irish Goodbye

Alice narrowed her eyes at Cait. "All of that is not even the point," she said. "What I'm trying to say is that having Luke here is hell for Mom. She'd been looking forward to spending time with you and the twins and you've turned this day into something else entirely."

Cait stiffened. "I don't even know where he is—"

"On the back porch with Finn and Kyle setting up some game with a tree trunk and a weird hammer."

"Hammerschlagen."

"Ha," Alice said. "As if his family hasn't done enough to nail us."

"Okay," Cait said. "You need a drink." She turned to the bartender. "Can you make her a—"

"I don't need a drink," Alice said. "I need you to help me."

Cait studied her sister. "Are you—" But before she could finish, Alice grabbed her arm and looked over her shoulder. "What's wrong with Maggie?"

15.

MAGGIE

"It's not exactly an *emergency*," Maggie said to her mother. "It's more like a situation."

They stood in the foyer, and she tried to keep her voice low so no one in the living room heard her fumble through an excuse for why Isabel was leaving early.

Her mother frowned. "But what happened?"

Maggie caught herself in the mirror at the foot of the stairs. She hadn't had time to wash the conditioner out in the shower, and her hair was now plastered to her head. When she and Isabel had returned to her room, she'd quickly thrown on her clothes from yesterday, but she'd mismatched the buttons on her shirt and her right collar stood up unevenly by her ear. She looked unhinged, but that was the least of her worries. As she adjusted the buttons and turned back to her mother, Alice and Cait walked into the room. She motioned them away—the whole thing was miserable enough without an audience—but they ignored her.

"What's wrong?" Alice asked.

The Irish Goodbye

"Isabel needs to leave," Maggie mumbled.

They all turned at once toward the stairs as Isabel made her way down, her coat already on. At the sight of her, Maggie's eyes welled. The look on Isabel's face was grim—as though there really was an emergency.

"Is everything okay?" Nora asked when Isabel reached the bottom stair. "I still don't understand what happened."

Isabel started to answer, but Maggie interrupted her. "I told them you're leaving because there was a situation—you know, with your cousin."

Isabel adjusted the bag on her shoulder. "That's not what happened," she said.

Maggie stared at Isabel with a pleading look she hoped said, *Please don't make this worse than it needs to be*, but Isabel faced straight ahead.

"Maggie and I got into an argument," she said, "and I don't think it's a good idea for me to stay."

Everyone turned to Maggie, willing her to explain. All was quiet aside from the music and murmurs of the guests in the other room. Maggie wanted to assure them all was fine—*It wasn't an argument! A minor disagreement! Nothing to see here!*—but what was the use? Everything was falling apart. She'd only look like more of a fool if she pretended otherwise.

"I'm taking her to the train station," she said miserably.

Alice walked to the window. "Kyle can take her. It's pretty bad out there."

"I'm used to driving in this weather," Maggie said. She opened the front door. Even more than not wanting Isabel to leave, she did not want to stand there for a second longer as her mother and sisters witnessed her relationship implode. Or for anyone else at the party to find them—especially Father Kelly.

"Are you sure you can't stay the night?" Cait said to Isabel.

"We can make you a plate of food," Alice added, "and you can stay in the cottage if you want."

Maggie felt pathetic. Like a little kid who needed her big sisters to save her.

"That's really nice of you," Isabel said, her back to Maggie. "But I think it's better if I go. Thank you for everything. I'm sorry to be leaving like this." Then she turned and walked out the door.

Maggie waved halfheartedly to her mother and sisters and hurried after Isabel to the car. She cleaned the windows with a snow brush and didn't wait for the engine to warm before pulling out of the driveway. She had hoped to use the ride to persuade Isabel not to get on the train, but now she was annoyed with Isabel's whole performance in the foyer.

"You didn't have to say that to them," she said after a moment.

Isabel looked at her, baffled. "You mean apologize?"

"No, you didn't have to tell them we got into a fight! As if this doesn't suck enough already."

Isabel guffawed. "It's called being honest," she said. "You should try it sometime. You might find it makes things easier rather than harder."

It didn't feel that way, but Maggie knew she shouldn't say that, so she said nothing. She steered the Jeep onto the road, grateful it had been plowed.

16.

ALICE

Alice closed the front door and turned to her mother and Cait. Could this day get any worse?

"Poor Maggie," Cait said.

Yes, yes, Alice thought, *poor Maggie*. And yet, she didn't want her older sister to forget that the bigger problem was not who'd just left but who was still there. Luke. She was so annoyed at Cait's willful obliviousness that she could hardly stand to look at her.

"Did we do something?" Nora asked, peering out the window.

"I don't know," Alice said. "Did you?" Her tone was harsher than she'd intended, but she wasn't entirely sure Maggie and Isabel's fight *hadn't* had something to do with their mother.

"Not that I'm aware of," Nora said.

A server walked by with a platter of deviled eggs. "Can I offer you—"

"No, thank you," Alice said, and when he presented the platter to her mother, she was more direct. "Can we have a minute, please?"

The server apologized as he backed out of the foyer and into the living room. Alice felt like a jerk. She turned to Cait. "Remind me again why this was necessary?"

Cait ignored her and to their mother said, "You didn't do anything."

Alice waited for her sister to elaborate—obviously she knew something that they didn't—but Cait just stayed quiet and sipped her drink.

"Well," their mother said eventually, "I'll have Beth remove Isabel's place setting, then." She headed toward the kitchen, back stiff, without looking at Alice.

Oh, sure, Alice thought. *Be offended by me because I was short with you. Don't question Cait for her unwelcome guest or Maggie for her abrupt departure. Lay it all on me!*

Alone now in the foyer, Alice turned to Cait. "Do you know what happened with them? Why she left?"

Cait shrugged, and Alice immediately regretted asking the question and giving her sister the power to refuse to answer. She started to walk away, but Cait stopped her. She looked around, then said, "Are you pregnant?"

Alice flinched. "Why are you asking me that? Do I look pregnant?"

"Augustus found a test when the raccoons got into the garbage."

Oh, God. How could she have been so careless? Of course someone was going to find the test in the damn garbage. "I'm not sure," she said.

"The test was positive."

"I don't know if it's accurate. I might not be."

"Are you okay?"

Alice nodded. "Just don't tell Mom—or anyone, really."

"I would never do that," Cait said, slighted.

As Cait made her way to the back patio, Alice sat on the Shaker chair near the grandfather clock under the stairs. She'd managed to stop obsessing over the pregnancy in the whirlwind of Luke's arrival and Isabel's leaving, but now that Cait knew, her dread returned. *This is happening,* she thought. *It does not matter what you want.* How strange the longing for the early days of her pregnancy with Finn. Though Topher had just died, and the family was in a state of shock and grief, at least then she knew what she wanted, and she wasn't afraid of her own body.

*   *   *

On the morning of Topher's memorial, Alice had invited her sisters to breakfast at Captain's Diner to make a plan to take care of their parents, especially their mother, who refused to leave the bedroom on most days or even open the drapes to the bay. Earlier that week, Nora had told Alice she would have joined a convent and spent the rest of her life in prayer if it weren't for Alice and her sisters. When Alice asked, "What about Dad?" Nora looked at her as though she didn't understand the question. Alice had always thought her parents had a closer relationship with each other than they did with any of their kids, and her mother's distance from him worried her. Her mother believed the Larkins' lawsuit had caused Topher to unravel, and it was an unspoken understanding that she blamed their father for agreeing to settle the case.

Alice had also planned to use the breakfast to tell Maggie and Cait about her pregnancy. But before she could mention her concerns about their mother or announce her pregnancy, Cait revealed her own surprise. Bram had proposed and she was planning to say yes and accept a job in London that would start in September.

"You're moving out of the country in two months?" Alice asked in disbelief.

Cait turned stony. "I'll take that as a congratulations?"

When Alice got around to telling them her news, the energy at the table was strained. Though her sisters seemed happy for her and the pregnancy, it was clear to Alice that she would be the one left to manage their parents. Maggie was still in college, and now Cait was moving to another continent.

Later that afternoon, they attended the service at Saint Mary's, where Father Kelly spoke about Topher's sense of humor and adventurous spirit, his capacity to spin a tale (that was one way to put it), and the tragedy of his untimely death. Nothing was mentioned about the tragedy of his life itself, Alice remembered. About his involvement in the accident that took Daniel Larkin's life. How he'd dropped out of college before the end of his first year. Drank himself into oblivion. Grew out his strawberry-blond hair, which everyone loved until he stopped combing it, so it formed uneven dreads. About how he drove his Jeep across the country, drifting from one menial job to the next. How he overstayed his welcome on friends' and friends of friends' couches—a detail Alice was embarrassed to learn from a childhood neighbor Topher had visited in New Mexico—and grew his hair even longer and wore it in a knot at the top of his head. How he sent postcards with knock-knock jokes that made Alice laugh despite her concerns he was becoming more distant. How he made Alice and Kyle a wind chime for their wedding with shells and driftwood he'd collected somewhere along the Pacific seaboard.

Father Kelly called him a wanderer.

On a Sisyphean journey to forget, Alice had thought. *Or to forgive himself.*

There was no letter to explain or to say goodbye. Only the torn sheet of paper duct-taped to the outside of his bedroom door instructing Maggie to get help. When Alice read the note, she wished she'd been the one to find him.

In the investigation, the detective found a sketch pad on Topher's desk with a note asking that his body be cremated. Yet another blow to their mother, who'd hoped to bury him at Saint Mary's.

The request didn't specify where Topher wanted his ashes scattered, but they all agreed on the bay outside the Folly, where they gathered after the service, just the family and Father Kelly, standing in a semicircle along the shore.

It was late afternoon. The sun hung low and heavy in the bruise-colored sky, and it was chilly for July. Everything was familiar to Alice—the sulfuric stench of low tide, the seagulls pecking the sand for crabs, the lobster buoy for the summer harvest—and yet, utterly surreal.

The Irish Goodbye

Father Kelly spoke first. "Let us pray."

Alice had recited the prayer thousands of times, but words that had once comforted her now seemed suspect, useless. Another way life would be divided into before and after.

Her father opened the canvas sack, and Alice was sickened to see the remains were not the fine soot she'd expected but a gravel of sharp bones. *Remember you are dust and to dust you shall return.* Everyone, except their mother, who said she just couldn't, took a handful to scatter.

Because no one else did, Alice stepped forward to go first. In her clenched hand, the ashes felt like the remains of something destroyed. She brought them to her face, inhaled the smell of incense, then tossed them quickly and without ceremony, where they gathered on a strand of seaweed, then dissolved into the sand and foam. She took Kyle's hand. Her longing for more—to be held—assailed her, and for the first time in their relationship, she thought: *This loneliness will be with me always.*

Maggie followed. The last to see Topher alive and the first to find him dead. Whenever Alice thought about that, she felt an anger toward her brother that nearly obliterated the sadness.

Their father went next. He'd lost several pounds over the week, and his suit hung loose on his shoulders and hips. What it must feel like to hold your child's ashes in your hand, to return them to the earth. Alice shivered, and the anger she felt toward Topher turned into a grief that made her want to howl.

After Cait's turn, she walked back without saying a word, and they all stood along the base of the seawall watching the tide creep closer, gently turning, as reliable as ever. Father Kelly passed around a handkerchief to clean the sticky ash from their hands. Alice wiped her palms on her black pants, streaking her thighs gray. Her heels sunk into the wet sand. Her belly pressed against her waistband, and the reason brought her comfort.

Their mother let out a sob.

"He's home," Father Kelly said. "He's at peace."

Alice was sure they were all tired of the meaningless platitudes, even their mother, but they nodded anyway.

Except for Cait. "That must be nice for him," she said.

Alice had done her best to ignore Cait's constant display of pain for most of the day, but she'd had enough. "Do you ever not think about yourself when you open your mouth?" she said to her sister.

Cait's expression hardened. "I'm just saying what we're all thinking," she said. Then she turned and marched up the seaworn stairs back toward the house.

No one said anything, and after a moment, they all followed. On the lawn, the geese scattered and honked. Kyle started to chase them off, but Alice reached for his hand and told him to let them be. The sun disappeared into the horizon as the tide carried Topher away.

Inside, everyone dispersed. As Father Kelly instructed—finally offering something useful, if not macabre—Alice used vinegar to wash the ash from her hands. She kicked off her heels and unbuttoned her pants, her belly swelling like a balloon. She collapsed onto the leather sofa in the sitting room and closed her eyes, which stung with exhaustion. When she woke an hour later, the house was dark, and her temples pounded.

She found Kyle outside on the back porch, rocking in the wicker chair and drinking a beer. She climbed onto his lap and pressed her face into the crook of his neck, breathing in the cologne she hadn't smelled on him since their wedding. That was the last time she'd seen Topher. He'd returned a few weeks before the rehearsal dinner, his skin weathered from a winter on a fishing boat in Maine, but his face no longer hidden beneath a scraggly beard. Their mother disapproved of the beard, and Alice was touched when he'd shaved it off for the occasion. After their honeymoon, Kyle hung the wind chime on the fire escape outside their apartment in Brooklyn Heights. A few weeks later, their landlord complained about the tinkling from the shells, and they removed the chime and stored it in the box of things they planned to take when they moved out of the city.

"Have you eaten?" Kyle asked her. Aside from a plate of oatmeal cookies, they'd mostly ignored the food platters covering the island in the kitchen. No one was hungry. No one had the energy to make room in the refrigerator for another casserole.

"No," she said.

He placed his hand on her belly. "Let me make you something," he said.

He shifted her to the side and went to stand, but she nudged him back. "Stay for a few more minutes," she said.

They settled back into each other and listened to the waves they could no longer see. Kyle pressed her head, still throbbing, to his chest. She was drained from all the crying, but her eyes welled again with hot tears. The chair creaked as he rocked them back and forth, and Alice looked at the sky, starless from clouds.

"Cait's moving to London," she said. "For a job and Bram. I think they're getting married."

"Really?" Kyle said. "I didn't realize they were that serious."

"I didn't either," Alice said. "She's leaving in September."

"That's soon."

Alice sat up. "Would you ever consider moving to Port Haven? To be closer to my parents. Now with the baby and everything?"

Kyle had just finished his master's in education, and they'd planned on moving to Asheville, North Carolina, where he'd gone to summer camp as a kid.

"I would," he said.

Relief flooded Alice. She wasn't used to Kyle being so flexible. Of the two, she'd always been the one to make concessions, and the reversal didn't feel natural. She was grateful, but asking this of him was hard—almost but not enough to make her backpedal. Immediately, she let herself imagine breaking their lease in Brooklyn and finding a small house near her parents, where their first child would be born that spring. Maybe this would make the unbearable bearable, a new measure for life.

She lowered her head to his chest again, and her mind shifted to the question that had been troubling her all week. She held her belly. "What if I carry it somewhere inside me?" she asked.

"Carry what?"

"Topher's ability to just—" She stopped.

Someone turned on a light inside the house, and they heard murmurings, the tea kettle whistle.

"Your brother had a lot to deal with," Kyle said. "A lot that he never learned how to deal with. That's not you."

Alice nodded. She did not clarify her question. Pregnant, it scared her too much to say it aloud.

Kyle patted her thigh. "Let me make you a tuna fish sandwich," he said.

"I can't eat tuna fish."

They walked inside together, but then Kyle helped her father with the firewood, so Alice made her own sandwich from the chicken and rolls Father Kelly had brought yesterday. Instead of satisfying an appetite she didn't know she had, the sandwich woke her hunger, and she assembled a second one before she finished the first. After, she made her mother a sugar-and-butter sandwich and a cup of tea and headed upstairs. In the hallway, she passed Cait, who had changed out of her black dress and into jeans and a sweater, her makeup refreshed. They walked by each other without a word until Cait said, "Your pants are unzipped," and marched down the stairs.

Behind Maggie's door, Alice heard music. She placed the tea on the floor, plate on top to keep it warm, and fastened her zipper as she knocked. When Maggie told her to come in, she stepped inside and found her sister sprawled across her bed reading.

"How are you doing?" she asked.

Maggie snapped her book shut and gave a thumbs-down.

"Yeah, me, too." Alice leaned against the door frame. "Do you want to talk?"

She worried how finding Topher would impact her younger sister. She'd already spoken to her about meeting with a counselor back at school, but Maggie hadn't shared anything with her about the experience.

"I don't want to ever walk by his room again," Maggie said.

"I don't either."

"Why do you think he did it?"

"I don't know," Alice said.

"And why here?"

Alice stared at the reflection of herself and Maggie in the window. "I don't know," she said again.

She'd been asking herself these questions since last week, when Father Kelly called from the hospital to say he had bad news. Her gut told her it was impulsive. Even the detective's investigation said there was no evidence Topher had planned his death in advance. But Alice didn't want to say that now, because she knew Maggie believed she could have made a difference had she arrived home earlier. And maybe she could have, but it hadn't been Maggie's job to keep their brother alive. Alice had worshipped her brother when they were kids, but as they got older, they grew apart, as seemed to happen with most of Topher's relationships. Over the past few years, Alice avoided answering most of his calls—a call, as opposed to an email or his signature postcard, usually meant he was asking for money. He hadn't called that afternoon, but had he, there was a good chance she wouldn't have answered.

"I keep imagining him like a wounded animal," Maggie said. "You know how they come home to die—"

A burp bubbled in Alice's chest, and though she tried to swallow it, a loud belch released from her mouth. "My God," she said, clutching her throat, which burned with indigestion.

Maggie laughed. "I can't believe I'm going to be an aunt."

"You are," Alice said. "And Kyle and I are moving back to Port Haven."

"That'll help Mom," Maggie said. "All of it will help."

Alice hoped she was right.

The shades were drawn and the lights were off in her parents' bedroom when Alice walked in, but her mother was awake. Alice placed the tea and sandwich on the bedside table and turned on the lamp.

"Thank you," her mother said, and she adjusted herself against the pillows. She hadn't changed out of her skirt suit, and dark circles of mascara made her look like she had two black eyes.

"How are you?" Alice asked.

Her mother closed the bible that had been spread across her chest and placed it on the bed. "Father Kelly gave me a list of scriptures to read, but—" She shook her head. "Cait had a point. Topher may be at peace, but we're all in hell, aren't we?"

"Maybe," Alice said. It was easier for her to admit this when her mother said it rather than Cait. She sat on the edge of the bed and picked up the picture on the nightstand. The photo was of Alice and her siblings standing on the beach as kids. At the bottom of the frame, *The Folly's Crew* was written in a sailor's rope. She placed the picture back and turned to her mother. "But we still have each other," she said.

Nora sat up and took a sip of her tea. "You know, after Maggie was born and I had the four of you, I used to count the years ahead to when you'd all be grown."

She had shared this story before, or some version of it, but she said it now as though for the first time, and anyway, Alice heard it differently. Not as a funny anecdote about the exhaustions of motherhood but as a confession of sorts.

Nora blew her nose in a handkerchief. "I even wrote out a timeline—" She reached for her bible again and opened it to the back cover. Alice leaned closer to look. "All of your ages listed next to the year. I would refer to it when things were hard." She blew her nose again. "Isn't that silly? I thought things would get . . . oh, I don't know, easier, I suppose."

The Irish Goodbye

Alice tried to see how far the timeline went, but her mother closed the book. What Alice hoped to find, she wasn't sure. Her mother had always said you're only as happy as your least happy child, but was that really true? What happens when there's no possibility of that child ever being happy again?

The sound of a car pulling into the pebbled driveway distracted her from the question, and they both turned toward the window. Alice slid off the bed and pulled the curtain to the side, and she watched Cait approach an SUV. The driver, a man Alice didn't recognize at first but then realized was Luke Larkin, got out and embraced her. Then Luke opened the passenger-side door, and Cait hopped in. A moment later, they pulled out of the driveway.

"Who is it?" Nora asked.

"No one," Alice said as they drove off. What was her sister doing with Luke when she'd just announced she was moving to London to be with Bram? "It must have been the wrong house. They've left."

* * *

Sitting in the foyer now and watching Cait on the back porch with Luke, Alice suddenly understood why she'd invited him to dinner.

This didn't surprise her as much as she'd have expected. She was a master at not knowing what she knew.

17.

CAIT

Cait watched as Luke, with an easy flick of his wrist, slammed the nail half an inch deeper into the tree log using the thin wedge of a strangely shaped hammer.

"That was sick," Finn said.

Luke gave Finn a fist bump like they were best buds. If Luke hadn't brought a date, Cait might have appreciated how at ease he was at the house and with her family. Now he just seemed arrogant and clueless.

"Let me try again," Finn said.

Luke handed him the hammer.

The goal of Hammerschlagen—to level your nail first—didn't seem all that difficult, but Luke was the only one who'd even managed to make contact with his nail so far, so Cait supposed she must be missing something. Luke claimed to have learned the game while rock climbing in Joshua Tree.

Cait didn't really care. She was tired of waiting for him to offer her more than a breezy "Hey," as though she wasn't the person he'd come here

The Irish Goodbye

to see. She stood on her toes and leaned into his ear as inconspicuously as she could manage. The smell of his skin, an almost woodsy aftershave, sent a thrill through her body. "Can we go somewhere to talk?"

"Of course," Luke said, but his eyes were on Finn.

Finn pounded his nail's head, but the shank bent sharply to the right, and the whole group laughed.

"It's all good," Luke said, clapping him on the back.

As Luke showed Finn how to align his nail, Kyle sidled up to Cait. "Have you talked to Mukesh yet?" he asked her.

"You just introduced us. Remember?"

"I meant, he's moving to London. Maybe you can help him settle in. Introduce him to people. He's a lawyer, too. Or is it a solicitor?"

"Please don't."

"Barrister?"

Cait rolled her eyes but smiled.

"Sorry." Kyle laughed. "Anyway, he's a great guy—"

Cait pivoted to Kyle and said this loud enough for Luke to hear. "Are you trying to set us up?"

"Not necessarily, but—"

"Okay, everyone," Luke said. He held on to Finn's shoulders, infuriatingly oblivious to Kyle and Cait's conversation. "It's my boy's turn. Pay attention."

Finn raised the hammer and slammed it on the tree stump a good three inches away from the nail.

"Aw!" Luke handed the hammer to Kyle. "It's all right. Next time."

Cait grabbed the hammer from Kyle's hand. "My turn," she said. "What is this thing anyway?"

"A blacksmith's hammer," Luke said.

"How do you play?"

"You use the wedge side to whack the nail," Luke said. "No lining it up. Just hold it in the air like this. Girls can use two hands, so—"

"I'll bypass the sexist rules, thanks." She raised the hammer and smacked it dead-on the head of her nail, lowering it a good half an inch into the wood. It was complete beginner's luck, but she handed the hammer back to Kyle as though she knew exactly what she was doing.

Luke whistled in admiration.

"How'd you do that?" Finn asked, almost affronted.

Cait gestured as though she was polishing her fingernails on her lapel. Through the window, Nicole walked toward the bar, probably trying to find Luke. Cait leaned into Luke's ear again. "Now," she said, somewhere between a question and a demand. Kyle eyed them, but she didn't care.

Instead of responding to Cait directly, Luke pointed at Finn with his beer glass. "Take my turn, buddy. I'll be right back."

Once alone, they stepped into the house, and Luke wrapped his arm around Cait's waist and pulled her closer. She thought he would kiss her, and looked forward to rebuffing him, but then he walked down the hallway. At the far end, he stopped at a collection of her mother's paintings. They were primarily landscapes from her garden, with a few she'd painted of Ireland. Taking up the other side of the wall was a framed pencil sketch of the original plans for the Folly from 1912.

"I can't believe your family held on to these," Luke said.

Cait had never noticed the handwritten note in the corner, which read, *Crafted for the Ryan family*. She hoped Alice's warning about their parents having to leave the house was just her sister being overly dramatic. Could things be that bad and she didn't know?

Luke looked at her. "It's really nice being back here," he said. "Just like old times."

The comment didn't sit well with Cait. How could it possibly feel like old times? Despite Alice's accusations, Cait understood the significance of inviting him to the house, and she didn't like how nonchalant he was being about everything.

"Like old times when?" she asked. Luke let out a laugh. He didn't get it, which annoyed her even more, and she heard herself say, "Like when our brothers were alive?"

The Irish Goodbye

Now he did get it. He tightened his jaw and stuffed his hand in his pocket. "That's where you want to go?"

That was *not* where Cait wanted to go. But she'd said it after all, and her mind returned to the day after Daniel died when she and Topher met Luke on the seawall outside the Folly, and Luke told them his mom didn't want anyone from the Ryan family attending the wake. Cait could still remember the shame she felt for hoping that she and Luke might carry on with their romance despite all evidence that would never happen. And yet, here they were.

Instead of responding to Luke's question, she pulled him through the door and closed it behind them.

Luke looked around at the wood-paneled walls. "What is this?"

"My mom's painting studio."

"I've never been in here." He studied a miniature painting of geese on the dresser. "I remember seeing her paintings in high school and thinking it was cool that your mom was an artist."

He stepped closer, and Cait took a step back. "What's with you bringing a date?" she asked.

Luke shook his head. "We work together. I told you yesterday I had plans with a friend, and you said to bring her." He held Cait lightly by the elbows. "I'm here to see you. Nothing's going on with Nicole. I actually thought it might make things easier having her here."

"Easier? For whom?"

Luke put his hands on his hips. "Look, it's no secret what your parents think about me—"

"It was never about *you*."

"Fine. What they feel—or felt?—about my parents. I didn't want them thinking I was coming back into your life to, I don't know, disrupt things."

"Oh, come on."

You are disrupting things! You're disrupting everything!

"Besides, you're the one who said we should keep things quiet," Luke said. "Until we know what's even going on here."

There was a knock, and before they could answer, the groan of the door opening.

"We need more nails," Finn announced behind Cait's back. "James wants to play."

"He can use my nail," Luke said.

"But then he'll be winning before he even starts—"

"Finn," Cait said. "Please?"

When Finn left, she turned back to Luke. "What *is* even going on here?" she said.

Luke seemed unnerved by the question. "I don't know," he said. "I thought we were trying to figure that out, but you're making things complicated by—"

"Me?" she said, taken aback. "How am I the one making things complicated?"

Luke reached for her again, but now the door was open, and from the other room, Nora was announcing that dinner was served and where was everyone.

18.

MAGGIE

"Maybe we got the time wrong," Maggie said. She and Isabel were the only two people standing on the platform at the Port Haven station, and there was no train in sight. "They probably have a holiday schedule."

"Well, they just sold me a ticket," Isabel said. "So I'm sure the—"

Before Isabel could finish, the train rounded the corner, and a voice crackled over the loudspeaker, bored and New York–accented, announcing the 3:24 to Penn Station now arriving.

Maggie's throat tightened as Isabel grabbed her bag. She no longer cared that Isabel had revealed their fight to her whole family. She just wanted her to stay. Even after she'd parked the car, Maggie did not believe Isabel would go through with it.

The snow fell harder, and Isabel stepped closer to the platform's yellow-bordered edge as the train slowed to a halt. Maggie held Isabel's elbow. "Don't go," she said.

Isabel's eyes were teary, and her nose was red—from the cold or crying, Maggie wasn't sure. As awful as it had been to leave the house, the expression on Isabel's face now, a sort of stony resignation, was even worse. The train settled, the doors opened, and Isabel stepped inside without saying a word. Through the fogged-up, streaked windows, Maggie watched her slump into a seat in the back of the car.

A shot of panic charged through Maggie's body, and as the doors were closing, she jumped inside the train. She stood in the corridor to get her bearings. When the train lurched forward, she nearly lost her balance and had to hold on to the backs of the seats as she strode down the aisle.

Isabel startled when she found Maggie standing beside her seat.

The only other passenger in the car—a teenager dressed in all black sitting near the rank-smelling bathroom—looked up from his phone.

"Why are you here?" Isabel asked.

Maggie didn't know exactly. She hadn't planned on doing this. All she knew was she didn't want to be away from Isabel; if they separated now, that would be the end. And so here she was, fairly certain Isabel would insist she get off at the next stop and that she looked like a complete fool to someone who'd already decided, perhaps accurately, that she was no longer worth the effort. When she opened her mouth, nothing came out.

Isabel turned toward the window, but she moved her bag off the seat next to her, and Maggie was relieved at the small gesture. As she sat, she felt the green caboose that she'd taken from Augustus and James earlier in her pocket.

The train pulled away from the station. They faced backward, and within minutes, she'd be motion sick, but she didn't dare move. She deserved to be ill.

"I'm going to ride with you to Penn," she said. She wished she'd worn a jacket. The heat didn't seem to be working in the car, and she could see her breath as she spoke. "Just to make sure you get there okay. If that's all right?"

Isabel nodded, then returned to the window to watch the snow-covered rooftops and trees passing by backward.

"Actually, that's not true," Maggie said, and Isabel turned to face her. "I'm here because I don't want to let you go. That's the real reason."

Isabel drew her knees to her chest. After a moment, she said, "What did you expect would happen?"

"That you'd tell me to get off the train."

Isabel looked at her, annoyed, and pulled her hair back into a ponytail, exposing her long, elegant neck. "I meant, when you went to her house," she said. "What did you think would happen?"

Maggie sensed Isabel was giving her another opening, an opportunity to explain, and she was desperate to get it right. "I guess I was hoping for some resolution," she said.

"So you weren't over her yet."

Maggie sat up. "No," she said. "That's not it." How could she explain? "Things ended so suddenly it was disorienting. She was the person I spoke to every day, all day, and then without a warning, she was completely out of my life."

There had been so much shame about the relationship—everything hidden—that Maggie rarely talked about it with anyone. Sharing this with Isabel now was edifying, and she wished she'd done so earlier and in different circumstances. For the first time in the last hour, Isabel didn't seem upset. Curious, maybe.

"It fucked me up," Maggie continued. "By the time I met you, I had no interest in getting back together with her. It was a pretty shitty relationship, to be honest. Like every relationship I've had besides you. But the whole thing still felt unresolved. When she invited me over, I thought—well, I never had the chance to look her in the eyes and say—I don't even know. Goodbye? Nice knowing you? I hope it's not awkward when I see you at Oliver's graduation? That's all I was looking for."

Isabel grimaced. "But instead you kissed her."

"She kissed me—"

"See, that's the problem." Isabel crossed her arms. "That's why I left your parents' house. You won't take any responsibility. Kisses don't just *happen*. There's generally a lead-up."

She was right, but Maggie figured it was safer not to say anything at all.

Isabel turned to her again. "You know, it's not like I haven't been in my own messy situations."

"Like what?" Isabel's dating history had always struck Maggie as almost irritatingly healthy and upright—no infidelity or toxicity. It was one of the reasons Maggie hadn't shared details of her own muddled past. Now she was wildly curious.

"I'll tell you another time," Isabel said. "The point is, you can't just say sorry and make it all go away. Your experiences, your life—you have to deal with things. I mean, no offense, but she doesn't sound like she was all that great. Why were you even with her?"

The answer to this question was easy. "I was lonely," Maggie said. Maybe that sounded lame, but she had been, profoundly so, and she had a feeling she would be again very soon.

Isabel sighed, as if the answer didn't quite satisfy, and stretched her legs out on the seat in front of her.

Maggie tried again. "It's always been easy for me to be with people who wanted to keep me a secret. I've been doing it my whole life."

"You can't just blame other people," Isabel said, but her face softened. "You've done that to yourself, too. You've kept yourself a secret here with me. You've withheld so much."

Maggie did not want this to be true, but she knew it was, so she nodded.

The interior train doors opened, and the conductor entered the car. "Tickets! Have your tickets ready!"

Fuck.

Isabel handed the conductor her ticket, and as he punched the holes, Maggie said, "I'm so sorry, sir. I don't have a ticket. I caught the train last minute and—"

The Irish Goodbye

"It's three dollars more if you didn't buy ahead."

Finally, a problem she could solve. "Sure. Of course." It was then she realized she'd left her bag in the car. She turned to Isabel. "I don't have my wallet."

Isabel paid for Maggie's ticket, and the conductor made his way toward the teenager.

"I'll pay you back," Maggie said.

Isabel waved her hand and slid her wallet into her bag.

After a moment, Maggie said, "I wish there was a way I could show you that what happened—it wasn't about us."

"Actually, you're not the one who gets to decide that," Isabel said. "It *was* about us. Look at how it's impacted us. Look at where we are now." She paused, then continued. "You've never even talked to me about your relationship with Sarah. You just mentioned it offhandedly when we first met."

"I know."

Isabel seemed to think of something. "Can I see a picture of her?"

Maggie wasn't expecting this. She took her phone out of her back pocket, relieved there wasn't another text from Sarah, and scrolled through her pictures for the first photo she could find that was just Sarah and not the two of them together. She finally found one from a year ago. A dinner at a restaurant in Amherst. They'd shared a plate of gnocchi and a bottle of pinot noir as they sketched different layout options for Maggie's new cabin on the back of the menu. A different life. She handed the phone to Isabel and watched her study the photo. She wasn't sure if this disclosure would make things better or worse. Sarah was objectively beautiful, but she wasn't someone Maggie could ever imagine Isabel finding attractive.

"She just seems so . . ." Isabel said, then stopped.

"So?"

"Like a mom from Grove."

"Well, she is."

Isabel let out a laugh, and Maggie smiled a little. She didn't want Isabel to think she was making light of it all.

"She couldn't be more different from me." Isabel handed the phone back to Maggie.

Maggie sat on the edge of her seat. "She couldn't. Everything is different with you. And that's the point. I want *you*." She reached for Isabel's hand again and entangled their fingers. It might as well have been their entire bodies reconnecting, and her chest tightened as desire coursed through her. "You're the one I want to be with."

Isabel pulled her hand away and turned back to the window. "I wish you had known that last weekend."

"I did know." Maggie scooted closer. "That's never been in question."

She was trying to be as honest as possible, but she'd already obliterated Isabel's trust, and when Isabel didn't respond, she worried it was too late.

The storm was quickening, and the train swayed with the wind. They rode along in silence.

Then Isabel turned back to face Maggie. "What about the other texts? When I scrolled, there weren't others—"

"I erased them," Maggie blurted out before she lost her nerve.

Isabel nodded, as though this confirmed something for her that was troubling. Maggie imagined her thinking she and Sarah had been sending flirty texts since that night in Boston, perhaps before then.

"I hadn't talked to Sarah since you and I met," Maggie said, "and I didn't talk to her after I left her house. When I got her message on Wednesday, I panicked and erased the whole thread."

"That's convenient."

Nothing about any of this felt convenient.

"And, you know, this isn't just about us," Isabel said. "A student's parent? Who's married to a board member?"

"About that."

Isabel looked up.

"Cunningham asked me to come to his office on Monday. I'm worried it has to do with what happened."

Isabel shook her head. "I just can't believe you were so reckless. It's not like you. Even with your job—which you love so much."

And you, Maggie thought. *I love you.* She wished she could say the words—she'd known this for some time, but she feared it would only come off as desperate to say it now.

Instead, she said, "It didn't feel reckless at the time. Obviously I see it that way now. But then—I was in a sort of haze."

The train was slowly pulling into the first station when it jerked to a stop. Maggie and Isabel looked at each other. The power switched off, and they could hear the *thump, thump* of the teenager's music blaring from his headphones in the silence. Then the power returned and a voice over the loudspeaker reported that they'd suspended service on the line due to frozen tracks. The conductor came through to let them know a van would be arriving soon to transport riders to a bus terminal in a nearby town, where they could use their tickets for a ride to Penn Station.

The teenager stormed out of the car.

The lights flickered again, and the conductor emerged through the back doors. "Let's go, ladies. Your chariot awaits."

Maggie stood and carried Isabel's bag. They followed the conductor onto the snowy platform, where Maggie called Kyle to ask for a ride. As reliable as always, her brother-in-law was the most likely to be sober and the least likely to demand anything more than small talk. They waited in silence, and Maggie hoped Isabel would agree to go with her, so she might have another chance to make things if not right, then at least better.

19.

CAIT

Cait stood next to the kids' table, pretending to ignore Luke and Nicole as they walked into the dining room, laughing. It was like being in high school again and going from party to party trying to track him down, only to find him hanging out with another girl or getting wasted with Topher. *Just like old times.* Had she really thought he'd changed? Had she really thought she'd changed?

Her hands shook as she cut the twins' slices of turkey into tiny pieces. There was no chance in hell they'd eat any of it, but she made them promise to take what Ruthie called a "thank-you bite," though the phrase always irked her. Poppy had woken about a half hour ago, but the Benadryl still seemed to be working to chill her out, and for that, Cait felt not an ounce of guilt.

The front door opened, and a moment later, Maggie and Kyle entered the dining room, bringing the cold air with them. Isabel followed, bag in hand, and gave a half wave. This could not be an easy room to walk back into, Cait thought. When Kyle left to pick them up, Cait tried texting

The Irish Goodbye

Maggie from Alice's phone to get the scoop—*Did you and Isabel make up? Did she decide to stay?*—but her sister never responded. She tried to assess the situation now. Maggie was still in her clothes from yesterday, and her hair was pulled back in a messy bun—but then, yes, they were holding hands. Or no, Maggie was reaching to take Isabel's bag. Cait looked for Luke again, but he was nowhere to be found, and Nicole was chatting with Alice about Finn's basketball team.

"How were the roads?" their father asked.

Cait appreciated that he was trying to make the situation less awkward. Certainly no one else knew what to say.

"Icy," Kyle said as he unzipped his jacket.

Nora welcomed Isabel and Maggie back and said, "Sit, please, sit," to everyone around the table. Then she dashed off to check on the caterers, and Cait watched her father follow after her to help.

She found her place card between Alice and Nicole and sat. Alice had asked the caterers to return Isabel's table setting, but they'd put Maggie and Isabel right next to Father Kelly. How'd that one slip by Alice? Maggie had said she felt more pity for Father Kelly, trapped in his own closet, than anger about how he'd tried to "save her" back in high school, but Cait still believed her sister was owed an apology.

"Maggie, dear," Father Kelly said, as he hugged her hello. He reached his hand out to Isabel. "And this is your friend—"

"Isabel," Maggie said.

Oh, for fuck's sake.

"She's not her friend," Cait called from across the table.

Father Kelly turned.

"She's her *girlfriend*," Cait said. "As in, they share a bed and—" She went to scissor her fingers, but Alice grabbed her hands and said, "We get it!"

Isabel and Cait shared a quick smile, but Maggie flashed Cait a look of complete horror. Cait didn't know if it was because of what she'd said to Father Kelly—and, okay, maybe the gesture had been too much—or because Isabel was no longer, in fact, her girlfriend.

Father Kelly's cheeks glowed as he went to sit.

"Do we get it?" Cait asked him.

"Yes, Cait, I believe we do."

Nora walked back into the dining room. "Isn't this lovely," she said of the table spread. She was avoiding her cane—out of vanity, Cait knew—and instead gripped Robert's thin arm for support. What good that would do, Cait wasn't sure. She'd been catching moments like this between them all day—her frail father supporting her frail mother, neither strong enough to be alone.

Luke reappeared holding two bottles of Malbec. He walked around the table, filling each glass, maddeningly at ease as he explained that he was friends with the vintner. Cait busied herself unfolding her napkin. She refused to make eye contact with him even as he gave her a generous pour and placed a half-empty bottle in front of her place setting.

Father Kelly finished saying grace, and the platters made their way clockwise from hand to hand. By the time everyone began eating, Cait had already downed her first glass of wine—it was fabulous, she was loath to admit—and so she poured another for herself and topped off Alice's and Nicole's, though hers was the only one in need of a refill. By the second glass, her hands no longer trembled, but whenever she'd catch Luke across the table chatting with Father Kelly or laughing with Mukesh, she'd think to herself: *I hate him*. It was not the kind of hatred that came with love. She knew that hatred. This was pure. Even more complicated than pure. Maybe it wasn't even hatred at all. Unless it was hatred for herself. Or for them both. The two flawed people they'd become who could never get back to the innocent kids they once were. The hatred was confounding. It meant she did not know the version of herself who'd invited him there in the first place, who'd been lovesick over him since she was sixteen. Who, then, sat here now? She tried taking a long sip of wine to calm herself.

"It's all delicious," Nicole said, and everyone mumbled their agreement before breaking off into their own conversations.

The Irish Goodbye

Cait picked at the kale salad on her plate and turned to Nicole. "So you know Luke from Saint Mary's?"

Nicole smiled and fanned her hand in front of her mouth to indicate she needed to finish chewing; then she swallowed dramatically. "We didn't actually know each other then," she said. "But I was friends with Danny."

The casual evocation of Luke's brother's nickname startled Cait, and her whole body stiffened. Not everyone called Daniel *Danny*. Just like not everyone called Christopher *Topher*. She looked to see who'd heard and caught her mother's eye.

"Daniel was a sweet boy," her mother said now.

Did her accent sound thicker? There was an unsettling intensity to it. Luke raised his glass, but his smile faltered. "He was."

Cait watched as the room absorbed this all in silence. Outside, the wind whipped the snow. The room darkened, and the candles flickered.

As the table resumed its chatter, Nicole turned to Cait. "Luke and I met again at an angel investment lunch two years ago when I was getting my NGO off the ground."

Alice leaned over Cait. "What does your organization do?"

"We work with women entrepreneurs in Nigeria." Nicole spoke now to Alice, over Cait's shoulder. "We provide grants and microloans to help them launch their own businesses."

Oh, the virtue. Cait wanted to barf.

"That's incredible," Alice said.

"Did you have a fundraiser in London a few months ago?" Cait asked.

"We did," Nicole said, taken aback. "How did you—"

Cait waved her hand. "Luke mentioned something about it."

She felt ill. The room blurred in a kaleidoscope of colors and sounds. She sipped her water, and when she reemerged, Nicole was talking about how they'd recently appointed Luke as the director of major gifts at her organization, the name of which Cait hadn't caught. She could see Luke watching them from across the table. Nicole seemed to notice as well.

"He helped us with the seed money," Nicole continued, smiling at Luke. "And now he leads our fundraising efforts."

"Nicole, could you pass me the gravy?" Maggie said. "And did I hear you say you ran track at Saint Mary's?"

Thank you, Maggie.

"Oh," Nicole said, handing her the saucer. "Yes, long distance. I wasn't very fast so—"

Mukesh turned to Luke. "I sit on a board for an aid organization that does similar work in rural India. Mostly Chhattisgarh. We should talk."

"Anytime," Luke said, too proudly, Cait thought.

Nicole took a delicate sip of her wine. "You should," she said to Mukesh. "He's brilliant. Whenever he comes to speak to the women, they're all inspired by what a self-starter he was—"

Cait snorted, and the table quieted.

"Sorry." Nicole sat up straight. "Did I say something funny?"

Alice pinched Cait's arm. "Not at all."

Cait knew she should stop, but she could not let go of the idea of someone—no, not just *someone*; his date!—referring to Luke as a "self-starter" in present company.

"I don't like the turkey," Poppy said from the kids' table.

"You don't have to eat it," Cait said, then turned back to Nicole. "You didn't say anything funny. Untrue, maybe, but not funny."

Alice squeezed Cait's arm again, but Cait yanked it away, nearly spilling her wine but catching it at the last second. She took a sip as though the whole thing was intentional.

"I don't get it," Nicole said, setting down her fork and knife.

Luke coughed into his napkin. "I'm not sure I do either."

Cait propped her elbows on the table and rested her chin on her entwined fingers. She fixed her eyes on Luke and felt strangely assured. "Of course you do," she said.

"I'd love to hear more about the women's businesses," Alice said. "And what kind of—"

The Irish Goodbye

"Just stop," Cait said to her sister. She turned to Nicole. "What I meant is Luke's far from a self-starter. Unless starting with"—she glared at him, challenging him to disagree with her—"what was it exactly?" Her face grew hot. "One million? Two—"

"One million thirty-four thousand," Nora said matter-of-factly.

Everyone at the table turned to Nora. Cait could hardly believe it. Her parents had never revealed the number—they didn't want Topher to know.

"That was the final amount," Nora continued. "When everything was settled."

Cait turned back to Luke. "That had to help, no?"

Luke shook his head slowly.

"What was a *million* dollars?" James asked.

"We do not need to discuss this right now," Robert said.

Cait turned back to Nicole. "You're from around here," she said. "You know what we're talking about."

Nicole looked up at Luke but stayed quiet.

Mukesh jumped in. "Is this about the NGO?"

"It's not," Maggie said.

"We're talking about—" Cait began but stopped when her father slammed his open palm on the table, the dishes and silverware clattering.

The room fell silent.

"Why's Papa so mad?" Poppy whispered to her cousins, her voice loud enough for everyone to hear.

Alice cleared her throat. "James, why don't you tell everyone what you learned at the turkey farm with your class last week."

James stood. "You can tell if a turkey is a boy or a girl by their poop," he squealed.

Augustus and Poppy burst into laughter.

"That's not what your mother meant," Kyle said.

"You're gross," Finn said.

Poppy jumped up from the kids' table. "Mummy," she shouted to Cait, and pointed to the window. "The raccoon!"

"That's Brew." Alice sighed. "The Callahans' beagle that howls all night."

As everyone watched the floppy-eared dog run home through the snow, Cait met Luke's gaze. He looked hurt, maybe embarrassed, but she felt vindicated in calling him out. What had he expected?

Alice turned back to the table. "Ah, holidays," she said with a nervous laugh. "Always something!" Then: "Father Kelly, what were holidays like for you growing up?"

Father Kelly heeded the call and sat up, dabbing his mouth with his napkin. "Oh, sure," he said. "Right, well, when I was a kid, every holiday, my father would spend time with each of us children in the sitting room while mother prepared a special meal. We'd go in age order, and as the second youngest of eleven, I could always see that he was tired by the time I sat in the chair across from him. But this was important for him and for us. He worked long hours as a hotel manager and rarely got to see us throughout the week. He'd smoke his pipe and inquire about our marks at school and were we being helpful to mother and the like. Then, at the end, he'd always ask the same question—"

Luke stood and tossed his napkin down beside his plate.

"I never wanted that money," he said to Cait. Then he turned to her parents. "You know that, don't you?"

Nora did not answer him, and Cait wasn't sure if that was because she disagreed with what he said or if she was just trying to keep it together, but then a strange look flickered between Luke and her father.

After a moment, her father said, "We know."

Suddenly Luke was standing next to Cait. At first she assumed he was there to get Nicole so they could leave, but then he announced to the table, "Please give us a minute. Cait?" He nodded toward the door.

Cait sensed everyone watching them as they crossed the room, Luke's hand on the small of her back guiding her, and she felt a flutter of exhil-

The Irish Goodbye

aration at finally being claimed by him publicly. She let him steer her past the kitchen, where the caterers ate their dinner at the center island, through the foyer, and then out the front door and into the November snowstorm, where a strange combination of grim satisfaction and remorse hit her immediately and hard.

20.

ALICE

Everyone at the table was stunned, trying to figure out what had just happened. All Alice knew was that Cait had detonated a bomb, and once again it was her job to clean up the mess. She had no idea where Cait and Luke had gone, but she was furious.

She turned to check on her mother, but Nora dropped her eyes, her hands clasped in her lap like a timid schoolgirl. Mukesh sneezed into his napkin, and Father Kelly said, "Bless you."

Alice exchanged glances with Maggie, but she knew her younger sister wasn't going to be of any use. Since returning from the train station, she'd looked on the verge of tears herself.

Poppy stood, hands on her hips. "Where'd my mummy go?" Before anyone could answer, she set off to follow Cait, but Isabel scooped her up as she walked by and plopped her onto her lap, distracting her with questions about her charm bracelets.

Alice winked at the boys to assure them everything was fine, though they knew it wasn't, even if Poppy was easy enough to distract and Augustus was busy driving a model train car through his mashed potatoes.

Finally, Nora looked up from her lap and spoke. "I'm sorry about that," she said. She adjusted the collar on her blazer, and the gesture sank Alice's heart. All the effort her mother had put into the day, and now this.

"I didn't mean to upset her," Nicole said.

Father Kelly refilled his wine and passed the bottle. "No, love," he said. "She's just a bit jet-lagged, our Cait."

"That's right," Nora said, and dabbed the corners of her eyes with her napkin.

Alice scrambled to find something to fill the silence, but then Kyle turned to Father Kelly and said, "You were about to share the question that your father asked you every holiday."

Alice offered Kyle a half smile to thank him.

"Yes, that's right." Father Kelly shifted in his seat. "Well, I'd later learn from mother that father spent this extra time with us because when he was a child, holidays were often ruined by his parents' feuding. He didn't have many happy memories, I'll say. And so the question he would ask us was simply 'Are you happy?'"

Father Kelly sat back, and for a long moment, everyone at the table seemed to consider the question. He meant the story to be heartwarming, of course, but Alice thought it was horrible. How was a child supposed to answer a question like that other than to placate their parent? *Yes, yes, I'm happy. You've done your job.*

Finally, Nora said, "Cheers," and they all raised their glasses with weary gusto. No one was convinced.

"Shall we?" Alice said, gesturing to the food. "Before it gets cold?"

Relieved to have someone tell them what to do, they all gradually resumed eating, and soon the scraping of forks and knives on china plates replaced the awful silence. Still, the empty chairs stood out at the festive table, and no one spoke.

"Maybe we can go around and say what we're most thankful for?" Alice said, desperate to shift the energy in the room. When no one volunteered, she asked Finn to go first.

Finn glanced up from his plate. He was still upset about not being able to go to Leo's house after dinner, and for a split second, Alice worried he might try to humiliate or punish her. But then he gave a half shrug and said, "My friends," his voice cracking.

When it was Augustus's turn, instead of saying what he was most thankful for, he stood up and in his proper British accent asked, "But how come Americans wanted to leave England to become Indians?"

James nearly fell off his chair. "They were Pilgrims!"

Augustus frowned in disappointment. "Oh," he said, and returned to his train.

After Kyle gave Augustus a brief history lesson on Thanksgiving—for once, Alice didn't mind his Mr. Principal voice—they went around the rest of the room, and Alice did her best to laugh or nod thoughtfully, trying to help restore some sense of normalcy to the day. As the servers—*the servers!*—refilled water and wineglasses, she wondered if they missed spending the day with their families or if they were grateful to be distracted by the drama of someone else's. She pushed her turkey, which was dry and tasted strangely like orange, to the side of her plate and picked at the bits—were they pomegranate seeds and crushed walnuts?—in the brussels sprouts. Nothing felt as it should.

"May I be excused?" Finn asked, standing up.

All day Alice had wanted to tell him to stop with the surliness—have a conversation with one of the adults! Help out your grandmother! Play with your cousins!—but mostly she'd just let him be, because she knew that any request beyond sharing a meal with the family would only make him more surly. And yet, she still wanted him there.

"What about pie?" she asked him.

"I'm okay," Finn said. "Can I just go to the attic to watch a movie?" He held his belly. "I think I'm getting the stomach bug, too."

The Irish Goodbye

"Oh no," Nora said.

Nicole leaned subtly away from the kids' table.

"I didn't have a stomach bug," Alice assured the table, avoiding Kyle's eyes. "Just some food poisoning."

"Can I watch a movie, too?" James asked, hopping off his chair.

Finn put James in a gentle headlock. "I'm not feeling well, buddy, so I'm going to go up by myself, but I'll hang out with you guys later. I promise."

Finn was acting weird—not just pretending to be sick, but now being nice to his brother. Alice wasn't sure what he was up to but figured as long as he was hanging out in the attic, at least she wouldn't have to worry about his sulking.

"I'll flatten some warm 7UP to take with you," Nora said.

"I'll get it myself," Finn said, and before anyone could answer, he turned the corner to the kitchen.

As the caterers cleared the plates, Father Kelly launched into another story, this time about catching mice at his grandfather's farm as a kid, and Alice grew more and more irritated with all of them. Why was she always the one who had to stay behind to deal with the fallout? The caterers served coffee and Earl Grey tea, and the conversation drifted to the raccoons. It was all Alice had been hearing about from her father for weeks. Cait should be the one sitting here listening. And with that, her irritation turned to a sort of rage. Not at her father and his fixation on the raccoons scarfing his garbage. Or at her mother, who was clearly upset by Cait's disappearing act and the drama of Maggie's exit and reentrance, but who would never be able to admit her own role in the unraveling. Or at her brother, forever gone. It was at herself, and it was not new. It had been there for almost as long as she could remember. Slowly, a truth emerged. Every important decision she'd ever made in her life had been in the service of taking care of her family.

She eyed the glass of red wine Cait had poured for her earlier, then picked it up and took a long sip. Before she finished swallowing, she caught

Kyle watching her and quickly placed the glass back onto the table. Then, in a rush of defiance, she raised the glass again and took another sip.

"Alice," Kyle said. A bark.

The table grew silent. Alice returned the glass again to the table. The wine burned her throat and unsettled her stomach, and she regretted it immediately. She set her fork on the left side of her plate in the four o'clock position, tines up, as her mother had drilled into her as a kid. She suddenly felt desperate to get out of the room. To be anywhere but there. She looked at Maggie and motioned to have her keep an eye on Nora, then stood and said, "I should check on Cait."

Kyle stood. "I'll come with you."

"I don't need help." Alice pushed her chair in against the table and fixed the linen tablecloth, which had gotten ruffled when Cait stood to leave with Luke. "I'll see how dessert's coming along, too."

Alice averted her eyes from Kyle and her mother and turned to leave.

When she got to the hallway, Kyle appeared behind her.

"I just told you I don't need help," she said. "Why don't you ever listen?"

"Because you're pregnant and were drinking wine," Kyle said sharply.

Alice looked into his dark eyes, then turned away. "I forgot. For a second—I just forgot." She gripped the wooden railing to the stairs. "I need to find Cait."

Kyle scoffed.

"What?"

"Cait's not looking to be found."

This was true, but she headed up the stairs anyway.

Kyle caught up with her at the landing. "Did you know something was going on between her and Luke?"

"Of course I knew." She did not mention she'd only just figured this out.

"Then why did you tell me it was a good idea to invite Mukesh?"

Alice turned. "I believe I told you the opposite."

Her heels clicked along the wooden floor of the hallway, Kyle following close behind her. She didn't actually want to find Cait, but now she felt like she had to go through the motions to pretend that's why she'd left the table, and she hoped the effort would at least help shed Kyle's presence. Downstairs, she could hear the kids getting their snow clothes back on. "Can you please go sit with my parents or take the kids outside?" she asked Kyle.

"I will," he said. "But at least tell me what that was all about. With the wine?"

Alice wrapped her arms around herself. "It was a mistake! This whole day has been a mistake, and I made one as well. Can you let it go?"

She wanted to scream when Kyle continued to follow her.

At Cait's door, Kyle jiggled the glass doorknob. "Stop," Alice said, but he opened the door anyway. The room was empty.

"It wasn't a mistake," Kyle said. "I know you."

Alice stopped short of the attic, assuming Cait and Luke weren't up there hanging out with Finn. "Then what was it?" she said. "Whatever you're implying, just say it—"

"I'm not implying anything. I'm asking a question."

"No," Alice shot back. "You're badgering me."

Kyle snorted. "Sorry if I find it hard to believe you just *forgot* you were pregnant."

Alice buried her face in her hands for a moment of reprieve. When she looked up again, Kyle expounded upon all the ways she'd obsessively protected her body when she was pregnant with Finn and James. "You wouldn't even eat tuna fish!" She half listened as she stared at the painting on the wall behind him—a watercolor of a fishing village her mother had visited once with the nuns. The night Alice and Kyle returned to the Folly from the hospital after Topher died, she'd noticed the picture had fallen to the floor. At first, she'd been confused, but then Kyle explained it was probably from the EMTs trying to maneuver Topher's body down the stairs in the carrier. She was newly pregnant then, too—Finn a cluster of cells dividing and dividing within her—but filled with a sense of hope for that child that she could not gather here and now.

She thought of what had just transpired at the table—not just Cait's outburst, but her determination to stand up for herself, however sloppily— and looked at Kyle. "I want to go back to school," she said.

Kyle's face settled instantly. "For design?" he asked.

"Yes," she said, exacerbated. "And maybe business."

"Then do that."

"I can't. I mean, I won't. Not if we have another baby."

"Of course you can," Kyle said. "You're my Alice the Invincible!"

Alice had to stop herself from rolling her eyes. "Do you know how much money we have in the bank at the moment?" she asked him. "Before you're paid next week?"

Kyle shifted. "More than we had when either of the boys was born, I imagine. We made it work."

"I made it work," she said, "for everyone but me."

"What's the point in even—"

"And we can't have three kids in a two-bedroom house. Do you know how much a house even slightly bigger than ours costs in Port Haven these days?"

Kyle cupped her elbows. "These are all problems with a solution," he said. Then his grip tightened. "There's a baby coming in nine months, so we need to stop focusing on—"

Alice turned away. She knew he wouldn't understand what this meant to her, not now, not ever. "I can't be more than six weeks along," she said.

Finally, it seemed to click. "Oh," he said quietly. "Okay. I see." Then: "We can't."

Though he didn't use the word, the evocation shifted something within her. By saying they *couldn't*, he was acknowledging they *could*. Or she could.

Below them, the chatter in the kitchen stopped. A moment later, it resumed, and so did Kyle. "There are logistics we'll need to work out, sure. But once the baby's born, you won't even remember these things."

She shot him a look, and he shrank away. His tone enraged her—*I'm the man*, he seemed to say, *the decider, and your feelings are irrelevant.* He was trying to talk himself into accepting this.

"Look," he said more evenly. "You're in shock. I am, too. And with everything"—he gestured downstairs—"you're overwhelmed. I told you that earlier. And today's not helping."

"I am in shock," Alice admitted. "But that's not—"

"I'll get an extra job. My dad couldn't afford to send three kids to college on a cop's salary, but he made it work. So can we."

Alice shook her head. "No, you don't understand—"

"And we'll talk to Dr. Chen about the risk factors. There must be something we can do. I know you're scared."

"Stop interrupting me and telling me what I am!" Her head felt like it would explode, and she pinched the space between her eyes. She knew he was upset, but she could not stand to listen to more of his assumptions and false assurances.

Kyle composed himself, but it seemed to take everything in him not to say more.

"I want to keep working," she said. "I don't want our lives to go back to sleepless nights, and I don't want to be changing diapers while trying to figure out how we'll ever be able to afford to send Finn to college, and—my God, how can you ask this of me? Why is another kid more important than your wife?"

Downstairs, someone opened the front door, and James's voice echoed through the house. "Papa, the raccoon's back in the garbage!"

Alice headed toward the stairs to see what was happening, but Kyle held her back and called down to James, "Stay away from the raccoon!" A second later, they could hear her father walking out the front door. "I got it," he yelled.

Kyle turned back to Alice. "I am not saying that this baby is more important than you," he said.

"But if you want me to go through with the pregnancy, then you are."

"No, we need to keep you safe, of course. But the sooner we accept what's actually happening and move forward—"

"That's not what I'm doing."

Kyle stared at her. "What *are* you doing?"

Here, the word caught in her throat. She knew that what she was saying—or not saying—was a devastating, heartbreaking thing. For her, but also for Kyle. An attack on his faith, his authority, his fathering. But she couldn't turn back.

"Maybe we shouldn't talk about this now," Kyle said.

The memory came to Alice unexpectedly. An article in the—was it *Newsday*? Maybe one of the Catholic publications always arriving in their mailbox for Kyle? Whichever it was, the article talked about how next year was the Holy Year of Mercy. And with it, Pope Francis's offering of absolution to women who'd had an abortion. She'd thought it a just thing to offer women forgiveness, though she wasn't sure forgiveness was warranted for her now, considering her intention.

"I want to have it done as quickly as possible," she said. "Before the . . . It's still an embryo. It's not even a fetus yet. It's almost like women who go through in vitro and then don't implant all the—"

"This *is* implanted—by the hand of God!" Kyle said, struggling to keep his voice down. "And if we left it alone, it would grow into our baby."

Alice crossed her arms over her chest. She'd been waiting for him to evoke the ultimate higher authority in his attempt to win this argument, and there it was. "Does God intend to kill me?" she said.

"That's not—"

"I'm almost forty. You may have forgotten about my preeclampsia—at twenty-nine weeks, for James—but I most certainly haven't. Now our risk—*my* risk—is close to forty percent."

Kyle lowered his head.

"You were in the room with Dr. Chen—"

"I know, I know." Then he looked up and said, "You're forcing me to choose between you and our child. How can I possibly do that?"

"You don't understand," she said. "I'm not asking for your permission. I'm telling you what I've decided." As soon as she said it, a surprising calmness came over her.

"So I have no say. In any of this?"

"No," she said. "I have to choose between my well-being and the . . . embryo . . . I'm choosing me."

Oh fuck, she thought. *That's my decision.* A flash of certainty but also fear moved through her. Kyle was used to being the one in charge—at work and at home—and did not seem to register her answer. A shift in power was unfolding in the fabric of their relationship, and she could see that it was disorienting to them both. Part of her found it liberating, but another part of her was terrified and mourned the loss of the baby already. She could cry tears of relief and tears of heartache all at once.

Either way, she was starting to realize, they would be her tears to manage on her own. She could hardly believe it when she looked up at him and heard herself saying, "You're absolved."

Kyle looked at her. "What's that supposed to mean?"

"It means all you have to do is object"—she paused, straightening her back—"and you don't have to bear any guilt or responsibility, while still getting what you want."

"And what is it you think I want?"

"To maintain the moral high ground," she said. "And to not have another baby."

21.

CAIT

Cait expected to find the cottage empty aside from her mother's old paintings and the bags of donations her parents perpetually collected for the parish. Instead, she noted the porcelain water pitcher on the dresser next to the sleigh bed and the red-petaled flower in a turquoise vase that looked out of place against the snow piled along the windowsill. Then she remembered her mother insisting that Isabel stay in the cottage.

Luke closed the door behind him and turned to face her. He was pissed, but then, so was she.

"So this is why you invited me?" he said, his eyes bright and serious. "To humiliate me?"

This surprised her. "Humiliate *you*? You're the one who showed up with your girlfriend!"

The thrill of walking out of the room with Luke was passing. What a joke she was. She imagined her family sitting around the table, her parents totally bewildered and her sisters ready to pounce. She'd gone too far. Why was she always going too far? She needed to go back and apologize. She stepped toward the door, but Luke blocked her with his arm.

"I already told you that Nicole is *not* my girlfriend," he said. "She has a fiancé in Tanzania."

"Of course she does."

Luke clenched his jaw. "I shouldn't have come here," he said.

This stung, and Cait shot back, "I shouldn't have invited you. I should have known."

"Known what?"

"That this could never work."

Luke let out a bitter laugh, and she wanted to hit him.

"Why are you laughing?"

He poured himself a glass of water and leaned against the dresser as he took a few sips, closing his eyes. This pleased her. Just like that, back to the pathetic teenager thrilled to have his attention. *He wants to stay! He cares!* She could hardly stand herself.

"I didn't mean to laugh," he said finally. "I'm not laughing now."

Cait turned to the door. *You need to go back to your family. To your kids.*

"I shouldn't have stopped you." He gestured toward the door. "If you want to leave . . ."

Cait faced him. She didn't want to leave, regardless of what she knew she should do. She'd have to do it eventually, but the thought of returning to the dining room filled her with shame. It was now obvious that something more was going on between her and Luke and that that was why she'd invited him to dinner. She had so much to explain and no idea where to begin—or finish, for that matter. She sat on the bench at the end of the bed.

Luke switched on the lamp next to the water pitcher, and a warm light softened the room. Then he sat next to her.

"Clearly you have things to say to me," he said. "We're alone now. Let's have it." He crossed his arms. "Or is it not as fun when there's no audience?"

Cait looked at his blue eyes and recognized her own age in the creases across his furrowed brow. Not her youth or what had already passed, but the years stretched out before her. She had so much life left to live. And what was she doing with it all? Billing three-hundred-hour months while a woman she didn't even like raised her children? Living so far away, alone and miserable in London? Expecting Alice to take care of their parents all by herself? Assuming the Folly would somehow be passed down to the next generation even though no one was stepping up to claim it? And what was she doing in this room, here and now, with Luke?

She did have things to say to him. She had *years* of things to say to him. But there was one question that stood out most. "Why are you here?" she asked.

Luke thought about this. "For whatever reason, we always seem to find our way back to each other."

"Or we always seem to let go," Cait said.

"I suppose it's a matter of how you look at it."

Is it?

"You like this game we play, don't you?" Cait said. "I used to think the push and pull with you had to do with our families and everything that happened, but you get off on this."

"And you don't?"

"It's miserable," she said, aware she wasn't answering his question.

Luke stood and walked to the window. He stared outside. "When you reached out to me after my mom died," he said, turning to face her, "I wasn't sure what to expect, seeing you in London. Then you invited me here, and I guess I thought maybe enough time had passed."

"Enough time had passed for what?"

He turned again to the window and pressed his forehead to the glass and exhaled. Then he stepped back and ran the tip of his finger across the patch of fog from his breath. Outside, evening fell. She stopped herself from walking up behind him and wrapping her arms around his waist. She needed to hear what he had to say before she was willing to expose herself anymore.

Finally, she tried to answer for him. "For us to be together? For everyone to have just forgotten what happened?"

He was quiet for a moment, then turned back to her and said, "For the record, I told my parents not to pursue the lawsuit. I don't know if you know that."

Cait did not know that, and it immediately raised another question. "Did you tell them why? That it wasn't just Topher's fault?"

"We were kids," he said. "It was an accident!"

"That we could have stopped. All we had to do was tell him—"

"You don't think I know that? That I don't think about that every day?"

"How would I know what you think about every day?"

"Of course I do!" He was pacing the room now. "But I've forgiven myself. I've had to—" He looked at her. "Have you not?"

"No," Cait said. "I haven't. I don't think I ever will."

Luke stopped pacing and turned to her. "Topher would not have wanted you to blame yourself."

"Well, he fucking killed himself, so he doesn't get a say."

Luke hung his head low. Then he looked up at her again. "You need to forgive him," he said. "And me. And yourself."

Cait didn't know what to say. Topher had taken responsibility. Cait and Luke hadn't had to admit a thing. Still, even during the long stretches when she and Luke didn't speak, every time she thought about him, she knew that there was at least one person in the world who understood and shared her crippling sense of guilt. This had almost been a balm for her distress. But she was wrong. He didn't share her blame. And maybe that made sense; he had less to assume.

It's all mine to hold.

A new wave of shame coursed through her, until suddenly she thought of something.

"Why not give their money back if you disagreed with the lawsuit?" she asked. "You've got plenty now, don't you?" She knew this wasn't fair. It wasn't about the money or even her parents not having to worry about the house. It was a sad and desperate hope that in doing so, Luke might make her parents see him differently and mend the one thing that had any shot at repair.

Luke sat next to her on the bench. "I tried to," he said.

"I don't know what that means."

"I called your dad, years ago, and told him I wanted to write him a check."

Cait stood. "What'd he say?"

"No."

"*No?* That's it?"

Luke uncrossed his legs and leaned forward. "He said that Topher made a mistake, and he didn't want the money back."

Topher made a mistake.

Cait was shocked into silence. Her father had never said it directly, but she'd always suspected he believed the lawsuit was just. She assumed her mother did not know about this conversation. That was the look Luke and her father had exchanged at dinner—Robert was asking him not to say anything.

Regardless, hearing that her father accepted this truth released something in her. She felt it in her body. As though this thing inside of her that had crystalized so long ago was undergoing a slight but definite shift.

Luke continued. "He also said that if I had that much hanging around, then good for me. Put it to good use. Which I have."

Now Cait understood. "So *that's* why you brought Nicole here—"

"Yes," Luke said. "To show your dad, if nothing else, that I'm a man of my word."

Cait shook her head. "And you didn't think to tell me any of this?"

Luke shot up. "When are you going to stop feeling so goddamn sorry for yourself?" he said, his face and neck flushed. "I've lost my entire family. Do you not get that? Do you not see what you still have?" He gestured to the main house, but instead of gratitude, Cait felt sick at the reminder that

The Irish Goodbye

she would have to go back there soon and face everyone. "Or are you going to spend the rest of your life stuck on what's been lost?"

Before Cait could answer, cold air swept in from the open door, and she turned to find James rushing to the closet. "I have to get the shells for Papa," he said as he used a chair to reach the top shelf. "The raccoon's in the garbage. It's okay. I know how to handle them safely."

"Wait," Cait said. "Where are the twins?"

"In the house eating pie."

"Tell them they are absolutely not allowed outside."

James nodded and shut the door behind himself.

"I have to go back," Cait said to Luke. She did not want to, but they'd been gone for too long as it was, and she had to find the twins if her father was going to be raccoon hunting with James.

Luke nodded, but then took a step closer, placing his hands on her waist. *Is he going to kiss me?* she wondered, almost confused. *Why now?* He looked at her for a moment, then leaned in, and she felt his lips on hers. She'd been waiting for this since she last saw him in London, desperate to be held by him, but now she worried about everything happening outside the cottage. The stubble along his cheek chafed her skin and the scar on his lip tickled her as it once had, but his mouth tasted like wine and sage, not beer and weed and Bazooka gum, like she'd expected him to still taste, as though twenty-five years of life wouldn't change that, too. His lips moved to her neck as he pulled her to him—

And that's when they heard the crack from the shotgun. Outside the window, the sound was dampened by the freshly fallen snow, but was as unmistakable as the scream that followed.

22.

ALICE

Alice jumped up, spilling her tea on the table, and rushed to the front door. As she flung it open, she found her father standing in the driveway with his shotgun raised and aimed at the garbage can.

"We got 'em!" he shouted.

"What are you doing?" Alice yelled. "Put that down!" She hurried over to James, who stood wide-eyed next to his grandfather, and wrapped her arms around him as she pulled him away from the garbage can.

The rest of the dinner party gathered on the front porch, and Cait appeared from the cottage door—*so that's where they went*—to scoop up Poppy, who was hysterical. Luke followed after her.

"My God, Dad," Cait said. Then, looking around, she added, "Where's Augustus?"

"Mummy?" Augustus said from the front door. "I thought I wasn't allowed to go outside?"

"Stay there," Cait said to him.

"He hurt the raccoon." Poppy sobbed, burying her face in Cait's shoulder.

"He had rabies," James said. He was unsure of himself but trying to act tough, and that made Alice even angrier at her father.

"We don't actually know that," Cait said to James.

James turned to his grandfather for confirmation, but Robert just lowered the muzzle toward the ground and stared at the garbage can.

"Let's put down the gun," Kyle said as he stepped off the porch. He held out his hands, but Robert stood stock-still with the shotgun in his grip.

Was he in shock?

No one moved. The whole scene looked like one of her father's train dioramas. Everyone frozen eternally in time.

Alice looked up at the attic window. Finn hadn't come down to see what was happening, but she figured he was probably wearing his headphones and playing a video game.

Nora started to walk down the porch steps, but Maggie stopped her.

"Robert," Nora said from the top step, "are you not well?"

"Where's the raccoon?" Father Kelly asked, standing next to Nora and Maggie.

James squirmed out of Alice's arms and pointed to the green plastic garbage can. There was a single tattered hole, and the air smelled like burnt paper. "He got stuck and"—he glanced at Poppy and lowered his voice—"Papa shot him."

Poppy wailed again.

Alice's stomach turned.

"Are you sure he's dead?" Father Kelly asked.

Everyone stopped to listen. Alice braced herself for the sound of the poor creature whimpering, but there was nothing.

Suddenly, Robert called out to James, "Topher, lift the lid!"

There was a moment of confused silence as though, Alice thought, they were all waiting for her father to correct himself, to take it back. When he didn't, Alice said, "Dad?" But he didn't seem to hear her.

"Go on," he said to James, and gestured toward the can.

James turned to Alice in a panic. "Is he calling *me* Topher?"

Alice didn't know if her father had mistakenly referred to James as Topher or genuinely believed he was addressing him. "Dad," she said, again, warily, "that isn't Topher. That's James."

"Bobby," Nora said. "Are you all right? What's going on?"

Alice hadn't heard her mother call her father that in years. It was a nickname she'd used when they were younger. If he walked by and pinched her waist or stole a kiss, she'd slap his hand and say, "Oh, Bobby!"

Finally, Robert looked up at them. His face was red, and his hands trembled. He shifted his attention back to James and shook his head. "I'm sorry," he said. "You just—" He stopped and let out a long exhale that billowed his lips.

Alice waited for someone, anyone, to do something. Then it hit her that they were all waiting as well.

Finally, Kyle inched closer to her father, hands still out before him, the crunch of snow beneath his steps echoing in the strange quiet of the day. *He will keep us safe*, she thought, regretting their argument just moments before, *like he always does*.

"Robert," Kyle said in a voice so tender and steady, it nearly made Alice cry. "The gun."

Robert looked down at his hands. "Oh," he said. "Oh. Yes." And then he let the shotgun slide through his fingers as though, it seemed to Alice, it was made of air, and it slammed onto the pebbled driveway and fired off another round.

There was a collective scream, and Alice heard herself yell "No!" as she huddled over James and pressed him to her chest. When she looked up, she saw snow flurrying from the sycamore by the garage, where the bullet had landed. Her knees nearly buckled in relief when Kyle retrieved the shotgun and said, "It hit the tree. Everyone's okay."

Alice grabbed James's face and smooshed his cheeks, smothering him with what felt like every cell of motherhood she had left. After checking the gun to make sure there were no more shells, Kyle placed it back in the cottage and then ran over to hug Alice and James.

Robert sat on the porch step. His white hair, yellowed along the sides, stood straight up as though he'd been electrocuted. His face was drained of color now, ashen against the bright snow, and his thin lips looked even thinner.

Alice sat next to him.

Cait brought Poppy up to the porch, then sat on the other side of their father. "Are you hurt?" she asked him.

Robert examined his hands. "I don't think so." Then he turned to Alice with an expression that made him look like a frightened child, and with quivering lips, said, "I don't know why I called him Topher."

Alice wrapped her arm around his shoulders. "It's okay, Dad."

He nodded, and his hazel eyes glistened with tears. Now he no longer reminded Alice of a child—he was an old man. His cheeks were hollowed. Her mind flashed to a hike he'd taken her on somewhere in the Catskills decades ago. She must have been about sixteen, because it was near the time Topher disappeared in Mexico City, and no one could track him down. It was a clear day, but when she and her father reached the mountain summit, they were swiftly immersed in a fog so thick they could barely see a few inches ahead. He guided Alice to sit on the ground, and as quickly as the fog appeared, it vanished. Alice had been paralyzed with fear, but her father sat there in awe. After a moment, he clapped his hands and stood, saying, "It's not every day you get caught up in a cloud."

Without speaking, Alice and Cait reached for either side of their father's upper arms to help him stand.

"Come on, Dad," Alice said. "It's cold out here."

He shifted his gaze upward, past them, toward the sky. "It is," he said, and shivered.

As they walked back inside, a police car pulled into the driveway with its lights flashing.

Alice guided her mother from behind by the back of her shoulders, the boniness of her slender body adding to the unease. Everything felt vulnerable, breakable.

"A neighbor probably called about the gunshots," Kyle said. "I'll talk to him."

The officer opened his door and stepped out. He regarded Kyle standing by the garbage can, then turned to the rest of the family on the porch.

"We're sorry, Officer," Kyle said. "We had an incident with a rabid raccoon, but it's all taken care of. We didn't mean to disturb anyone. You can look in the garbage if you'd like to check—"

The officer shook his head. "I'm not here about a gunshot," he said. "Are you the family of a boy named Finn?"

23.
MAGGIE

"Okay, time to settle down now," Maggie said in mock seriousness, though she *was* serious. James had been showing her his karate moves for the past half hour, and she had no idea how to get him to stop. Teaching privileged kids at an elite boarding school was one thing—trying to get her nephew to brush his teeth and put on his pajamas was another.

Isabel poked her head through the doorway. "Whoever gets into bed in under five seconds gets a cookie!"

James froze mid-kick, then vaulted onto the bed.

Maggie didn't care that James would be eating a cookie after having just brushed his teeth—cavities be damned, anything to get him to sleep. She turned to Isabel and said, "You're good at this."

Isabel shrugged. "Younger cousins."

As James changed into his pajamas, Isabel whispered into Maggie's ear, "Any update?"

Maggie checked her phone again and shook her head no. She'd been trying to keep it together because she didn't want to upset James even more, but it wasn't easy.

When the officer explained that someone driving by had seen Finn slip on the ice farther down the street, everyone was confused. Wasn't he upstairs in the attic sick with a stomach bug? But Alice understood quickly that he'd snuck out and must have been on his way to his friend's house when he fell. He'd hurt his collarbone and had a concussion that prevented him from remembering where he'd come from and where he was going. After the ambulance brought him to the hospital, the officer had been going around to every house on the street trying to find Finn's family.

While Alice and Kyle frantically jumped into the car to follow the police officer to the hospital, Maggie and Cait stayed behind to help the caterers pack up and to say goodbye to their guests. James was worried not only about Finn but also about his grandfather, both of whom he'd always seen as superheroes. When Cait took the twins upstairs for a bath, Isabel suggested a movie. She and Maggie sat on opposite sides of the sofa in the attic TV room, with James fidgeting in between them. Periodically throughout the movie, James would sit up and ask one question after another about Finn—Why didn't he tell us he was going to Leo's? Is he going to be in trouble?—that Maggie did her best to answer.

Since returning from the train station, Maggie and Isabel had not had a chance to finish their discussion. Throughout the evening, Maggie kept apologizing to Isabel—not just for her mistake with Sarah but for everything that had happened with her family—and Isabel would say, "I know." Maggie was grateful that Isabel hadn't just locked herself in the cottage, but she had no idea where things stood between them.

As Isabel went downstairs to get some cookies, James asked Maggie if she'd read him a story, so she grabbed an old book about a soccer team from the shelf and slumped onto the bottom bunk next to him. She read the words on the page—even adding in some inflection—but her mind was so distracted with worry about Finn and where things stood between her and Isabel that she had absolutely no idea what the story was about.

The Irish Goodbye

Halfway through, Isabel returned holding a tray filled with glasses of milk and a plate of the Mikado biscuits Nora kept stashed away.

"Thank you," Maggie said, trying to keep the emotion out of her voice. "I'm so grateful you're here."

Isabel nodded, but her expression was inscrutable.

"Keep reading," James said, dunking his cookie into his milk.

After she finished the book and the cookies were eaten, Maggie finally received a text from Kyle on the family thread reporting that Finn's CAT scan had come out clean, but he'd broken his collarbone and they needed to stay for a few more hours until he passed the final neuro exam.

"That's a relief," Isabel said.

Maggie agreed. She gave James the news, then kissed him good night, praying he'd actually go to bed as she turned off the desk lamp.

"Can you keep it on?" he asked.

Maggie turned the light back on. "Are you scared?" she asked. She was doing her best to keep her patience. "I was always scared as a kid."

"No," he said. "I want to wait up for Finn."

"He's going to be fine," Maggie assured him.

James sat up on his elbow. "Why did Papa call me Topher? Who is that?"

"Your uncle," Maggie said. "Do you not know about him?"

"The one who died?"

The matter-of-factness of James's delivery was like a punch to Maggie's gut. "Yes," she said. "He was my brother. And your mom's."

"Do I look like him?" James asked.

So, so much, Maggie thought. But before she could answer, James chimed in again.

"I think there's a picture of him on our refrigerator," he said, "but I'm not sure."

Maggie handed the tray to Isabel and sat back down on the bed next to James. "There are lots more pictures here, too. Your mom will show you in the morning."

James looked at Maggie again. "How come he died?"

"Well," Maggie said, feeling entirely out of her depth, "everyone dies, so, you know—"

"Finn said it was suicide, but I don't know what that is."

"That's when someone ends their own life," Maggie said.

"On purpose?"

"Yes."

James thought about this for a moment. "Is that like an Irish goodbye?"

Maggie stopped herself from laughing. Topher would have found that hilarious. "No," she said. "Where did you learn that?"

"Finn said an Irish goodbye is when you leave without saying goodbye."

"Well, I mean, yes, but—"

"Did Topher say goodbye?"

"No," Maggie said. "He didn't. So, yeah, maybe you're right."

James nodded and, in a soft voice, said, "But *why* did he do it?"

Maggie paused. When were you supposed to tell kids about this kind of family history? How were you supposed to tell them? Certainly *she* wasn't the right one to reveal it all. She turned to Isabel, but unlike the cookie bribe, she didn't seem to have an answer here. "That, I don't know," she said finally. "No one does. He made a terrible decision without thinking."

James was quiet, then said, "Do you miss him?"

"Every day."

James bit at a loose piece of cuticle on his thumb. "I don't want to look like him," he said.

This saddened Maggie, but she also understood. She wanted to tell her nephew something good about her brother to show him that he was more than the story of his death, but she worried that would only lead to more questions, and that she might have already gone too far. Instead, she brushed the reddish flop of hair from his forehead and said, "I always thought you looked more like your mom, not Topher."

James lowered his head onto the pillow. "Yeah," he said. "People tell me that all the time."

Before she and Isabel left, Maggie turned to say good night once more. "Everyone gets scared sometimes," she said. "But we're safe here."

Isabel went to the bathroom, and Maggie was heading back to her room when she ran into her mother.

"Why are you wearing your coat?" she asked her.

"I'm going to meet your sister at the hospital," Nora said, her voice tired.

"I'll come with you—"

"No, we don't need to crowd the room. But can you check on your father in a bit? Maybe bring him a cup of tea? He's resting but he feels awful about the stupid raccoon."

As he should, Maggie thought, but instead, she said, "Of course."

"Thank you, love."

As her mother turned away, Cait appeared from the dark hallway and asked if she could speak to Nora quickly before she left for the hospital. From her bedroom, Maggie tried to listen to their murmurs, and when she heard Nora gasp, she hopped out of bed and found them in Cait's room.

"What happened?" she asked. "Is Finn all right?"

Her mother turned, and to Maggie's surprise, she was smiling. "Oh, yes," she said. "Cait just had something to share with me."

Cait looked at Maggie. "I'll tell you later," she said. "Big news, but too early to go viral. I have some things to figure out yet."

On a normal evening, Maggie would have pumped her sister for more information, but Isabel had emerged from the bathroom. All Maggie wanted was to shut their door, take Isabel into her arms, if Isabel allowed her, and not have to deal with anyone or anything for the rest of the evening.

24.

ALICE

"I hate this place," Alice said, pacing the small room.

By the time they'd arrived at the hospital, Finn's memory had returned completely, but she was still terrified about the impact of the fall. They'd found him in the trauma room with a neck collar and a shoulder wrap and a blooming black eye; the transport team had just returned him from a CAT scan. Whether he was ashamed or worried he'd be getting into trouble, he could barely look at them as the nurse hooked him up to the monitor. Finally, when the nurse left, he broke down and couldn't stop crying and apologizing. Even when he tried to blame Alice—*if only you'd let me go, I wouldn't have had to sneak out*—she just held his hand and nodded, wiping the tears from her face. Nothing mattered to her beyond the fact that he was okay.

After the scans came back normal, and the doctor and radiologist assured them that there was no bleeding or skull fracture, Alice's nerves still couldn't settle. They ignited every time Finn groaned about his collarbone or a doctor stopped by to do yet another neuro check—*person, place, time?*

The Irish Goodbye

"Sit, love," Nora said to Alice. "You're driving yourself mad. And us."

From the bed, Finn looked up at them and began crying again. "I'm sorry," he sobbed, wiping his nose on the hospital gown.

Alice rushed over to kiss his forehead, but he pulled away from her. He didn't like to be fussed over. She was trying to give him the space she knew he needed, but all she wanted was to hug him and ask a million questions about what happened and how he was feeling. Instead, she refilled his paper cup with ice chips and handed it to him. "We know," she said. "Shush. Just lie back down."

Nora pulled out the chair next to her, and Alice sat again. She picked up the *Reader's Digest* on the table and skimmed its pages, looking for something that might distract her from annoying everyone in the room or, God help her, her own thoughts. She scanned an article on whether apple cider vinegar was actually good for you, then tossed the magazine back onto the table.

Nora scooted her seat closer. She reached for Alice's hand and pressed her rosary beads to her palm. "Try this," she said.

Alice clutched the beads in her closed fist. She envied her mother's and Kyle's faith and the solace it offered.

A nurse popped in to check Finn's vitals, and he said he needed to use the bathroom.

"Pee or poo?" she asked, and Finn blushed.

"Pee," he said, mortified.

He tried to sit up, but the nurse stopped him. "You can't get up until you've passed the final neuro," she said. "I'll bring the urinal for you to pee in."

"Here?" Finn said. "In the bed?"

Instead of answering him, the nurse left and a moment later returned holding a skinny plastic jug with a handle. Finn looked like he was going to cry.

"Do you want us to stay?" Alice asked him.

"No!"

"Poor thing," Nora said once they were in the hallway. "He is suffering."

Alice felt her nerves flare again. "I knew something was off when he left dinner without having dessert," she said. "Why didn't I listen to myself?" She was just as angry at herself for not stopping him as she was at him for sneaking out.

Back in the room, Finn could barely look at them again. Alice stood by the window and stared out into the night. The parking lot was filled with cars, and she felt an unexpected kinship with the tribe of people at the hospital that evening instead of at home watching holiday movies and eating leftover-turkey-and-cranberry sandwiches. In the window's reflection, she stared at Finn, the sling for his collarbone wrapped around his shoulder. He scratched at something under his neck collar, then let out a deep sigh that sounded like it came from an old man instead of a teenage boy. When he was younger, she always seemed to know what he needed. It came more naturally to her than knowing what she needed for herself. Whenever there was a problem, she could tell by just looking at his face if the remedy was a snack, a bathroom, a nap, or a hug. Now she wasn't so sure. And even when she did think she knew the answer, he often pushed her away. *It is easier with a baby*, she thought. *You pick them up, feed them, and burp them.* She wished she could do that again with Finn, but also knew with certainty that she couldn't with another baby. She wouldn't.

Kyle appeared in the doorway. He had been at the front desk dealing with the insurance paperwork, and gratitude flooded Alice as she walked over to hug him.

"Does anyone want coffee?" he asked.

Nora, jacket draped around her shoulders to keep her warm, raised her Styrofoam cup to show she already had tea. "But you two go grab some and take a break," she said. "I'll stay with Finn."

Kyle led Alice out of the room. This was the hospital where her mother had given birth to her and her siblings. It was where Alice had spent countless hours as a kid when she broke her arm and Topher needed stitches and Maggie had her appendix removed. As she and Kyle walked to the lounge, the blinding fluorescent lights, the beeps and trolleys, and the antiseptic smell all brought forth a cascade of shared memories. The surreal first hours after Topher's death. The birth of Finn, terrifying enough, and then of James, when she was convinced she was going to die, and nearly did.

The lounge was empty and decorated for Thanksgiving with cutout turkeys and pumpkins taped along the walls.

"I can't drink coffee," Alice said. "My nerves are already frayed."

"I'll get you a hot chocolate," Kyle said.

Alice sat across from the vending machines. She watched him examine the selection of snacks, and though she wanted something simple and bland like popcorn, she waited to see what he'd choose. He was doing everything right—dealing with the doctors and insurance, being patient with Finn—but the distance between them was vast and, it seemed to her, growing.

He handed her a cup filled with watery hot chocolate and a snack-size bag of Cheez-Its. "Sweet and savory," he said.

She smiled and took a sip.

"Any good?"

"Shockingly bad."

They both laughed, which helped ease some of the terribleness of the day and of this thing hanging between them.

She sat with him for a bit, slowly sipping the hot, bad drink. And because she'd been so consumed with concern about Finn for the past few hours, what came out next surprised her. "I'm worried about my dad," she said.

Kyle nodded, which made it worse. Somehow, she'd hoped he would assure her that nothing was wrong.

"Why did we let him walk around the house with a shotgun in the first place?" she asked. It felt easier to believe that it had been their fault, something they could have stopped if only they'd been more vigilant.

Kyle sighed. "Maybe it was just the pressure of it all. Cait's visit. Luke's resurfacing. Trying to keep up with the house—the cost of the roof and everything."

"The roof?"

"He didn't tell you? The estimate was over thirty grand."

"When I brought it up yesterday," she said, "he claimed the roof was fine. When did he tell you this?"

"Last week at the trivia tournament. He didn't want to bother any of you about it."

It wasn't the first time her father had been more forthcoming with Kyle than with her about her parents' financial difficulties, and she was never sure how she felt about that.

"I guess he couldn't take this rabid raccoon coming in and causing even more chaos," Kyle continued. "He's getting old."

Alice handed him her cup, and he placed it on a table.

"He is," she said. "So is my mom."

He nodded.

Earlier that year, her mother had forgotten to take her statins for weeks, and she didn't figure it out until her annual revealed a dangerous spike in her cholesterol. Alice didn't want to bring it up now, but she planned to take charge of her parents' weekly pill organizers and talk to her father's physician about stress management. She was proud to take care of her parents—and she was going to be there for them, they deserved it—but she hadn't expected to have to do it alone. The role had unfolded slowly enough that she never noticed it all that much, but, lately, she'd averaged five to six doctor or physical therapy appointments each month between the two of them. Sometimes, she realized, it felt like they were more like her children than her parents.

"Their care will fall to me," she said.

She wished Kyle would piece together what she meant—that this was another reason she did not want a new baby or to risk her life with another pregnancy, but it went over his head.

"It's always fallen to us," he said.

"Not us, Kyle," she said, aware of the edge in her voice. "*Me*. Mostly. You clean their gutters, but it's not the same, the emotional labor of caretaking."

Kyle reached for her hand, but she brushed him away. She wanted to say something that would jolt him into listening to her for a change, but when she opened her mouth to speak, something between a sob and a gasp burst out of her. Her chest heaved as she tried to compose herself, and Kyle wrapped his arms around her shoulders and pulled her to him.

"Hey," he said. "Look at me." He held her by the chin. "We'll be okay. We always are, right?"

She wasn't sure what to believe, and she was too exhausted to tiptoe around false promises. She knew he felt like she was betraying him, and to be the cause of his sadness was unbearable. But what about her sadness? Her resentment? She was starting to see that they would not survive if he could not accept her choice. And she didn't know if he could.

"I don't want this pregnancy to be another before and after," she said.

Kyle started to say something, but a nurse came into the lounge to tell them that the doctor was performing the final neuro exam on Finn and needed them to be in the room. They stood, and Kyle handed her the unopened bag of Cheez-Its. She followed him down the hall, his hands in his pockets and head bowed.

As the doctor explained the post-discharge care instructions, Finn grew weepy again. Not only would he not be allowed to play basketball for a while, but his brain needed to rest because of the concussion, and so he couldn't use screens or even read his comics for a few weeks. A forced break from everything sounded heavenly to Alice, but she understood why it made Finn even more upset.

"We can't let him sleep, right?" she asked the doctor. "How long does he need to stay awake?"

"That's actually a myth," the doctor said. "He's going to be tired."

Kyle would take Finn back to the Folly, but Alice insisted on driving her mother back in Nora's car. The roads were still a mess, and the last thing they needed was her mother getting into an accident.

As they pulled out of the hospital parking lot, Nora turned to Alice and said, "I know you're tired, but could I ask one favor from you?"

"What is it?"

"Would you take me to Saint Mary's?"

"Tomorrow?"

"Now," Nora said. "Kyle can handle Finn for a minute. I'll make it quick."

Alice pushed open the church's wooden doors, surprised to find the lights on in the vestibule, and let her mother in first. She felt like they were doing something wrong, sneaking in after hours, but Nora walked straight down the nave toward the pulpit without hesitation, as if she did this all the time. Maybe she did. Alice dropped a few dollars into the collection box and followed after her, their footsteps disparate and echoing in the emptiness of the small cathedral.

Alice had spent nearly every Sunday morning of her life at the church, singing in the choir, and had had periods of devotion as a teenager, but over the past few years, her attendance was mainly for Kyle, a sort of performance for the families of his students—and maybe even for him. But being there now with her mother, just the two of them, she felt a peace she hadn't experienced in the limestone and stained-glass walls of the cathedral since she and Kyle used to attend mass on Friday nights in Brooklyn.

There were several votives already lit, which Alice also hadn't expected. She handed her mother a box of matches from the nearby table, and they each picked a candle to light, then knelt before the altar. When she was pregnant with Finn and James, Alice would constantly say novenas to Saint Monica, but now she called on Mary directly. Her prayers began with Finn but quickly meandered to a defensive plea for the choice she was prepared to make about the pregnancy. She was not looking for understanding or even acceptance, just forgiveness.

Who are you to tell me this isn't right for my life? And then, *Oh, but please have mercy on me, please forgive me.*

She opened her eyes, and her mother patted her on the shoulder and handed her a tissue. "Finn is going to be all right," she assured her.

The Irish Goodbye

Alice straightened. She imagined sharing with her mother the other source of her pain, but that wasn't possible, that would never be possible. Instead, she looked at her mother and said, "Have you ever done something you couldn't forgive yourself for?"

Nora didn't seem surprised by the question, which intrigued Alice. She looked up at a fresco of Mother Mary on the ceiling, then back at Alice. "I couldn't protect him," she said. She fidgeted with the Saint Christopher pendant at her throat, which she'd worn every day since Topher's death. "I'll never be able to forgive myself for that."

Alice turned to the flickering votives, and the clarity of her decision dropped like a stone inside her. She buttoned her jacket, wrapped her arm around Nora, and gestured toward the door. "Let's go," she said.

25.

CAIT

That night, the twins insisted on sleeping in bed with Cait instead of in the bunk room because they were sad about the dead raccoon and worried about Finn. Cait couldn't blame them. As she snuggled between their warm bodies to read a story, she remembered being a kid and sneaking into her parents' bed when she was scared or sick. It still sometimes amazed her that she was now the one who had the power to make other people, her own children, feel that safe.

In her first therapy session, Dr. Wagner had asked why she'd married Bram if she recognized early on that he wasn't right for her. It was a fair question, but when she said it was a good excuse to move to London, he pointed out that she could have done that without getting married, and asked if it might have something to do with her relationship with her father. Cait rejected that interpretation as too easy, practically boring. Plus, her father and Bram could not have been more different.

A year out from the divorce, it bothered her that she still didn't know how to answer Dr. Wagner's question. Watching her father mistake James

The Irish Goodbye

for Topher earlier that evening, though, she'd had a flicker of insight. It wasn't her relationship with her father that she'd been trying to repair. It was her relationship with Topher.

Then again, wasn't that true for all of them?

It wasn't just her father mistaking James for Topher. It was her mother, still determined to believe that it was the Larkins' lawsuit that set Topher on the downward spiral that took his life. It was Maggie's inability to accept the sudden breakup with Sarah. And, of course, it was Alice and her enduring anger toward Cait for leaving right after Topher died.

For years, Cait had resented Alice's anger in part because she knew that it was warranted. She had defended herself by saying she had no choice but to go to London, but the truth was more complicated. She'd wanted to leave.

During their session last week, Dr. Wagner questioned whether Cait's plan to see Luke on her visit home might be a way to distract herself from her family. Again, she'd dismissed the suggestion right away, annoyed by his reluctance to entertain the possibility that Luke was the person she was meant to be with all along.

To admit otherwise, she'd long believed, would mean their brothers' deaths had been meaningless.

* * *

The day after Cait lost her virginity, she sat on Topher's boat as they pulled up to Luke's Boston Whaler, anchored near the lighthouse. It was already noon, but none of their other friends had arrived yet for the boat party, which made her happy. Their brothers would be hanging around, but hopefully she'd get some time to chat with Luke before everyone else showed up.

Luke's Whaler was so shiny and new, it made Topher's beat-up skiff look even worse. Topher had purchased his boat that spring from a bankrupt local charter out east—and now Cait knew where he'd gotten the money. The boat had been in need of serious repair. If Cait had to guess,

Topher had maybe taken it out fishing less than half a dozen times that summer because the motor kept breaking down. Their parents had been so proud of him for buying it with his own money, and as she watched him adjust the fenders to tie up to the Whaler, she remembered with annoyance how he'd basked in their admiration.

Notes from a saxophone tuning carried over the water as a jazz band readied itself on the lighthouse balcony for the Port Haven Lighthouse annual fundraiser. Cait tugged on her cutoffs as she stood. She smiled at Luke, but he was distracted by Daniel stealing a cigarette from the pack in his back pocket.

That morning, as she tried to pick out the perfect bikini, she couldn't stop smiling. She knew Luke wasn't going to ask her to be his girlfriend or anything—he was leaving for college tomorrow—but something between them had changed. How could it not have? It wasn't just that they'd had sex—though that had made her feel like she was part of the world in an entirely new way—but now she knew what his sheets smelled like and that he listened to "Footloose" when no one was around.

Standing there and waiting for him to acknowledge her, though, it felt like nothing had changed. She leaned against the boat's console, pretending to listen to Luke's story about a baby sand shark Daniel had caught that morning while fishing for stripers and blues. While he talked, he grabbed three cans of Budweiser from the dirty Styrofoam cooler by his engine and tossed two to Topher, who then handed one to Cait.

"Where's mine?" Daniel asked.

Daniel was fourteen, Alice's age, but he was skinny and had a high-pitched voice that made him sound like he hadn't hit puberty yet. It was just a few years ago that she'd been his camp counselor at the beach club, and she'd nominated him for the "Jokester" award at the end-of-summer dinner.

Luke looked at Daniel over his sunglasses. "Dude, chill. You've already had two." Then he tossed him another one anyway.

As Daniel caught the beer, he stumbled over the tackle box, and

The Irish Goodbye

Topher and Luke laughed, as if he'd done it on purpose. Cait wasn't sure if he was trying to be funny or was really that wasted before noon. As his former camp counselor, she wanted to tell him to get it together, but another part of her knew that hanging out with guys meant letting go of those kinds of things. Besides, Daniel was Luke's brother. Let him deal with it.

Instead, she cracked open her can and took a gulp of the cold beer, enjoying the chill running down her throat. She waited for Luke to at least smile in her direction, but he seemed more interested in arguing with Daniel about why he wasn't allowed to drive the Whaler.

Luke put his hands on Daniel's shoulders. "Want to drive the boat?" he said. "Stop crossing the no-wake zones like a dumbass. It's not that hard."

Daniel pretended to tremble as though he was terrified, then said, "Whatever," and took another gulp of his beer.

Finally, Luke turned to Cait. What he said—"Watch it"—confused her until she followed his gaze to a thread from her cutoffs that was caught on a hook. Embarrassed, she tried to untangle it, any sense of coolness she'd been attempting ruined by her clumsy hands, and finally just tore off the thread.

Luke smiled, but she couldn't tell what that meant. She was desperate for more information. Like a forensic scientist, she analyzed his every move while he tidied the fishing gear and tossed the bait away into the water, the fish all rising to the surface to feed.

The band at the lighthouse started playing, and Luke turned off the Led Zeppelin song on the portable radio attached to the window above the wheel. When Daniel turned it back on, Luke slapped his hand away and turned it off again.

"Everyone's here to listen to the band," Luke said.

"Zeppelin! Zeppelin! Zeppelin!" Daniel yelled through cupped hands. Then he performed a sloppy air guitar.

"I vote for the band," Cait said.

Daniel took a swig of his beer. "Well, chicks don't get a vote, so."

"Excuse me?"

Luke punched Daniel on the arm. "Ignore him," he said. Then he nodded to a hand-painted sign on the dashboard that read, BOYS ONLY CLUB. "It's from a clubhouse we had when we were younger."

"Aw, and here I was thinking you were a bunch of New Age, sensitive guys," Cait said.

Topher was lounging on the boat's bow, a frayed Grateful Dead hat pulled over his face. Luke did a cannonball into the water to splash him, and Daniel followed after. Their yelps echoed across the bay as they swam toward the lighthouse. Once they reached the rocks, they clambered on top of them.

Topher propped himself up on his elbows to wipe his face and take a sip of beer.

"What's up with you and Luke?" he asked.

"Why? Did he say something to you?"

Topher slapped the boat railing. "I knew you were into him!"

Cait rolled her eyes. "Is that why you fart when we're all in the car together and blame it on me?"

Topher laughed.

"Anyway, it's nothing," she said, and watched Luke and Daniel skip rocks along the lighthouse peninsula.

Topher shrugged. "If you say so." He grabbed Luke's pack of Marlboros off the console and stuck an unlit cigarette between his lips.

Cait waited for him to offer more, and when he didn't, she added, "I think he's weirded out that I'm your sister."

"I don't care what you guys do."

"Can you tell him that?"

Topher twirled his Zippo, then lit his cigarette. "I don't want to get involved," he said, exhaling rings of smoke. "If he liked you, he wouldn't care what I think. Sorry."

"Why are you such an asshole?"

The Irish Goodbye

Topher raised his hands. "Just looking out for you, kid!"

Cait yanked the pull tab off her beer and threw it at him, but he just dodged it and laughed.

As Luke and Daniel swam back to the boats, splashing each other along the way, more of their friends arrived. Cait overheard Luke directing them to raft up alongside Topher's boat instead of his. Luke and Daniel had to head out by four to meet up with their mom. Cait hadn't realized this. As the afternoon waned, their friends wandered between the line of boats like rooms at a house party, and she felt even more desperate to get a minute alone with Luke before he left.

Eventually she found Topher on his boat, showing off his juggling skills with balls made from nylon rope. She pulled him aside. "Can we leave at four with Luke and Daniel?" she asked. "I want to say goodbye to Luke without everyone around."

Topher tossed the balls in the air and caught them with one hand. "Why do I have to go?" he asked. "Just hitch a ride with them."

"But then Daniel will be on the boat with us, and he's annoying as shit."

Topher whistled. "You've got it bad."

"Shut up. Can you just give Daniel a ride?"

"It's a stupid idea," he said, tossing the balls again. "I'm telling you. Don't do it. Spare yourself."

Cait opened her mouth to challenge him, but before she could, a bunch of guys kicked off a game of spades on Luke's boat and shouted to Topher to join them. She grudgingly found her girlfriends on a neighboring boat, lounging in their bikinis and flipping through the latest J.Crew catalogue.

By late afternoon, Cait and Luke had barely spoken beyond the brief exchanges earlier in the day. When it got closer to four, she made her way to his boat, where the guys were now playing hacky sack and doing flips off the bow. She cornered Topher to ask him one more time to head back early and take Daniel with him.

"The fireworks haven't even started!" Topher laughed, his eyes barely open. He was stoned out of his mind.

Cait imagined him sitting in Marcus's basement and weighing out little dime bags of bunk weed on a scale. She leaned in closer so no one could hear her. "Do me this one favor," she said, "and I won't tell Mom and Dad how you got the money to buy your boat."

The disgust on Topher's face made her regret the words immediately. He leaned back and shook his head. "That's fucked up, kid."

It was fucked up. She knew that. She'd just betrayed the most sacred rule of their siblinghood—to never snitch on one another—and she wasn't proud of that, but she'd already gone too far to back down. Besides, his response only confirmed what Luke had said last night about Topher dealing, and this emboldened her.

"Talk about fucked up," she shot back. "I can't believe you're doing this shit. I should tell them anyway. What are you even selling?"

Topher ignored her question and hopped up. "Daniel," he shouted over the heads of their friends.

Daniel was assembling a fishing rod, though Cait had heard Luke yell at him throughout the day to stow it away because there were too many people around. Topher waved him over.

"You're riding back with me," Topher said.

Daniel furrowed his brow. "Why?"

Topher snapped and pointed to Cait. "Ask the boss."

Cait felt her cheeks redden. She watched Luke saying goodbye to their friends on another boat, then turned back to Daniel. "I just need to talk to your brother alone for a second," she said.

Daniel rubbed his hands together conspiratorially. "What do I get out of it?"

Cait glanced at Topher, then back at Daniel. "He'll let you drive," she said.

Daniel's eyes brightened. "Hell yeah."

"Try hell no," Topher said, and flicked his cigarette butt into the water.

"Come on," Cait said. "It's a couple hundred feet to the dock." She squeezed Topher's shoulder, but he jerked away.

When Luke came over, Topher refused to acknowledge her. Instead, he tossed Daniel the keys and said to Luke, "Cait's going with you," and he untied his boat from the rest of the party.

Luke looked back and forth between them. Cait hoped he wouldn't ask why and silently begged their brothers not to sell her out, but Luke just turned to Daniel and said, "Don't fuck around. We're already late."

Daniel saluted Luke with two fingers and flashed a dopey grin. Suddenly, Cait realized he might not be okay to drive. She looked at her brother and Luke, but neither seemed concerned, and, she supposed, it wasn't like Topher was in better shape. When Luke asked, "You coming?" she hopped onto his boat.

Next to them, Daniel reversed Topher's boat and set off a bunch of waves that disturbed the other boats, knocking over beers and ruining a game of spades by sliding all the cards onto the wet floor.

"Dipshit," Luke shouted as Daniel took off.

Luke and Cait led the way, navigating the boats near the lighthouse. Cait stood next to him at the wheel, and as she watched him fiddle with his sailor's bracelet, she remembered its slightly pungent smell from last night. Her skin stung with a fresh sunburn. She waited for him to speak, and when he didn't, she wondered if this time she should be the one to say it had all been a mistake. Let him see how it felt. But she'd never do that. She couldn't let go of the hope that it *hadn't* been a mistake. Finally, she said, "Last night was fun."

Luke looked over her shoulder and frowned, and when she turned, she saw what was bothering him. Instead of following them and heading back to the dock, Topher and Daniel were doing loops around the lighthouse.

"Fucking Topher," Cait said.

No doubt he was keeping Daniel out on the boat to annoy Luke and therefore punish her for threatening to rat him out to their parents.

Luke waved them off and turned back to her. "Last night *was* fun," he said, but there was something in his tone, a seriousness that made her uneasy. Then he said, "You know, I'm leaving tomorrow, so—"

Cait forced a laugh. "No, of course." She swallowed hard. "We're friends. Same old."

Luke nodded and smiled, his obvious relief upsetting her even more. "Exactly," he said. "Yeah, that's what I was thinking."

It's what she'd expected but also hoped he wouldn't say. His shoulders were sunburned and peeling, his wet hair pushed back, and his blue eyes shimmered against the bay's light. He'd never looked so beautiful. Her anger faded, this time back into the ache she always carried during these conversations. She felt trapped on the boat with him now, worried she'd cry if she let her guard down for even a second.

When they approached the beach club, she spotted Maggie and her friends building sandcastles along the shore. She waved, but her youngest sister didn't see her.

While Luke cut the engine and dropped the anchor, signaling to the dock attendant to pick them up, Cait watched Topher's boat. Just as it seemed they were finally heading to the dock, Daniel pulled another sharp turn and circled back toward the lighthouse. She hoped a police boat wasn't around to pull them over, amazed one hadn't already.

"You could come visit me," Luke said. "If you wanted to."

He stood on the bow, waiting for the attendant to approach in his dinghy. His eyelashes were so thick and black, it was like he was wearing mascara. "Boston's not that far," he continued. "I think there's a cheap bus from Chinatown or something."

She didn't even try to hide her excitement. "I would definitely do that."

"Cool," Luke said. Then he hopped off the bow and leaned over the steering wheel to kiss her. His lips were chapped and salty from swimming all day, but when he opened his mouth and their tongues met, she felt a dizzying, almost sickening longing for more.

The attendant pulled up and connected the boats with a hook. As he helped Luke transfer his cooler, fishing gear, and a garbage bag filled with

The Irish Goodbye

empty beer cans from the afternoon, she checked again to see what was happening with Daniel and Topher.

They were being jerks, and Topher would definitely still be annoyed at her when they got back to the beach club, but she didn't care anymore. Let them have their stupid fun. Luke had asked her to visit him in Boston. It had all worked out better than she'd expected.

* * *

Cait was reading in bed, the twins sound asleep next to her, when she heard the first thump. But it wasn't until the pine cone hit her window directly, rather than the side of the house, that she sat up and saw what was happening. From the window, she waved at Luke, standing in the center of the driveway next to his Range Rover.

"Hey—" Luke half whispered when she opened the front door.

"What are you doing here?"

Luke smiled and tossed a handful of extra pine cones onto the snow-covered rose bushes by the front porch.

"You don't have a phone," he said. "I wanted to see if everything was okay. If you're okay." He paused. "And I didn't want to leave things like that with you."

She didn't either.

"It's not that late," he said, checking his watch. "How about a glass of something at O'Reilly's?"

Cait made sure the twins were still asleep as she grabbed her coat and lipstick. She popped into Maggie's room to ask her to keep an ear out just in case the twins woke, and then snuck back down the stairs.

Luke lowered the music and turned up the heat when she climbed into the car.

26.

MAGGIE

Maggie was lying in bed when she grabbed her phone and opened her work calendar. She'd been avoiding reading the invite from Cunningham out of fear that it might mention Sarah, but after all the surprises that day, the uncertainty was almost worse. The Wi-Fi connection at the Folly was terrible, but there it was. She knew—well, she'd hoped—Cunningham would provide context, and she found just that.

> Meeting between Maggie Ryan and Headmaster Cunningham
> Monday, November 30, 2015
> 10 a.m.
> Headmaster Cunningham's office
> Topic for discussion: Chair position for the English department

She placed the phone on her chest and closed her eyes. Instead of immediate relief, she felt a deep sense of regret, again, at how she'd put herself in such a position that she even had to worry about losing her job.

When Isabel returned to the room from brushing her teeth, Maggie handed her the phone.

"I don't think I'm getting fired."

Isabel read the email, then handed the phone back. "Isn't that a good thing?"

"I guess," Maggie said. "Yes, of course it is. I just have a lot hitting me at once."

Isabel nodded. She picked up *Anna Karenina* off the bedside table and noted the paperclip Maggie had used as a bookmark. "You've already read a hundred pages?" she said. Maggie shrugged. Isabel placed the book back on the table. "I didn't think you were. Getting fired, I mean."

"You didn't?"

"I doubted Frank would go running to the school board about his wife having an affair with a woman. I wouldn't."

Somehow, the answer disappointed Maggie. Isabel might have mentioned how she was beloved and had been named Teacher of the Year four out of the seven years of her tenure. But maybe that wasn't fair.

She watched Isabel brush her hair into a ponytail and sit on the far end of the bed. She ached to hold her, to be held by her. She didn't want to misinterpret Isabel's staying as anything beyond logistics—the trains were still out of service—or, she supposed, kindness. Was she really going to leave while Maggie's nephew was in the hospital? She was about to ask if she wanted to pick up where they'd left off in their conversation on the train when Isabel posed her own question.

"How was Topher a liar?" she asked. "That was the word you chose for him yesterday in the car. What did you mean by that?"

Was that really only yesterday?

Maggie sat up. "Well, he was always lying," she said. "Mostly small stuff, but still, the last thing he ever told me was a lie, and it was a big one."

"What'd he tell you?"

Maggie pulled her legs to her chest and wrapped her arms around her knees. "He dropped me off at the dentist and told me that he'd come pick me up after the procedure and we'd get ice cream," she said. "Like it was nothing. For years, I beat myself up because I didn't notice that anything was off about him that morning, but there wasn't. There really wasn't."

"I believe you," Isabel said. Then, "Maybe he meant to come back. Maybe he didn't know he was lying?"

Maggie had never considered that possibility. But what did it change? He hadn't come back. Either way, he'd lied.

Isabel's question brought up the other question that had troubled her since his death—why had he chosen her to be the one to find him?—but the question emerged as something different now: Why *not* her?

Cait and Alice had both been living in the city at the time. Who else would have been there to find him? Their parents. Most likely, their mother. Given that option, Maggie would never have wanted to trade places with her. And then there was the more difficult thought: that he had no choice— that he was in so much pain that he couldn't stand it a moment longer and it didn't matter who found him.

"Maybe his word is *haunted*," Maggie said to Isabel.

Isabel nodded. "That sounds right."

Maggie shifted to Isabel's side of the bed and reached for her hand, pressing her knuckles to her lips. "Do you still want to leave?" she asked.

"I don't know," Isabel said. "What do you want?"

"For you to stay," Maggie said. She wished Isabel would curl up next to her and say that's what she wanted, too, but she stayed put, so Maggie continued. "I want never to have met Sarah. To have never gone to her house in Boston last weekend. I want not to have ruined things with you. Like the text thread, I just want to erase it all. That's what I want. But I can't have that. I can't do that."

"You can't," Isabel said. "Besides, that would be like erasing yourself."

Would it? Maggie wasn't sure.

"I should have told you about her," she said. "About everything. But I was ashamed and wanted to forget it ever happened."

Isabel leaned against the wooden bed frame and picked at the green polish on her nails. "That's kind of your family's thing, isn't it?" she said finally. "Pretend everything's okay, even when it's not."

"Isn't that every family's thing?"

"Maybe, but it's not *my* thing. And it doesn't have to be yours. Imagine if we had to keep pretending that I had had some family emergency like you tried to tell your mom earlier. How weird would that be now?"

Maggie felt her defenses rise. "I didn't want to make things worse."

"Don't you see that doesn't work?" Isabel asked, exasperated. "The lying and avoiding are what make things worse."

Maggie stared out the window, the bottom corners covered in snow. She remembered one summer night when she was younger and she and Topher stood on the back porch watching a sailboat try to make its way back to shore during a storm. Lightning flashed around the bay, and Maggie worried it would hit the boat even though Topher assured her they probably had some kind of grounding conductor. Besides, he said, the weather report had warned of storms, so the sailor should've known better. He lost interest soon after, but Maggie couldn't turn away until the boat finally reached the dock. After Daniel's accident, she recalled that sailboat and Topher's comment and thought, *Why hadn't you known better?* And later, of course: *Why hadn't we known better?* Maybe Isabel was right. *Pretend everything's okay, even when it's not.* But who had been the one pretending? Topher? Their family? All of them?

She knew Isabel was offering her a warning here, and that it was her choice to listen or ignore it.

"I do see," Maggie said.

Isabel looked at her. Flecks of gold speckled her brown eyes. "If we're going to be together," she said, "you have to open up. You have to share yourself. Your whole self, you know? Otherwise, this won't work. *We* won't work."

"That sounds true enough," Maggie said, "though I'm not sure I actually know how to do that."

For a moment, Isabel was very still. Then she offered a shrug and a small, surprising smile. "Well," she said, "I guess that's a good place to start, right?"

27.

ALICE

Alice drove her mother through the half-plowed, nearly empty streets of Port Haven village in silence. The roads were slick with ice, and she gripped the steering wheel tightly as though that might stop them from veering off the road. Shattered from the day, she pulled into the driveway hoping the boys and Kyle were already asleep so that she wouldn't have to talk. Still, there was something she needed to say to her mother before they went inside.

"What happened with Topher was not your fault," she said. "You tried to protect him."

Nora stared straight ahead as she nodded, and though Alice knew she probably didn't believe her, she was glad to have said it anyway.

"Ready?" Alice asked.

Nora reached for her bag, but then, still not looking Alice in the eyes, said, "Are you happy?"

A sharp annoyance rose up within Alice as she recalled the last forty-eight hours. An unwanted pregnancy. Cait's blowup at dinner. Finn sneaking out and getting sent to the hospital. Her father seeing the ghost of her dead brother. Kyle being angry at her, without an end in sight. *Happy* wasn't exactly the word she would have used. Then again, just like she thought when Father Kelly told his story at dinner, her mother wasn't exactly asking a genuine question. What she sought was reassurance. Alice had played this role countless times before. She was the daughter her mother didn't have to worry about. The one in a stable marriage, with kids enrolled in Catholic school. The one who still attended mass herself, whatever her reasons. The child who'd come back and would never leave. However wearying, Alice prided herself on that role, because it was an act of love none of her other siblings were deemed capable of offering.

"I'm happy," Alice lied. "But I'm also tired. Can we go inside?"

Nora unbuckled her seat belt and reached for the door handle, then stopped again. "What about your sisters? Are they happy, do you think?"

Alice rubbed her temples. She could feel a headache coming on. "I don't know," she said. "What do you think?"

"Cait's lonely."

"She won't be forever."

"And Maggie, well, she doesn't let me know what's going on in her life anyway, so—"

Here we go. Alice had lost count of the times she'd talked to her mother about how to repair her relationship with Maggie. Mostly it was useless, as Nora just wanted to be soothed, to know that it wasn't all her fault, but Alice did not have that in her now.

"You could ask her," she said.

Nora shifted in her seat. "You don't think I've tried?"

Alice looked up at the house, imagining everyone inside, asleep in their respective rooms, just as her mother had hoped for this weekend. Her parents had always wanted a big family. They'd had lonely childhoods in their own ways, and this shared dream was one of the things that had brought them together. Her mother always said that if they hadn't started so late, she would have had more children. Now they'd lost a son, and two of their daughters rarely returned home. But if Alice found Cait's distance frustrating, she understood why Maggie stayed away.

She met her mother's stare and tilted her head as if to challenge her defense. "I know today was hard, but I think Maggie seems happy—and in love." Then she said, "But I'm not sure you see that, and she knows it, and she suffers because of it."

Nora received these words with a tiny escaped gasp, but Alice didn't take them back. They needed to be said. She should have said them a long time ago. And if she could not share her own truth with her mother, at least she could share her sister's.

"You will lose her," she continued. "You have to know that. Eventually you will lose her if you can't accept her."

They sat in silence. The storm had passed, and the moon shone brightly on the snow-covered evergreen bushes and the garbage bin with the dead raccoon in front of the house. Tomorrow morning, Kyle would deal with animal control and take her parents to the parish for the food drive. But where would things stand between them?

"Maggie knows I love her," Nora said finally. "I love her very much."

"But do you respect her?" Alice asked. "The life she's living? Who she is? The choices she's made?"

"I see."

Alice wasn't sure she did. Ever since Topher's death, Nora had insisted on believing that he'd been destined for greatness had he not been derailed. Who could say either way? Still, Alice knew that Daniel's accident and the admission of guilt in the settlement were not the only things that had determined Topher's life. She'd always assumed allowing her mother to maintain this belief was both kind and harmless, but she was starting to see that there had been a price. It had allowed Nora to stay in a world of fantasy, where none of her other children could possibly compete, and where their lives and choices were held to a false standard.

But she'd already said enough. She grabbed her bag. "I need to check on Finn."

"Wait, and what about the boys? Are they happy? I mean, I know Finn made a mistake, but is he doing okay?"

Alice slumped back into her seat. "They're fine. You see them nearly every day."

"And Kyle?"

"We're all fine, Mom. What's this about?"

Nora shook her head. "I just seem to—" She stopped.

"To what?"

"To miss everything."

"What's *everything*?"

"I don't know," Nora said. "That's it. I don't see the problem, or no one tells me until a full-blown crisis is under way."

It was getting cold in the car, but something in Alice wanted to reveal everything she'd grappled with earlier in the church. To lay it out for her mother. To tell her how she'd found a certain affirmation that ending the pregnancy was the right decision for her, no matter how it broke her heart, no matter how much Kyle might not see it that way, but that she was still desperate for someone to give her permission to have a life beyond motherhood, wifehood, and even daughterhood.

"I'm not in a crisis," Alice said evenly.

Nora nodded. "Right, well. If you say so."

She knows, Alice suddenly realized. She turned to face her. "Who told you?" she asked. "Cait? Kyle?"

Nora reached for her arm. "I heard you talking to Cait earlier today in the hallway. I didn't mean to pry. Oh, love, I'm thrilled for you—"

"I may not keep it," Alice heard herself say. She knew her mother could influence her decision, and she was cautious about giving over that power. "I love being a mother, but I don't want to take that chance with my body." Then, choosing her words carefully, she said, "I don't want to leave the boys motherless."

Alice understood Nora thought she was committing not only a crime against nature but one against her soul. That she wanted more grandchildren. That this was, in fact, one of her biggest hang-ups with Maggie being gay—her fear that her youngest would never have children and, therefore, never live a full life.

For a long time, Nora said nothing. Finally, she said, very quietly, "I understand."

"You do?" Alice said. She was so stunned, she wondered if her mother had misunderstood her.

Nora pressed her hands together and held them to her lips. "I had a miscarriage before Topher was born," she said.

"I didn't know that."

"It was early on. I didn't even know I was pregnant. I should have, but I was naïve back then." She stopped and breathed into her hands to warm them from the cold. "Your father and I were just engaged—"

"This was before you were married?"

"It was."

Alice would never have guessed her parents had had sex before they were married. Growing up, the extent of sex education she and her siblings had received went something like: "Don't. Until you're married." She looked at her mother. "What happened?"

"I was at the grocery store and started gushing blood and fainted."

"Oh, Mom."

"They told me while I was at the hospital. I was deeply ashamed, and I believed it was my fault. Like a punishment of sorts."

Alice imagined her newly immigrated mother alone in the hospital, blaming herself for the loss. She couldn't believe Nora had never told them about the miscarriage, that she'd kept that to herself all these years, but she knew why: she was ashamed to have gotten pregnant before she was married.

"There was a young priest who came to talk to me," Nora continued. "He was so handsome. From somewhere in Italy. He told me how Saint Aquinas believed a fetus did not acquire a soul until further along in pregnancy."

"I've heard that," Alice said. Though she was pretty sure she'd read it in an op-ed against abortion, so she wasn't sure how the argument held up, exactly.

"I don't believe that's true," Nora said. "I believe human life begins at conception and is sacred."

Alice closed her eyes and nodded. She swallowed hard again, and this time, she could not hold back the tears.

Her mother reached for her hand. "But I also believe *your* life is sacred. And that you are a moral person who will follow her own conscience." Then she said in a soft voice, "And your boys do need you."

All at once, it felt like nearly every muscle in Alice's body released the tension it had been holding. The pregnancy had been like a relentless fist squeezing her heart all day. But the ache was not just for a child she knew, had known from the beginning, she would not keep. It was for Kyle. It would be difficult, but she would survive the abortion. What she did not want to lose was him. That had never been clearer to her than in this moment, with the gift of her mother's acceptance.

She could smell her mother's rose perfume across the seat. She clutched her hand, the skin cold and thin.

28.

CAIT

Cait and Luke grabbed stools at the long wooden bar, and he ordered them IPAs from Montauk. The younger crowd had dispersed, but the dive was filled with old-time locals with hoarse voices and raucous laughs. Not much about the place had changed since Cait started going there as a college student home on break: the wooden plank floors, the smell of greasy burgers and beer, and the walls adorned with neon signs, yellowed newspaper clippings about Port Haven, and vinyl album covers. She recognized one of Topher's old buddies slumped at the bar, but thankfully, he didn't seem to recognize them.

"To us," Luke said, and they clinked their glasses.

Cait took a sip, but the beer tasted sour. "I bet Topher never got to come here," she said. She didn't have to explain why. By the time he was old enough to get in with a fake ID, he'd dropped out of college and rarely came home, even for the holidays.

"Well, Daniel certainly never did," Luke said. Then, "But I once had a beer here with Topher."

"You did? When?"

"I think he was back for Alice's wedding. I was in town visiting my mom. We ran into each other at 7-Eleven."

"Did he tell you about the fight we'd gotten into?" Cait could see Topher standing in her studio apartment that cold morning, stunned as she screamed at him to get out.

"He mentioned seeing you in the city and you being pissed about something. He was kind of joking about it, though."

Of course he was.

Luke guided her chin toward him. "Hey, you all right?"

Cait straightened. "Yeah, sorry."

"He was wasted," Luke continued. "We both ended up apologizing for everything that went down between us. I told him I didn't blame him. I don't." After a moment, he continued. "He joked that sometimes he thought about driving his car into a ditch—" He stopped and wiped his cheeks. "Sorry."

Cait reached for his hand and gave it a squeeze. "Don't be. That sounds like something Topher would joke about."

Luke cleared his throat. "Yeah," he said. "I didn't take it seriously. I should have reached out to tell you. I don't know. Done something. But I just drove him back to the Folly. Before he left, I told him to go talk to someone, and he laughed again and said he was fine and that he'd call me the next time he was in town. He never did, of course."

"No," Cait said.

"And you know why I never reached out to him again?"

"I don't."

"Because every time I was around him, I couldn't forget that I was the one who spent that afternoon drinking with Danny. I was the one who bought the beer. I was as guilty as Topher. But that's not how the world works. It's not how my parents saw things, and it's definitely not how I wanted to see things. So I kept living my life." He paused, then said, "Do you know the last thing I said to Danny?"

Cait shook her head.

"I called him a dipshit for—"

"The waves."

Luke nodded. "He could be such a dipshit, though," he said, and laughed. "Anyway, not exactly what I thought would be my last words to my brother."

Cait wanted to laugh along, but she couldn't shake the image of Daniel reversing the boat while high-fiving Topher. The smell of the musty rope bracelet around Luke's tanned wrist as he clutched the steering wheel. The brassy notes of the trumpet off the lighthouse balcony. The conversation she was already rehearsing in her mind to convince her parents to let her visit Luke in Boston. Then the crash, ending all of that, and so much more.

"It was my fault Daniel drove Topher's boat," she said.

"It wasn't."

"You don't get it," she said, looking at him. "You'd ignored me all day. It was my idea for Daniel to drive Topher's boat, so you and I could be alone. I threatened to tell our parents all about Marcus and how Topher bought the boat. He didn't even want to leave the party. If I hadn't done that, Daniel would have gone home with you—"

Luke stopped her. "I know all of that," he said.

"You do?"

"I saw you and Topher fighting, and I assumed." Then he said, "But you're not the only reason Danny ended up on that boat. We all let him drive. You said it before and you were right. We all could have stopped him."

Cait tried to take in everything Luke was saying. It was the recognition she'd sought earlier in the cottage, had sought ever since they were teenagers and had made a stupid, stupid mistake.

"Topher and I never talked about it," she said. "He never called me out on my part in the accident and I never apologized to him for the threats I made."

"Speaking of apologies," Luke said, "I was a dick to you that day. I know I was. I liked you, I did, but I didn't want a girlfriend back home when I was going to college. And I felt guilty about that and didn't know what to say when I saw you the next day."

"You were a dick."

They shared a smile, and Luke nudged her with his knee. "Well, I am sorry," he said.

Cait took a sip of beer but could barely swallow. She felt hungover. Not just from the day of drinking but from the years of drinking. She pushed the glass away and turned to Luke. "I miss Topher," she said.

"I do, too. And Daniel. I'm not sure that'll ever change. Maybe it shouldn't."

"I guess not."

They watched the bartender swirl a pint of Guinness to make a shamrock in the foam, and then Luke looked at her again and said, "It feels good to talk about all of this."

"Does it?"

He laughed but continued. "I've been at my mom's all week by myself going through everything. It's been depressing."

"I'm sure."

"I was at a pretty low point when you showed up the other night and asked me to come to dinner. I'm not sure I would have said yes if I wasn't feeling so . . . Not that I didn't want to see you—"

"No, I get it."

Luke nodded and took another sip of his beer, then noticed something over her shoulder. "Pool table's open," he said. "You still a shark?"

"Maybe? It's been a while."

Luke racked the balls into the triangle as Cait tried to snag a decent cue from the dismal selection. She finally picked one that wasn't warped, then shot the white ball across the table on the break, nailing two stripes into corner pockets.

"I guess you are." Luke laughed. He took his shot but missed. "And I am still not!"

The Irish Goodbye

Cait strategized her next shot while he deposited a handful of change into the jukebox and browsed the albums, and then Billy Joel's "The Stranger" filled the bar. As Cait chalked her cue, Luke approached her from behind, but his presence did not make her swoon the way it once had. There had been so many times when she'd wanted to be the one to finally rebuff him—to punish him or to make him want her more. But that was not the reason she took a step away as he nuzzled against her neck.

Maybe it was too little too late. Or maybe this was where they were headed all along. Fresh out of a bad marriage and the mother of two high-spirited kids, she needed to find a job to support her family and keep her parents in their home. Nobody was looking to take all that on. And that was okay. More than okay. Her plate was full enough. She had no place for Luke in her life right now, other than as a friend.

She nudged him with her hip, then turned back to the pool table to line up her shot.

29.

MAGGIE

Maggie woke when she heard the front door downstairs open, then close. She listened to the footsteps cross the foyer and make their way into the kitchen. In bed next to her, Isabel stirred and curled onto her side. They'd fallen asleep on top of the comforter, and Maggie wasn't sure what time it was now. After a few moments, the door to the kids' bunk room across the hall opened, before all grew quiet again.

She had a sense of what would follow next, and there it was. Below the wooden floors of her bedroom, her mother moved about the painting studio. Maggie could almost smell the turpentine and see Nora perched on her stool immersed in whatever landscape she was currently working on. She heard the faint Gregorian chants from a CD someone had gifted her years ago.

Nora claimed to have been a lifelong insomniac. It stemmed, she said, from being frightened at having to go to bed earlier than all the other kids at the orphanage because she was so much younger; she never learned how to settle herself into sleep and was always worried about wetting the bed.

But in Maggie's memory, her mother only began staying up all night after Daniel died.

It was a crash that finally sent Maggie downstairs.

"Don't—" her mother said, holding up her hand. Her smock was drenched in water, and she crouched on the floor by the small dresser that held her paints. With a dust broom, she swept the shattered glass onto a sheet of cardboard. "You're barefoot."

"And you're in socks," Maggie said. "Plus, your knee."

Maggie slipped into Finn's old Vans that were by the mudroom and handed her mother a pair of her father's loafers; then she made two cups of tea in the kitchen, which she brought back to the studio. She sat in the armchair in the corner and watched her mother arrange tiny blue, black, and white paint droplets onto her glass palette. Before her, a half-finished painting of a seascape seemed to capture the time of day when it's not clear where the water ends and the sky begins, one mirroring the other. Her mother rarely allowed anyone to see her paintings before she finished. It was beautiful, but Maggie didn't want to say anything to draw attention to the rare viewing of a work in progress. When she was a kid, she was jealous of her mother's paintings and her time in the studio. As she got older and took a women's studies class in college, she assumed her mother had sublimated her creative passions for her motherly duties—and she not only felt bad for her for this decision, but she judged her for it. Sitting there now and looking at the seascape, she appreciated her mother's longing for selfhood despite her motherly obligations.

Nora gave her the latest update about Finn, then said, "And are things okay with you and Isabel?"

Maggie nodded. "They are," she said. It was nice to be asked. "We had some things to work out." Then she said, "I made a mistake, and I had to fix it."

Nora sipped her tea, her hands slender and fragile-looking. "We all make mistakes," she said.

"We do."

"Not all of them can be fixed, though."

"That's true." Maggie started to sip her tea, but it was too hot, so she placed it on the dresser. "I appreciate you asking, though."

This seemed to resonate, and her mother said, "Can I ask you something else?" She looked tired, older than Maggie could ever remember, her features delicate.

"Sure," Maggie said.

Nora turned to face her. "Are you happy?"

Maggie didn't hesitate. "I am," she said. "Do I not seem happy?"

"No, no, you do," her mother said. "I just want to make sure." Then she picked up her brush and studied something on the painting. Maggie could now see a lone figure on the horizon in the background. A man standing on a boat.

Her mother placed the brush on the side of the palette. Facing the painting, she said, "I worried you wouldn't be happy. That you'd spend your life alone."

Maggie was caught off guard by her mother's honesty. She felt that old urge to retreat, the very thing Isabel had accused her of. But that wasn't what she wanted—not for herself or her mother—and so she said, "There was a time when I did, too." Then she said, "That's why I needed you."

A noise upstairs, maybe someone going to the bathroom, startled them. When it was quiet again, her mother looked at her and nodded as though she understood. Then she reached for her brush again before turning back to the painting.

Maggie cradled her steaming mug of tea in her hands. She didn't need or even want her mother to say anything more. What she'd offered so far was almost too painful to accept, like the ache of cold hands thawing out in the warmth. She watched her paint. Nora was left-handed, and growing up, the nuns forced her to write with her right hand, and the older girls at the orphanage called her a *ciotóg*. Apparently it was an insult used against left-handed people and meant "awkward." Nora often shared the story of a kind nun who noticed her talent for art and once gifted her a pencil. She'd had nothing, and this meant the world to her. Now Nora switched hands naturally, from right to left, as she dipped the brush into the light blue paint splotch on her palette and capped the ripples on the water, bringing the waves to life. The man on the boat stood with his hands in his pockets, surrounded by the sea and sky.

Maggie didn't know what would happen when her parents had to sell the house, as surely they would eventually. Where would they go? What would happen to the generations' worth of stuff? She imagined these questions weighed more on her sisters than on her. She didn't have Cait's money to maintain the house and didn't live down the street like Alice, helping with the day-to-day. With her tenuous relationship with her mother, she hadn't considered what role she might be expected to play in their care, but perhaps it was time for that to change.

"You should get some rest," she said, and stood.

Surprisingly, her mother seemed to listen. She cleaned her brush and covered her canvas. "I'm tired," she admitted.

"I'll walk you to your room," Maggie said as she gathered the teacups.

Her mother tapped her cane on the floor. "What do you girls think I do when you're not around?"

Maggie walked her to her room anyway, and when she closed the door and turned around, she nearly screamed at the small, ghostlike figure floating toward her down the hallway.

"Where's my mum?" Poppy said. Red cheeked and sleepy eyed, she held one of Cait's old teddy bears in a headlock.

They checked the bathroom, which was empty, and Maggie considered looking downstairs but changed her mind because she suspected Cait was still out with Luke. She walked Poppy back to Cait's room, and said, "Don't worry. She'll be back soon."

"I want to sleep with you." Poppy's footie pajamas slapped the wooden floor as she walked out of the room.

"Oh," Maggie said. "Okay."

In the moonlight, Maggie made a bed on the floor with extra blankets and pillows, and Poppy closed her eyes and cuddled her teddy bear.

Isabel woke as soon as Maggie sat on the bed. "I can go to the cottage," she said.

Maggie pulled back the comforter and slipped beneath it. "Stay," she whispered.

"You sure?"

Maggie kissed Isabel's shoulder and lowered her onto the pillow.

They were drifting into sleep when Maggie heard a stirring and Poppy appeared on Isabel's side of the bed.

"I have to go to the bathroom," she declared. "Can you bring me? I'm scared."

"All right," Isabel said. She swung her legs off the bed and gathered Poppy into her arms. "But no phone privileges on the toilet. You have a reputation."

Poppy laughed.

"I love you," Maggie said, as they walked out of the room.

Isabel peeked her head back through the doorway. "You'd better," she teased.

When they returned a few minutes later, Isabel sang Poppy a Spanish lullaby until she fell asleep. After, she crawled into the bed and wrapped her arms around Maggie. "And I love you," she said, pulling her closer.

30.

ALICE

Alice sat at the foot of Finn's bed and watched him sleep. His face was sharpening with puberty, and he was so beautiful she could hardly believe he'd come from her body. The next week or so would be hard with him at home, but the day had given him a scare, and maybe that was needed. She hoped he was all right. Not just his body, but his spirit. She'd been annoyed by her mother's question in the car earlier, but she was no different. Of course Alice longed for him to be happy. And for herself to be as well.

On her way to her bedroom, she bumped into Isabel in the hallway.

"Hey," Isabel whispered. "I was just grabbing my sleep mask from the cottage. The moon's like a spotlight on all that snow. How's Finn?"

"He's hanging in there," Alice said. "Thanks for asking and for helping with everything today. I'm so sorry you had to deal with all that family drama—and I hope everything is okay with you and Maggie?"

Isabel smiled. "It is," she said.

Alice nodded, relieved. Then she said, "Do you remember what card I picked earlier today? Can you tell me?"

"Sure," Isabel said. "It was the Chariot."

"The Chariot?"

"I think it means you're the one holding the reins. Now you have to look ahead to determine the right road to take. That sort of thing."

"Hmm," Alice said.

"Some days the readings speak to me more than others—"

"No," Alice said. "It does speak to me. It's helpful, actually."

Alice returned to her room and found Kyle in bed reading. He rested his book on his chest and watched as she collapsed into the rocking chair, using her toes to rock back and forth.

"How was Finn when you got back?" she asked.

"Still weepy and apologetic, but he went straight to bed."

Alice nodded.

"But James was awake, and he had some questions about Topher."

"Did he? Like what?"

Kyle removed his glasses and placed them gently on the nightstand with his book. "He wanted to know what happened."

Alice stopped rocking. "Did you tell him? I mean everything about Daniel and—"

"Yes, everything."

"How'd he take it?"

"I kept it all high level, but he was fine."

Alice knew it was the right thing to do, and eventually, the boys would have to learn the truth, but she'd always imagined being the one to tell them.

She leaned back in the chair, again rocking gently on the tips of her toes. She was still surprised by the conversation with her mother in the car—not only learning about the miscarriage but Nora's unexpected offering of support. *See,* she wanted to say to Kyle, *even she gets it!*

"I'm going to Dr. Chen's on Monday," she said instead.

Kyle lowered his gaze and folded his hands in his lap.

"I know you'll need time," she said. "I can give that to you."

But would it be enough? Would he ever be able to forgive her—and, if not, would she ever be able to forgive him?

She stood and walked to the bed, sitting next to him.

"Will you be sick?" he asked, looking up at her. "I mean, will it hurt?"

Alice didn't know. She was afraid of what was to come, but she didn't want to worry Kyle or give him more ammunition to make his case. "It's early," she said, "so I'll probably take medication. I'm hoping I don't need a procedure."

"Will you share this in confession?"

"Yes," she said. She wasn't sure if she'd said this just to comfort him, but even if she had, she decided it was the least she could do.

Earlier that day, the thought of keeping the pregnancy from Kyle—from everyone, really, including her sisters—had seemed like a viable option. She could go to Dr. Chen's alone. Why did she owe this part of herself to anyone? But burying even more secrets felt ludicrous now.

"I'll go to confession," she continued. "And I'll ask for God's forgiveness. But I can't spend the rest of our lives together begging for your forgiveness. I can't carry that burden on top of everything else."

He reached for her, but she didn't move toward him.

"And the last thing I need from you is more distance," she said. "I need *more* of you—not less." He looked up at her, confused. "You don't even kiss me anymore."

He dropped his eyes again. She had no idea what he was thinking. Was he angry at her? How dare she say these things to him considering the pain her decision was causing?

Finally, he looked up again. "I'll go with you on Monday," he said. "I don't want you to go alone."

She lowered herself onto the bed next to him.

After a moment, he pressed his lips to the top of her head. "Maybe we've drifted," he said, "but that's not what I want either."

She reached under his shirt and rested her hand on his chest, playing with the silver cross that hung from his neck, something she hadn't done in a long time. His heart beat calm and steady against her palm, and she wept.

31.

CAIT

It was close to midnight when Cait returned to the Folly. She hadn't eaten anything beyond the oysters earlier that evening, and in the kitchen, she ventured a bite of the untouched vegan apple pie that Alice had begrudgingly baked for her. The filling was too sweet, but the taste ignited her hunger, and she cut an enormous slice of the regular apple pie and plopped it onto a plate. After taking a few bites standing at the counter, she topped the pie with a scoop of vanilla ice cream and sat at the table.

Through the window, the snow sparkled under the moonlight. Earlier that day, Maggie had pointed out the broken fence and warned her it wouldn't keep the twins away from the water. Cait could see the damage more clearly now. She'd have to get that fixed.

The house was quiet, but thinking about Luke alone in his nearly empty childhood bedroom, she felt its fullness with a new sense of gratitude. Her family, all asleep. The Tiffany table lamp on the desk in the foyer dimly lit as always. Her grandmother's gardening boots never moved from the mudroom. The doorway of the butler's pantry notched with generations of children growing taller each year, her measurements alongside her grandfather's and father's, her sisters' and brother's. She would have to remember to mark the twins' heights in the morning. When she was a kid, she'd sometimes sit in a room and try to imagine the lives that had been lived within these walls. *This is my home now*, she would think, and then daydream about the people who would live here after her.

As she stood to put her dish in the sink, Alice came into the kitchen for water. Cait tried to duck out with a quick good night, but Alice began speaking while she filled her glass. "About today," she said, and turned. "I am pregnant."

"Oh," Cait said. She knew her reaction was stilted, but she wasn't sure how to read her sister's tone. Her eyes were puffy, as though she'd been crying. "Are you . . . excited?"

Alice shook her head. "No," she said. "I'm talking with my doctor on Monday about how I can, you know . . ."

Cait wasn't entirely sure what her sister was trying to say. "Have an abortion?"

Alice winced at the word and crossed her arms. "I thought you should know, because you found the test and everything."

Cait tried to keep the shock out of her voice. "Thanks for telling me." Then she said, "And good for you."

"It's a pretty shitty situation. I'm not sure I need your congratulations."

"I didn't mean it like that—"

"No, I know," Alice said. "Sorry." She pointed to the cyst on her chin. "Anyway, that's what this is about, too."

"Hormones," Cait said. "They don't lie."

Alice laughed, then turned to the sink. "You ate the regular apple pie, didn't you?"

"It was *delicious*."

Alice huffed. "I'm never accommodating one of your diets again."

"Fair enough," Cait said. Then she shifted. "I had one. An abortion. I'm not sure if you knew that."

The Irish Goodbye

Alice stared at her.

"It was a few months before I took the bar exam. Bram and I were long-distance, and I knew I'd ruin all my plans if I became a mom then, so."

"I didn't know."

"I figured you wouldn't approve," Cait said. "Maggie took me to the appointment." The exclusion seemed to hurt Alice, which Cait hadn't intended, and so she added, "I never told Bram either."

"I understand why you would have thought that. There was a time when I wouldn't have approved, but I guess I see things differently now."

Cait nodded. "Life will do that to you."

Alice smiled. "I guess it will."

"How does Kyle feel about it?" Cait asked.

"Devastated, but he's supporting me. Or trying to?" Then she said, "I also told Mom."

"What the hell?" Cait said, almost incredulous. "What did she say?"

"That she understands."

Cait was staggered. She wanted to know more, but she could see that Alice was in a vulnerable place, so she just said, "Things have certainly changed around here since I left."

"Some things. It's been a while."

Cait looked out the window at the broken fence, then back at Alice. "I know you've had to deal with a lot here on your own."

Alice stood straighter. "I appreciate you acknowledging that."

"I'm not just acknowledging it. I see it. And that's going to change."

Alice looked skeptical, but then said, "Well, I have plenty of ideas for how you can help—"

"I'm sure you do," Cait said. She could see that Alice was annoyed at being cut off, so she added, "We can talk about it more tomorrow. I have some of my own ideas."

"Why does that make me nervous?"

"Don't be," Cait said, and headed toward the stairs.

Back in her room, Cait panicked when she discovered only Augustus in the bed. She tried to wake him to ask where Poppy had gone, but all he did was mumble incoherently and turn over. Shame overwhelmed her as she checked her parents' room, only to find them asleep. What had she been doing, hanging out with Luke all night, playing pool like a teenager? Next, she checked the kids' bunk room, where Finn and James slept as soundly as kids who *knew their parents were in the next room!* She was on the verge of waking everyone in the house when she finally discovered Poppy in Maggie's room, cuddled between Maggie and Isabel. She scooped her up, her heart finally settling, and put her back in the bed next to Augustus. Then she snuck downstairs and into her father's office. She closed the door behind her, sat at the desk, and picked up the phone. It was nearly six a.m. in Amsterdam, and Bram would be waking for work.

The morning was blinding, with the sun reflecting off the snow, but Cait slept late, and when she woke, Poppy was no longer in her bed and Augustus was sitting on the floor playing with her father's trains. The smell of coffee and bacon filled the old house.

Downstairs, Alice made pancakes, and the kids ran around pretending to be characters from a movie Cait didn't know.

"Why do I always have to be the princess?" Poppy yelled.

"Because you're the girl," Augustus said.

James raised his hand. "I'll be the princess."

"You can't be the princess!" Augustus said. "You're a boy."

"He most certainly can," Cait said.

"Ruthie says boys can't be princesses," Poppy explained.

"Well, Ruthie's wrong," Cait said. "Now scram."

Through the window, she watched her father and Kyle greet a van that read ANIMAL CONTROL.

In the kitchen, Maggie and Isabel set the table. Cait poured herself coffee. She felt clearer than she had in a long time.

As everyone took their seats, she sat and placed her napkin on her lap. "I have some news," she said.

"What is it?" Alice asked.

"I'm moving back home."

Alice was about to slide a pancake onto James's plate, but she paused with the spatula in midair and looked at Cait. "Back to Port Haven?"

"Back *here*." Cait tapped the table. "At least for a bit. Until I can plan our next move."

Their mother clapped. "Isn't it just grand?"

Alice forced a smile. "Sure," she said to Nora, then turned back to Cait. "But what about everything in London? Your job and—"

"I quit."

"Weren't you going for partner?"

"I didn't get it," Cait said. Admitting this stung less than she'd expected. "And I'm miserable there."

"I didn't know that," Maggie said.

"I'm not sure I did either," Cait said.

Alice continued to plate the pancakes, mechanically moving through the tasks of mothering, but she was clearly holding back as she asked more questions about the logistics. "What will you do? I mean for work and everything?"

Cait wanted to challenge her sister's lackluster response to what she thought would be welcome news, but after yesterday, she was trying not to cause a scene, and so instead, she said, "Half of my graduating class from Columbia is in the city. I'll find something."

"And what about Bram?"

Cait nodded toward the twins and raised her brow.

"Oh, sorry."

"I spoke with him last night. He comes to New York quarterly, so he'll see the twins just as much. And, master of the grand gesture, he'll take them on some extravagant summer holiday every year."

Alice put down the now-empty platter and looked at Cait. "So you'll live *here*?" she said. "In this house? With Mom and Dad?"

Cait squared up. "Yes," she said defensively. "I've thought about it, and we'll come in the summer after the twins finish school, then see what happens. Maybe get a place in the city. Or not. Maybe we'll stay on."

Alice was about to take a bite of pancake but put her fork down. She started to say something, then stopped.

"For God's sake," Cait said. "What?"

"Nothing," Alice said, shaking her head. "I'm just surprised, I guess."

Cait resisted making the barb that there were plenty of surprises going around this weekend, and relied on another truth instead. "I thought you'd appreciate it. Having some help around here?"

Their mother turned to Alice. "What do you need help with?"

"Nothing," Alice said.

"Why are you crying, Grammy?" James asked.

"I'm happy."

Poppy stood on the bench and stomped her feet. "You can't cry when you're happy."

Were all children this self-righteous, Cait wondered, or just hers?

"Oh, but you can," Nora said.

"That's silly." Poppy sat and drowned her pancake in a pool of syrup.

Cait took a sip of her coffee. "Isn't it, though?"

From the other end of the table, Finn pushed his empty plate away with his one good hand and leaned back in his chair. "I'm bored," he announced.

"Good for you," said Isabel, next to him. "You're on the path toward enlightenment."

Finn looked at her in confusion.

"You know," she said, "the whole 'do nothing' thing. Just be."

"Huh?" Finn said, but everyone else laughed.

Sensing the tension between Cait and Alice, Maggie turned to the kids. "How about a snowball fight?" She nodded to Finn in his shoulder wrap. "We'll take it easy on you."

After bundling up, Maggie and Isabel followed the kids outside, and Kyle came in to take Nora to the parish for the food drive.

"We need to get going," he said. "Father Kelly is expecting us."

Alone now, Cait and Alice navigated around each other, clearing the table and washing the dishes. Cait tried to wait to hear whatever problem Alice had with her decision to move back home, but finally, her patience worn, she crammed the syrup bottle into the crowded fridge alongside last night's leftovers and turned to Alice at the sink.

"If you have something to say to me, I'd prefer you just come out and say it."

Alice turned.

"I thought you wanted me here to help?" Cait continued. "Isn't that what you've been on me about all these years?"

Alice wrapped a dish towel around the faucet. "Not everything is about you."

"Okay," Cait said, trying to compose herself. "Then what is it about?"

Alice sighed. "I'm just worried about Finn. And Dad."

"Oh," Cait said. "Yeah. Well, you're not the only one."

"Do you really know what you're signing up for returning home and staying with them?"

So this wasn't entirely *not* about her. "As much as I can," Cait admitted.

"And Luke? I mean, you're not doing this to be closer to him?"

The only question Nora had asked when Cait checked if it was okay for them to move into the house was "How soon can you come?" Cait had hoped her intentions would be obvious to her sisters as well. That they would understand that she wanted to be a more hands-on daughter. To help their parents. To find a more sustainable work-life balance. That she missed them, all of them, even Alice. That she wanted the twins to grow up knowing their family. That she dreaded the Folly being sold off to some developer from the city who'd arrive the next day with a bulldozer. But considering how she'd behaved all these years, she supposed it made sense that Alice had some misgivings.

"Alice," she said quietly, and looked at her. "I'm doing this because I want to come home."

Alice nodded. She seemed to believe her. "So what's happening with Luke? Are you together?"

"We're friends," Cait said. "At least for now."

Alice thought about this for a moment. "There's something I want to show you before Mom and Dad get back."

"What is it?"

Alice didn't answer. Instead, she opened the back door and called for Maggie, then asked Isabel to watch the kids.

Isabel paused mid-throw and turned to the kids on the lawn. "Hey, everyone," she announced. "I'm in charge! Time to eat broccoli and do your homework."

Maggie came into the kitchen and kicked off her snow boots. "What's up?"

"Follow me," Alice said to them both.

Alice led them upstairs and into their parents' room, which was dark with the shades drawn and smelled of their mother's rose perfume. Cait switched on the lamp on the nightstand and watched as Alice opened the closet doors and reached for a shoebox on the top shelf. She placed the box on the bed and opened the lid to reveal a pile of yellowed envelopes addressed to *The Ryan Family*.

"They're cards," Alice explained. "From when Topher died. I found them yesterday when I was helping Mom get dressed."

Cait and Maggie looked at each other, trying to work out what they were missing.

"And?" Cait asked finally.

Alice continued. "Mrs. Larkin sent one, and Mom never opened it."

Now Cait was even more confused. "I thought she never reached out?"

"I guess it was sometime later."

Cait leafed through the pile. She recognized the names on the return addresses—families from town or Saint Mary's, a few of their father's colleagues.

The Irish Goodbye

"Why didn't she open it?"

"I don't know," Alice said. "I don't think she even knows. She doesn't want the cards anymore. They're making her miserable, but she doesn't feel like she can move them herself. Last night, when I fell asleep, all I could think about was this unopened card sitting here, stuck in time."

As they looked for the card, they stopped to read a few that had already been opened—to themselves and sometimes aloud. Most were generic sympathy cards—*I'm sorry for your loss*, *You're in our prayers*, that sort of thing. Cait shared a note from Topher's lacrosse coach. It was the only one they read that directly acknowledged their brother's struggles—*I know he was trying to get his life back on track*. Was he? Maggie read another from their aunt Brigid in Ireland. In the card, she referred to Topher by his full name—Christopher John—and called their mother *Baby sister*.

Maggie was the one to finally find Mrs. Larkin's card. She handed it to Cait deferentially.

Cait took a deep breath. "Should we open it?" The card was specifically addressed to their mother. "What if it's an angry rant? I don't want to read that."

"I don't either," Alice said.

"Just open it," Maggie said.

Cait unsealed the small, green envelope. She held up the front of the card, a picture of a field of yellow-petaled flowers, and read the note to herself and then aloud.

Dear Nora,
I know from experience that there are no words to bring you comfort.
So I offer here what I can: my sorrow.
    If I could offer more, I would.

Yours,
Connie

No one said a word as Cait returned the card to the box.

Alice passed a tissue to Maggie, then turned to them both. "Do you ever think about who we would be if none of this had ever happened?" she asked.

Maggie wiped the tears from her face and stood, irritated. "Of course," she said. "But maybe we'd be exactly the same. Maybe we've always been this way. We'll never know." She seemed upset in a way Cait didn't fully understand. Maggie picked up the card, then continued. "I mean, Mom let this sit in her closet and haunt her for years when she could've just faced it and maybe even found some healing in it. Instead, she hid it away, stuffed it down, you know? Like we all do, like Topher did, until"—she slapped her hands together—"everything implodes."

Cait and Alice flinched at the loud clap, then exchanged glances. They looked at their younger sister.

Maggie sat on the bed again. "Sorry," she said. "I'm just so tired of blaming everything on the past."

"I am, too," Alice said.

Cait wasn't sure what to say. She knew she was the cause of the most recent "implosion," but she also wanted to defend their mother. Nora had probably held on to the cards because she couldn't bear the guilt of letting the wound heal, and Cait could understand that. But she suspected this was something her sisters already knew. "I'm sorry for yesterday," she said.

"It's okay," Maggie said.

"It's not," Cait insisted. "I was terrible."

"You were," Alice agreed. Cait readied herself for more, but then Alice surprised her. "You inspired me, though. Your directness. It helped me tell Kyle I'm not going through with the pregnancy." Then she turned to Maggie. "I'm pregnant and having an abortion."

Maggie sat up. "You're what and you're doing what?"

"You didn't know?" Cait said.

Maggie turned to Alice. "Are you okay? What do you mean you're not going through with it? What about Kyle?"

Alice grabbed another tissue and removed her glasses to dab her eyes. "I'm not keeping—" She stopped. "It? The baby?" She blew her nose. "What's the right language to use?"

"Whatever language you want," Maggie said. "I can't believe this was all going on and you didn't tell me. What can I do?"

Well, that's a better way to respond, Cait thought, regretting her reaction in the kitchen last night.

"Nothing," Alice said. "I just want to get it over with."

"I'll go with you," Maggie said. "When is it?"

"It's okay. Kyle's coming. We're going on Monday."

"I'm staying another week," Cait said. "I can take care of Finn while you're there."

"That would be really helpful actually," Alice said. "I don't know if this will last, but right now, all I feel is relief. Like I've been given my life back. I didn't realize how much I liked my life the way it was until this happened."

Outside, they could hear the kids playing in the backyard.

Cait held Mrs. Larkin's card and rested against the pillows on her parents' bed. "Should we share this with Mom?"

"Maybe," Alice said. "Or maybe not? She kept that thing for thirteen years. If she wanted to read it, she'd have done it already."

"Let's at least take the box out of here," Maggie suggested. "Then we can figure out what to do with all the cards."

"I can take them back to my house," Alice said. "Store them in the basement."

"I say we burn them," Cait said, standing up. "Torch them all."

"That's too permanent," Maggie said. "She might change her mind."

Alice grabbed a handful of cards from the box. "We might want to reread them at some point, too."

"Why?" Cait asked. "Why would we ever want to reread these?"

"To remember he was here?" Alice said. "That he existed? That he was part of the world beyond us?"

No one said anything to that.

Finally, Maggie spoke. "And maybe the kids would want to read them someday? Get to know their uncle."

"Is this how they would get to know him?" Cait said.

"How about we keep the ones that mean something," Alice said, "and burn the 'thoughts and prayers' cards? Mom said that she didn't want them anymore."

Cait and Maggie agreed, and they spent some time sorting the cards that mattered from the burn pile.

Downstairs was quiet thanks to Isabel, who was still outside with the kids. On the fireplace hearth, Cait formed a tepee with a handful of twigs and tossed a lit match into its center. Soon, the fire warmed the kitchen, and the smell of burning oak reminded her of winter evenings when she was younger.

Maggie reached for the envelopes in the box. "Are we sure about this?"

"No," Alice said.

Cait peered outside again. The kids were sledding down the small hill by the garden. The sun shone brightly in the blue sky, but she could see from Poppy's red cheeks that it was still cold out. "Well, we don't have much time," she said. "The house will be full of maniacs begging for hot chocolate in a minute."

"We should do it," Maggie said, and when Cait and Alice nodded, she tossed a handful into the fire.

Cait watched the envelopes burn. There was something beautiful in their destruction, a transformation. She imagined them carried away with the smoke, eventually falling back to nourish the ground around the house for the next generation of Ryans to walk upon.

Mrs. Larkin's card was safe in her pocket. She would let her mother know that it was there whenever she was ready. She turned to her sisters. She would not get sentimental. They wouldn't like it, and there was no need anyway. She didn't have to say aloud what they all now understood: it was time to start letting go.

She used the brass fire poker to stuff the rest of the cards between the logs until they all burned to a gray soot. They heard honking and, when they looked out the window, saw Isabel and the kids chasing the geese on the lawn.

"That's probably not a good idea," Cait said. She grabbed the fire poker again, and they all headed outside.

"Be careful," Alice yelled. "They're vicious!" None of the kids—or Isabel—seemed to hear her. She turned to Maggie. "Does Isabel know they'll fight back?"

"The geese or the children?" Maggie asked.

"They're fine," Cait said as the geese retreated. "We used to do that."

"But Dad stood by with a golf club," Alice said.

Cait laughed. "Better than a shotgun." She held up the poker. "Besides, I have this."

"These are the great-great-great-grandkids of the geese we used to harass," Alice said. "They return home every year to nest."

"Remember when one of them went after Topher?" Cait said. "He had to run into the bay to get away."

Alice laughed. "That was me!"

"Was it?"

"Maybe it wasn't? Now I don't remember."

"It's all a blur."

Maggie sighed and stuffed her hands into her pockets. "I don't remember it at all."

"I remember it as Topher," Cait said.

"It probably was."

The kids resumed their chase, but they were far enough away that the geese, with their yearlings in the mix, didn't put up a fight. Instead, they made a big flap of their wings and honked at one another, as if trying to decide whether to stay or leave. Then the loudest of them took charge, and the rest of the flock lifted off the ground and ascended into the air, still bickering. They circled the Folly in a wide loop before assembling into a V formation and soaring over the snow-covered lawn and the dark blue water, heading to wherever they were going next.

Acknowledgments

Growing up in a large family is one of the defining experiences of my life, and I am so grateful for it.

To my mom, for your infinite support and for encouraging me to live freely, and to my dad, for teaching me to find my passion and never stop working hard.

To Meredith Hassett and Melanie Lynch, not only my sisters but the first people I call when I need advice or a good laugh. Also, thank you for marrying two of the greatest guys around, John Hassett and Brian Lynch, and for making me the proud aunt of Liam, Sean, Patrick, and Jacqueline.

To all my aunts, uncles, and cousins and my godmother, Peggy Gonser, I will forever love walking into a room as one of over a hundred of you.

To my grandmother, Mary Alice, who taught me how to read (it wasn't easy) and to see the world as an artist, and to my grandfather, Thomas, who moved through the world with more grace than anyone I know.

Acknowledgments

To Abbie Gonzalez, Tim Croneberger, and Glenn Finn—what a crew, I am so grateful the thread has held.

To Emily, Aubrey, and Durward Fisher for accepting me into your family with such open arms.

To Jessica Piazza, for inviting me to coffee after Eric McHenry's (hi, Eric!) poetry class so many years ago. Thank you for never failing to say, "Of course, love, send the pages." You are a gifted reader and an even better friend.

To Joy Abbott, for sprinkling your gems of insight and support over countless revisions—you are a true friend in need and celebration.

To Julia Fierro, for your friendship, unwavering encouragement, and for building a home for me and many other writers at the Sackett Street Writers' Workshop.

To Jane Mulkerrins, literary matchmaker extraordinaire who was there from the beginning. I still miss you in Brooklyn.

To my students, whose dedication, heart, and talent inspire me every day. Thank you for trusting me with your stories. Keep going.

To the F*t Kids (+1 Yogi), you're next!

To the friends who supported me along the way, especially Mauricio Merlo, Hilary Terk, Meg duPont, and the best neighbors around, Mike, Genevieve, and Josie Brennan Gaworecki.

To K. C., for your listening and wisdom.

To Mackenzie Stroh and Daniel D'Ottavio, for your photography.

To Nathan Bransford, Jessica Strawser, and Kate Garrick for providing feedback on earlier pages. Lynn Steger Strong, for your wise counsel. Natalie Serber, for being a trusted sounding board. Jen Louden, for your encouragement. And Scott Robson, for being a steady presence.

To everyone who offered me their unique expertise, including John Hassett, Jesse Capell, Melanie Lynch, Catherine Boshe, Heide Mason, Nami Soga, and Elizabeth O'Reilly. All mistakes are my own.

To Alexandra Shelly, teacher and friend, for your keen editorial eye and for giving me the confidence to keep going.

Acknowledgments

To Nancy Rawlinson, this book would not have been possible without your steadfast guidance.

To my teachers, especially Victoria Redel, Joshua Henkin, Ernesto Mestre-Reed, Peter Cameron, and Laure-Anne Bosselaar.

To my marvelous agent, Sharon Pelletier, for your steady and trustworthy hand, and to everyone at Dystel, Goderich & Bourret, including Nataly Gruender, Masie Ibrahim, and Kendall Berdinsky. And to Noah Ballard for your generosity and vision.

To my exceptional team at Henry Holt, most especially my brilliant editor, Serena Jones, for guiding me every step of the way with more care than I ever imagined possible; Emily Griffin for believing in the work; Andrew Miller for your warm welcome; Zoë Affron for always knowing the answer; Hannah Campbell for seamlessly keeping all the moving parts moving; Kathleen Cook for your sharp eye; Emily Mahar for the beautiful design; and Clarissa Long, Allegra Green, Sarah Bode, Amber Cherichetti, and Caitlin Mulrooney-Lyski for your thoughtful strategizing and advocating for this book.

To Madeline O'Shea of Mantle, for your infectious enthusiasm, invaluable edits, and for bringing the book to the UK.

To Tommy and Teo, what a privilege and honor it is to be (one of) your moms. As much as you think I love you, I love you more.

Lastly, to the love of my life, best friend, and wife, Caroline. Thank you for always keeping me laughing, holding my passport, calming my soul, and interrupting my writing to tell me that you love me.

I am so blessed.

* * *

This book was inspired in part by the work of the Jed Foundation, the nation's leading organization for young adult mental health and suicide prevention. You can learn more about them at https://jedfoundation.org. If you or anyone you know is struggling with suicidal ideation, call or text the Suicide and Crisis Lifeline at 988 or visit https://988lifeline.org. You are not alone.

About the Author

Heather Aimee O'Neill is a poet, a teacher, and the assistant director of the Sackett Street Writers' Workshop. She lives in Brooklyn with her wife and two sons. This is her first novel.